WARRIO
TELAN

The Last Shadow Epic, Book Six

by

AJ Cooper

THE EMPIRE

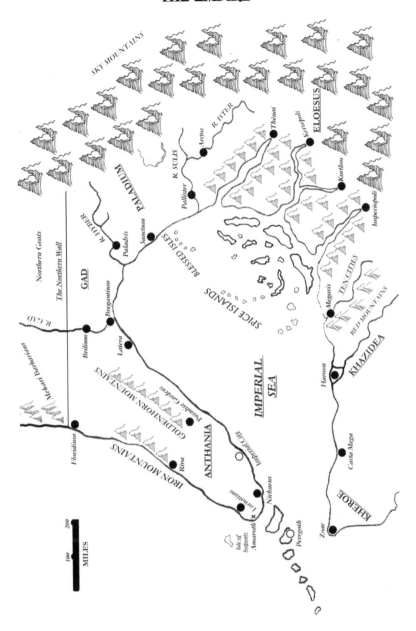

Imperial City

1 mile

WARDS (LABELED)
a. Armory District
b. Kings Terrace
c. Maxima
d. Villa Regis
e. Bulus Wharf
f. Market District
g. Canyon Row
h. Newmarket
i. Mud Bottom
j. Meridia
k. Mystia
l. Villa Mares
m. Loud Surf
n. Perrine
o. Gaboline
p. West Limes
q. East Limes
r. Terrentian
s. Majorian Markets
t. The Strand
u. Meletus
v. Urubus

THE CITY: ITS SIGHTS AND WONDERS
City Bounds: *No legions may enter. It is the law.*
Wagontown Settlement: *A Haunt of Halflings.*
Dualmis: *An island across the sea.*
Imperial Harbor: *A wonder of the world.*
1. Imperial Square: *The Imperial Palace, the Council House and the Hippodrome, among other wonders.*
2. Campus: *The city's most ancient boundary.*
3. Imperial Arena: *Glory. Honor. Blood.*
4. Walk of Triumph: *See the nation's heroes and be amazed.*

WAGONTOWN SETTLEMENT

THE RICCI

q.

p.

s.

t.

u.

v.

CELSUS HEIGHTS

o.

r.

n.

g.

f.

EMPORIA

l.

m.

h.

k.

WEST SIDE

4.

c.

d.

e.

a.

b.

SUBURRO

i.

1.

2.

AVEDICCUS

j.

3.

HARBOR DISTRICT

CLOACA

IMPERIAL HARBOR

CITY BOUNDS

PALLADIAN SWAMP

DUALMIS

Chapter One:
Which God Take Captive

How many days had Reev been at sea? He had lost count.

The skies had been blue, and then they had been gray.

They had been gray, and a rain began to pour, after Spyke had made for the hundredth time a stew of ship's biscuit, after Wrinn had looked out the deck for the thousandth time, longingly for shore.

The five of them, the five against Seymus — an elf, Wrinn, and the humans Spyke, Xan, Fortunato, and Reev — were headed to a land called *Naron Da*. There, prophecies said, Reev would crush the Dark One underfoot, though the prophecies said not how, only that Reev would do so when he got there.

Xan was a dark figure on the prow, his black hair wild as ever, to his back tied his famed butterfly blade. He, a former warlock, once the Dark One's thrall and now his foe, would lead them to *Naron Da*, for he alone knew the way.

The first stop, he said, was a port on the Empire's southern coast. There, they would begin their arduous trek by foot.

Or so they hoped.

The shore was long gone from them now, and all about them was grayish-blue waves under a gray sky. The sailing at first had been smooth, but of late, the waves were getting taller, and the ship had begun tossing and diving, upsetting Reev's stomach and his sense of direction.

Reev longed for shore. He wanted his two feet on the ground. There, he would feel sure. There, he would be at his most capable.

And yet, as he stood on the aft deck of the ship called *Velatari*, he saw the first sign he would not have to wait long.

The clouds were beginning to part, and the sun was casting its orange light on the seas below. Through the waves, and pelting rain, there was a break in the wind, and there was also a break in the sea. The shores of an island were in the distance, pristine sandy beaches and beyond them tangled trees, and beyond the green trees a towering mountain of blackish rock.

As he beheld the island, the coin necklace of Telantis about Reev's neck seemed to glitter in the sunlight. Reev said, "What is that?"

It was the first sign of land they had seen in surely weeks.

"The Isle of Serpents," Spyke called out from the ship's wheel. "We're deep into Imperial waters, now."

Reev stood on the aft transfixed. He gazed upon the black mountain and felt an inexplicable stirring in his heart. He looked at the golden shore and had an urging to leap off *Velatari* and swim into its embrace.

"Is there a harbor?" Reev said. "A port, where we could stretch our feet?"

"No one lives there, anymore," Spyke said. "Only lizards and snakes. You'll be liable to be their meal."

The air became still, but it was an uneasy stillness. The rain ceased, but Reev had a feeling the rain was waiting for something.

Reev gazed again at the black mountain, and saw, beyond them, a wall of clouds moving swiftly in from the northwest.

Spyke, on the ship's wheel, at once began to call out orders. "A Devil's Wind! Everyone, to their places!"

~

In the span of a moment, the stillness evaporated, and a howling wind began to blow. Spyke called out "We have to ride with it!" and the sails caught, and soon the ship called *Velatari* was blown off course, and before an hour had passed in the driving wind and rain and hail, the Isle of Serpents was no longer in sight.

The following day, they continued to succumb to the wind, as Reev began to wonder if Spyke was as supreme a sailor as he had boasted, as the ship was swept faster and faster in a direction they did not wish to go.

Fearing the sandbars "off the coast of Amaroth" Spyke began to order Wrinn and Reev to toss the crates of ship's biscuit overboard and empty the barrels of spring water. Spyke began eyeing Reev's prized Elvish horse Cobalt and Wrinn's Asté in a way Reev didn't like.

Yet the lighter load, now with only a few barrels of water left, and meager rations, did not seem to help them in the face of the overpowering Devil's Wind.

They passed in sight of "Amaroth," a glittering white city, on the third day since the Devil's Wind began to blow. They missed the sandbars, but the Devil's Wind was continuing to blow, even as it changed direction, and Spyke again unraveled the sails, and decided to ride with it.

The storms were only growing in strength, the pelting rain, the blazing lightning and the rolling thunder. Hailstones began to fall onto the deck, and it seemed they were the only ship at sea.

But as *Velatari* began another turn, another turn with the changing direction of the wind, and after Spyke's command to cut loose the rigging had failed, Reev began to sense that the water was growing shallower and shallower.

Where they were, Spyke seemed to have no idea. But they began to take soundings, and saw that the depth of the water was only two-hundred feet. On the second day since they had passed by Amaroth, the depth had lessened to fifty feet.

And then, as the Devil's Wind continued to swiftly speed them on, there was a loud and sundering crack, a sense of the wood giving out beneath Reev's feet. The next thing he knew he was in the water, amid the raging seas. He could see two shores on either side of him.

He could see the wreckage of the *Velatari*, run aground on a sandbar. He could hear Fortunato screaming in the wind.

And as he struggled in the water, he laid hold of a barrel of spring water he had emptied, now floating. He uttered prayers, but the mission now seemed to have failed, not long after it had begun.

~

"Where are we?" Fortunato called out to Spyke as he watched the ocean currents bear Reev swiftly away.

"I don't know," Spyke said. "The wind was driving us north. I —"

Spyke was looking about. *Some sailor you are*, Fortunato wished to say, but thought better of it.

The ship had split in two, and the lifeboat had come loose and was drifting off to sea. Wrinn was standing bruised and battered on the other side of the rent ship.

"The Sage is escaping us," Fortunato said.

The disappearing form of Reev was now a tiny dot in the distance.

"We have to get to shore," Spyke said, "then, we'll recover him…"

~

The water was so cold, Reev's body was growing numb, and he was finding it difficult to breathe. But amid the numbness, clinging to the barrel as he drifted, other senses began to come to him.

The first thing he noticed was an overpowering smell, the smell of human filth and tanneries, of smoke and smog. And another thing he noticed, amid the numbness and delirium — other ships patrolling the way.

They did not intervene, or stop to help him, though they surely saw him drifting. The ships were fishermen's vessels and thin sailing crafts, hugging the shore amid the raging waves.

And a third thing he noticed, as the barrel and the current drove him along — it was no ordinary shore. There were towering white buildings, and buildings built of tuff concrete. There were walkways and colonnades, and countless people walking along them. There was the smell of cooking food, and spices rich and peppery, and Reev's stomach growled despite his desperate situation, as he feared he would succumb to the cold.

He kicked his legs to stay warm, but found the freezing sensation only grew. And so he remained perfectly still, and clung to the barrel in a viselike grip, as it continued to float.

Reev had never been the best swimmer. He would flail his arms and legs to stay afloat, but not much better.

He thought — *Fortunato.*

He thought — *Xan, and Wrinn.*

And he saw that the barrel was drifting through a gray-stone sea-gate, and beyond him were piers and docs of unfathomable number.

Where was he?

It seemed he was in the city of the gods.

~

"Where are we?" Fortunato said again, knowing it would anger Spyke but no longer caring. The Sage, in whom the hopes of the mission rested, had been carried off to sea, and perhaps died.

"We must get to shore," Spyke said, "we'll find out. Somehow…"

There were two shores, one far and one close, one veiled in smoke or fog and one green with cypresses and palm trees beside a rocky beach. Fortunato took Cobalt and Asté by the reins and led them into the water, then clucked at Tyra Jade.

Then he dove into the water himself and began to swim toward the green shore.

~

The barrel was continuing to drift, but now there was no current. Reev was beginning to lose consciousness, and his eyes beginning to wink shut. He felt the barrel scrape against something — he opened his eyes and saw that the barrel had caught on one of the piers. He looked up, and as he succumbed to the cold, saw a cadre of Imperial soldiers with red half capes about their shoulders, and on their steel helmets red horsehair crests.

~

"Where are we?" Fortunato said a third time, and now Xan and Wrinn, Spyke and the horses, and his black wolf Tyra Jade, were on solid ground.

"There is a road," said Spyke, and pointed to a stone road that wound its way along the green shore. "The road will take us somewhere… We will learn where we are. We will rescue the Sage, Fortunato. That is my vow."

~

When Reev's eyes opened, a thick cloak was about his shoulders, and a fire was burning in a fireplace next to him. He was in a vast room, and on the plaster walls were painted marine scenes of squids and octopuses, dolphinfish, and on one wall, a portrait of the goddess Amara on the half-shell.

He was not alone.

A woman was sitting on a stool before him. The light of the fire reflected on a copper complexion, on gray hair hanging about in tresses from her head, on brown eyes and wrinkles that hinted of advanced age. She wore a gown of blue, and she was gazing at Reev worriedly, seemingly deeply concerned for his wellbeing. "You are awake," she said.

Reev said nothing. He realized he was continuing to shiver.

"Do you know where you are, young man?" she said.

Reev tried to shake his head, but all that emerged was a spasm of shivering.

"Perhaps, I should let the shock come to you later," she said. "And I think, young man, you should remove that amulet from your neck. For the True Empire shames the current one, and the glory of the True Empire will forever put the current one to shame. It will arouse jealousy if it is seen in this place."

Reev, to his surprise, did not resist as the woman removed the coin amulet from his neck.

"I will put it in a place of safekeeping," said the woman. "I will let you have it when you depart."

"And who are you?" Reev said.

"Astarthe," the woman answered. "The wife of a governor. The mother of two daughters. And now, an old woman."

"A governor?" Reev said.

"Appian," said Astarthe, "the love of my life. We shall not talk of him, now."

Reev gazed at Astarthe, overcome in confusion. "Where am I?" he insisted.

But Astarthe, it seemed, was not interested in telling him. "I was praying in the chapel," said Astarthe, "and I saw a vision of a boy clinging to a barrel in the harbor."

"Which harbor?" Reev said.

Astarthe smiled. "You are brave to sail in the month of Candlebright."

"Brave, or foolish," Reev said.

"Do you know that it is New Year's Eve?" said Astarthe.

"I know little, it seems," Reev said.

"And what is your name?" Astarthe said.

"Reev Nax," he dared say, realizing he was totally at this woman's mercy. "And where am I?" he continued to insist.

"There is a party tonight," said Astarthe, "with a guest you will do well to impress. Actually, you are *his* guest. I will have my servants get you out of those foreign clothes and put you into something proper. I will tell them you are my consort. How would you like to accompany the Queen of Khazidea? After all, that is my title, though it is now lost."

~

For an hour, Fortunato and Spyke had been walking down the road, followed by Wrinn and Xan, and the afternoon was growing late. Cobalt and Asté were following a step behind, and Tyra Jade Fortunato's black wolf was in the back of the train.

There were cypresses; there were palms. And though Fortunato believed they were in some part of the southern Empire, he could not be certain. Yet it was clear it was highly developed, and on the island there were vast spaces of farmland.

Yet there had been another shore.

Tyra began to bark, and the barking was answered. Dogs were approaching, and through the grass beyond the road, a coach flanked by men in armor.

In the distance were vineyards, and a white villa on a hilltop.

The dogs ceased their approach, but not their barking, as an elderly man in a long white tunic stepped out of the coach. His eyes seemed black and wrathful. He carried himself like a rich man, and it seemed certain to Fortunato that he owned this villa and this farm, and that the farm was worked by slaves.

"What do these four have as their purpose, intruding on the villa of Malchus?" said the old man.

Fortunato said, "We do not mean to intrude, my good signor," and his Imperial speech it seemed would help. "We are trying to find our way. We were shipwrecked..."

The hostility in the old man's eyes seemed to lessen, but not his pride. The slightest curl of a smile appeared on his lips. "A shipwreck," said Malchus. "It is treacherous to sail the Imperial Sea in Candlebright."

"Where are we?" said Fortunato.

"The isle of Dualmis."

Dualmis — the large island abutting the Imperial capital, the largest city in Varda, Imperial City... they had come to the capital of the world.

"There is a ferry that leaves every hour for Imperial City a mile north of here, in the town of Avento," said Malchus. "I suggest you go there with all due speed, before a less kindly farmer finds you. And report the shipwreck to the navy office as soon as you are ashore."

~

Not long after Astarthe had left Reev, servants had arrived and indeed dressed him in new clothes. They had given him fine trousers of fustian, and then a long white tunic that fell down to his knees. They had cinched his tunic with a gold rope, and then remarked among themselves in a foreign tongue before departing.

Reev was alone, trying to warm himself, wondering how Fortunato and Xan and Wrinn were faring, worrying about Cobalt, Asté, and Tyra Jade too.

There was the crackling sound of the fire.

Then, through some fault in the room, some architectural flaw overlooked, there was something else.

"I already told you, Verrus, the emperorship can help pay your way until your career as a kitharode takes off," said a woman's voice, clearly heard, in the room adjacent.

"But I always wanted to play the kithara," said a voice, nasal yet deep. "That's what I wanted above all, Mother."

"You have to be realistic," the woman's voice said.

And Reev felt a voyeur, that through some flaw in the room's construction, he was hearing this private conversation as if it were held right in front of him.

~

The horses were tired, and Tyra Jade was whining softly, when the town of Avento appeared. It was small, composed of only a few dozen buildings, but in the dark of night was lit by bronze street lamps, and its buildings were of brilliant yellow stone, and crowned in sparkling red tile. It was clearly a place of great wealth.

Just a short span across the waters was a titan, city lights so numerous they were like the stars of the sky, and despite the darkness, clearly something that had no equal in Varda. Even in the dark, the promise, the shadow, of Imperial City stole Fortunato's breath away.

A woman was approaching from the docks. "The last ferry has left," she said. "You'll have to wait until the morning."

~

It was dark outside Reev's window when Astarthe appeared again. She was no longer carrying Reev's coin amulet.

And she had spent these past hours getting ready. Her face had been powdered with chalk, and red ochre had been applied to her lips and eyes. She wore a gown of red dark silk, and now was wearing a gold necklace. On her hand was now a gold ring. She looked like the queen she had claimed to be, though there was no crown.

"Reev Nax, my consort," she said. "How shall we explain your presence? If anyone asks, say you are from a princely family of Gad."

It was not far off. Norwood, his hometown, was in the hinterlands of the province of Gad, and though he was not a prince, the elves had declared him the Sage, the Prince of the Dawn.

With Astarthe's arm hooked in his, Reev passed through gold corridors and silver antechambers, through halls trimmed in gold and painted with reliefs, beside gold-framed paintings that depicted grand battles of the civilized versus the barbarian or depictions of the gods enthroned. The truth of where he was had begun to dawn on him, but he thought if he admitted it, his heart might begin to race, and suspicion fall on him, and the mission be doomed from the start.

He had to get back to Fortunato, but he would not leave until he retrieved his coin amulet.

"Welcome," said Astarthe, "to the emperor's chambers."

And Reev supposed he could no longer deny the truth now.

Beyond an open door flanked by Imperial soldiers was a room Reev Nax had no place in. Beyond tables with red silk tablecloths, and tableware of platinum, was a window overlooking the lights of Imperial City, and the moonstruck waters of the harbor. Reev's heart began to race, and he tried to stay calm, as people he had no place getting close to began to take their seats amid the grandeur, which he still had not fully processed.

A dusky woman in a black gown sat down with her husband, an Imperial with short-cut brown hair. Her midnight-black eyes gleamed, looking to Astarthe and then to Reev, and wonder touched them.

"My girl," Astarthe said softly, "Appenina."

A swarthy young man was seated in the room's far corners, thin and muscular. Reev felt like a sword should be at his side, though there was no sword to be seen.

"Khando," Astharthe whispered, "the emperor's son."

Reev and Astarthe took their seats at the edge of the room, and as Reev settled into his seat, he saw there was one who had already arrived, whom he had not noticed.

He had not noticed him, perhaps, because his place in the room was so obvious, near the window, raised up above. He sat at a table with a purple tablecloth, and he himself was dressed all in purple. His body strained against the seat and spilled over it, so large was his belly. His complexion was ebon. His ulcer-spotted feet were set against a stool, gingerly, and the act of sitting itself seemed a strain to him. His eyes were cloudy. On his graying black hair was the simple crown that emperors wore intended for humility, but which had become a symbol of ultimate power due to the one who wore it — a circlet of silver.

"Khandaraeus," said Astarthe, "our emperor."

Beside him at the table was a petite Imperial woman with blond hair, garbed in a gown of scarlet.

"His wife," said Astarthe, "Flavia."

The doors opened.

A woman stepped out, dressed in a dark blue gown hinting at purple. Around her neck was a diamond brooch. She was strikingly beautiful, with black hair and dark eyes. She was pallid, strikingly so, but the effect of her dark hair and dark eyes, and her deep purplish gown, seemed to make her one of darkness rather than light.

"Valeria Verra!" called out the emperor's son, Khando.

The woman, Valeria Verra, smiled as if she were humoring one lesser than herself. She looked to the emperor sitting at the purple table. "My dearest emperor," she said, "Your Excellency. Long may you reign... The household of Valeria Verra has a most splendid gift for you this New Year's Eve, one you are certain to enjoy."

This was the woman Reev had heard.

"My son Verrus is an accomplished kitharode, a graduate of the Academies of Eloesus. He shall play a song for you and entertain you all. You are certain to enjoy it."

From the door stepped another, tall and red-haired. Verrus seemed large in places and thin in others, having overall a disjointed look. Yet he carried himself, and a presence emanated from him wherever he stepped. All eyes gazed at him when he walked, and Reev saw that there was a stage at the side of a room, and in his hand was a stringed instrument, what his mother had called a kithara.

He took to the stage and strummed a few notes. The effect of the instrument was resonant and haunting.

At once, he began to play and sing.

O Lunas, good Amara's son, I shall take heed
Glutted with Brecko's red wine
Mouth dripping red, red wine flowing down his bright cheeks
Dancing to Brecko's sharp song
He steps to dance, he steps to war; his face is changed

His skill was masterful, but there seemed to be little passion in his notes. The emperor seemed to be nodding off. Others were stirring uncomfortably.

Ye mad mortal ones, which god shall you take captive
And dare place on a dark shore?
Alabaster? Tyrus? He shall do worse to you
And slay you on a dark shore

Verrus took a bow and there was scattered applause. The emperor was motionless in his seat.

Valeria Verra eyed Verrus and seemed to utter a curse under her breath. They hastened to a seat next to the emperor's table.

~

"Where is Reev?" Wrinn said in the dark of night, on the outskirts of Avento.

More than the ferry had been closed. Every inn in Avento was full, and so they now would sleep or not sleep, and await the dawn in the fresh air.

"Where is Reev?" said Fortunato. "Swept off by a current. We will not stop searching until we find him."

"What if he is dead?" said Xan.

"He is not dead, Xan," Fortunato snarled. "Is there perhaps still something of a warlock in you?"

But Wrinn didn't think there was. Wrinn thought all evil had been purged from Xan. But perhaps Xan did not have as much hope for Reev's rescue as the others.

~

Reev observed the diners quietly as the New Year's Eve banquet progressed. There seemed to be tensions underlying the banquet, tensions a bumpkin from Norwood and later Galiope could not begin to understand. His eyes kept returning to Valeria Verra and her son, who looked so unlike each other. The performance had been a quiet disaster, and Verrus seemed to be nursing his wounds.

As Reev sat, servants began to come by and set platters of olives and cheese at each table. Then servants distributed glasses of wine.

Reev took a sip. "It tastes thin," he said.

Astarthe touched his hand. "In the Empire," she says, "it is considered barbaric not to water down your wine."

They ate the olives, they ate the cheese, as conversation endured. Servants were aiding the emperor in the consumption of his food, spooning it into his mouth or otherwise, while his petite wife sat by.

And then, the doors opened yet again, and there was the smell of food to roil the appetite, clay pots and in them, songbirds in a thin broth.

Reev had a thought that there would be no end to the courses. Yet after so long at sea, he was in a state to eat richly.

He had finished his watered down wine. He had picked apart and devoured what meat could be found on the songbirds. He looked to Verrus, to Valeria Verra.

He could not help but notice that Valeria Verra was continually eyeing the emperor's table.

As the servants removed the devoured songbirds and began to bring out new dishes in covered pots, there was a noise — a persistent cough of the emperor's wife… what was her name? Flavia.

And she stood up, coughing wildly, and Reev could see against the light scarlet gown, she was coughing up blood.

Panic seemed to seize the room in that moment. Valeria Verra wailed, as the coughing turned to hacking, and the hacking to vomiting of blood.

The emperor sat in his special seat, confused, and Reev realized he was blind.

"Get a physician!" howled Valeria Verra, as Verrus looked about, and various partygoers scrambled to Flavia's aid.

"You've picked quite a New Year's Eve to wash up in Imperial Harbor," said Astarthe softly. "Are you not telling me everything you know?"

~

"He could have washed to sea," said Wrinn. "He could be on Dualmis, where we are…"

But Fortunato had a feeling… the currents seemed to be drifting in the other way.

"Perhaps, a merchant ship would have taken him to shore," Spyke said. "And warships patrol the coast even in winter. They would have taken him to Imperial City and questioned him…"

Spyke, a former soldier, still had ties to that world. And Fortunato remembered, according to the government that sat just across that short span of water, in the city whose lights he could see, he was a traitor to his country. He had fought for the Gallians in war, and taken up arms against the Empire's legions.

Yet he would risk all for the Sage.

~

Astarthe quickly and quietly led Reev Nax back to his room. "I am sorry you witnessed that," she said. "I am afraid, I have witnessed it before, though not up close. The emperor, though, is normally the target, not his wife."

Reev Nax was still confused, and still fighting panic. He wondered if he had still not recovered from the icy water's grip.

"I will guard over you, Reev Nax," Astarthe said. "I won't let a hair of your head be touched."

"I really must depart," Reev said.

And as Astarthe made no reply, and turned, he realized how difficult it would be to escape without Astarthe's help. He was a prisoner in this palace, until he could find a way out.

~

The first ship was at sunrise, and Xan vowed he would board it. As Fortunato and Wrinn lay down to sleep in the grass, and Spyke seemed to nod off with one eye open, Xan stood watch. All he owed to the Prince of the Dawn. His life and his rescue he owed to Reev Nax, the Prince of the Dawn. He would not rest until Reev was safe, and they resumed their journey to *Naron Da*.

~

In a half-sleep on his cot, Reev stirred awake to voices.

"They hated my performance," said the voice of Verrus, as clearly as if he had spoken in Reev's ear.

"Oh, we have much more important things to worry about than your kithara," said Valeria Verra.

"Flavia? You didn't have anything to do with it, did you Mother?" said Verrus.

"Really, Verrus?" said Valeria Verra. "You say that about your own mother?"

Chapter Two:
A City of Gods and Giants

The ferry left at dawn, and Wrinn and Fortunato, Xan and Spyke, were the first to board.

Wrinn watched as the ferrymen gently rowed across the narrow waters, and through the sea-gate of Imperial Harbor.

What Wrinn was seeing did not seem possible. What the Imperials had built did not seem within the ability of human hands. A city of gods and giants stretched before him on all sides, buildings the size of Galiope itself, columns and colonnades so white they outshone a fresh Gallian snow. And in a city of gods and giants, Wrinn was less than an ant, and Wrinn wondered, in such a city, if Reev indeed had made his way here, how they could possibly find him amid such vastness.

Wrinn felt humbled that he had thought Galiope was a great city, or anything more than a town. For the Empire and the Imperials put it to shame. And it was a wonder that against a people who had built such a city, Galiope had lasted more than an hour in war.

"Welcome to Imperial City!" cried one of the ferrymen, as the ferry broached the pier, and the ferryman sealed it to the posts. "Keep a watchful eye! And revere the emperor!"

Would Wrinn revere the emperor? Which emperor now reigned?

~

Sailors and workmen unloaded crates and amphorae with antlike organization, loading them on carts and sending them on their way. The harbor was crowded, but there were also civilians darting from point to point in the light of the golden morning. Wrinn's heart raced at the breadth of such a city, and he wondered how many people it contained. He supposed all Galiope could be housed in one of Imperial City's blocks.

They pushed on through the crowds, past the dazzling white columns and colonnades, past temples with triangular roofs large enough to house a titan, and well might have. The people of Imperial City were richly arrayed in sumptuous tunics or gowns of brilliant green or sapphire blue or diamond white, and what's more it seemed every part of Varda was represented, that each people group from the far corners could be found, complexions ranging from dark to amber to fair, and everything in between. Wrinn even spotted a few elves walking about, but like him they were *dra'datsi*, born in the human world, as implied by the common tunics and trousers they wore.

Past more colonnades and monuments, past a titanic bronze statue of what the Imperials called the god of the sun, Fortunato, Xan, Wrinn and Spyke pushed, and for a moment it seemed their attention was no longer on finding Reev, but on marveling at this, what many called the greatest city in the world — and who could argue?

Here was the wealth of Varda, stored. From here all the military power of the world was projected. From here all legions were sent, all edicts were issued. And Wrinn could not help but marvel, to see this place and its grandeur, and know he was at the source of all Varda's triumphs and its woes.

"Look! Imperial Square!" Fortunato said, and the road opened up, and at last there was ample space for the raging crowds. There was a basilica that looked to Wrinn's eyes the size of Galiope itself, "Imperial Treasury" written over its great open doors. There was a titanic temple with a triangular roof, on its pediment inscribed in bold letters, "The Temple of Justice."

Ringing the square, and amid the square, were colored lanterns that glowed like starstones of brilliant brightness. On the walls of the high buildings were advertisements, "Regulo's Potions," "Madam

Laria's House: Enter and Enjoy," and a portrait of fighters in the sand, "Imperial Arena — Glory. Honor. Blood."

Wrinn found he couldn't walk, overcome with fascination. He heard Fortunato's voice calling out for him.

Both he and Xan were standing transfixed.

Spyke was smiling. He and Fortunato were standing up ahead. They beckoned them on.

~

No market vendors seemed to be set up in Imperial Square, but something else seemed to be for sale everywhere. Women in tight-fitting red tunics accosted Wrinn wherever he went, and Wrinn felt himself blush. It seemed everyone who sold such wares were ordered to wear the same uniform, to leave no doubt.

But now another woman was approaching, plump, dressed modestly. Her plain brown gown contrasted sharply with her dark brown hair. There was a bright smile on her face as she approached.

"Visitors?" she said. "Awestruck, I am sure, by the greatest city in the world. I can tell you are not from here."

Spyke and Fortunato had frozen in place. Wrinn recalled that Fortunato was not from Imperial City, but from another city called Ríva in this same province.

"Take a moment to catch your breath," said the woman.

She was proud of Imperial City. Was it her profession to be proud of Imperial City? Would there be a moment in their conversation where Wrinn would be expected to reach for his coinpurse?

"Pardon me, my signora," said Fortunato, and the way he said it seemed cutting, though his Imperial was more fluent and natural than any in their party. "You can see we have some unusual beasts on our hands…"

"In this city are pens for elephants and wild lions," said the woman. "Do you think in such a city there would be no place for a wolf? There is a wolf kennel in the Emporia, the fifth building on Crooked Street."

"And what of Elvish horses?" said Wrinn, pointing behind him, to Asté, to Cobalt.

"Do you think, in the greatest city in the world, we have not come into contact with such beasts?" the woman said. "In the west side, just outside the Suburro, there is a stable for the horses of the Elders. A marvel of engineering — an indoor pasture. Your two beasts will think they are frolicking in the steppe of Non."

And Wrinn saw, then, at her belt, was tied a wide-mouthed jar for tips. She wouldn't be getting any money from Wrinn, however.

Fortunato, however, tossed a copper coin in the jar as he walked away, and Tyra followed.

"Spyke," said Fortunato, "take care of the animals. Meet us here, outside the Imperial Treasury, at vespers.

"Our search begins. Reev couldn't have gone far."

But couldn't the currents of the ocean have swept him deep into the sea?

As Spyke departed with the animals in tow, Wrinn uttered a prayer for Reev under his breath.

~

The morning sunlight was spreading through Reev's room, and he stirred awake. Below him was a city stretching from the sea into the interminable horizon. He remembered where he was, and fought panic. But he had to keep a level head.

He was not alone, he noted then, as he removed his covers and sat up. Astarthe had been there while he slept, and a finger of distrust wormed his way through him. Yet Astarthe, he inexplicably trusted.

"You've been watching me sleep?" Reev said.

"Standing guard," Astarthe said, "over a guest. There's panic in the palace, Reev Nax, and I think it would be inadvisable to leave. You will draw suspicion, fleeing here."

But he had to get back to Fortunato. He had to continue his journey to *Naron Da.*

"Where is my amulet?" Reev said.

"In my room," Astarthe, "kept safe and also kept secret, as is wise."

Reev looked about, and his breaths were growing cold and shallow. Perhaps, he did not trust Astarthe after all.

And why would he? Why would he trust anyone in the Imperial Palace? Why, after the behavior he just witnessed? "Verrus," he blurted out, though he did not know why.

"Verrus and his mother are overstaying their welcome," said Astarthe. "Make of that what you will."

Chapter Three:
The Imperial

Giufrio Vallo was an Imperial, through and through.

He had been born and raised in the ward of Villa Regis, and his mother and father had lived in the province of Anthania their whole lives. His ancestry, if one was so diligent as to track it, would have been tied to Anthania's sandy soil from the very beginning.

This, he recalled, as he began his investigation, considering the death of the emperor's wife — the wife of the emperor, the barbarian that still ruled them. Khandaraeus, he was named, for his origins in the land of Khandara far away, which acknowledged tacitly the rule of the emperor on the White Throne but which ruled itself in all its barbarian frenzy and furor.

Giufrio longed for an emperor born and raised, as he eyed the body of Flavia, his examination complete, loaded onto a gurney and ferried away from the scene of the crime — the Imperial banquet hall.

"What do you think?" said Barcho, Giufrio's second-in-command, his lieutenant in the Imperial Guard.

Giufrio was the Marshal of the Guard and he wouldn't let anyone forget it. "If that was natural," said Giufrio, "I'll give up my Imperial citizenship and set sail for Fharas."

For a man such as Giufrio, it was an oath of certainty.

"I'm inclined to agree with you," said Barcho.

Now came an examination of every inhabitant of the Imperial Palace. Giufrio had his suspicions, but he wouldn't let his biases and dislike of certain members of Khandaraeus's court poison him, one way or the other.

Poison... he was certain, that was Flavia's method of death. The motivation, he knew, would lead him to the killer.

~

Astarthe had brought a guest to the New Year's Eve banquet. He had been the youngest consort Giufrio had seen, but Giufrio knew that before Astarthe married Appian, she had played the part of a Khazidean queen, and engaged in countless indiscretions and torrid romances. That was what a Khazidean queen was meant to do.

Fertility cults had no place in Imperial City, but a lot of things had no place in Imperial City which had come to it. Ruling the world had invited in all sorts of influences that Giufrio's ancestors would have disapproved of and condemned. It was the Imperials' burden to bear.

At least, it was for now.

But Giufrio did not believe such a young man, an invited guest, would have any part in Flavia's death. Besides his youth, what would he stand to gain?

Astarthe would not stand to gain either.

Valeria Verra was a woman that Giufrio had never liked. During her stays in the palace, she had made countless advances toward him that Giufrio had rebuffed. Giufrio's bias was likely to lead him directly to her. She was a natural subject of his suspicion, a tireless schemer, one who wanted power above all else, who had married and divorced and remarried her way up into the Imperial elite's highest echelons, who would not stop now.

But perhaps, an investigator should start at the beginning.

The beginning, as far as Giufrio knew, was the meal itself. No meal was served to the emperor or the emperor's family without a food taster.

The food taster would determine by his own survival whether food was poisoned or not. The poison that had killed Flavia, née Karbo, was fast acting, causing a hemorrhage of blood.

Thus, the food taster had either skipped the meal, or had had a hand in the poison itself. And in Khandaraeus's court, a nest of vipers for certain, there was no evil intent or selfish move too evil or selfish to believe.

Giufrio made a bee line for the kitchen.

~

The chef was an Eloesian, an Easterner, as was typical, but the kitchen maestro was the one ultimately in charge.

The scullions were scurrying about, and there was the smell of frying eggs and the scent of yogurt left out to strain. Giufrio realized breakfast had not been served.

The kitchen maestro, what was his name? Giufrio had forgotten. It had slipped him by. And Giufrio realized he had not met him before.

There was a scullion a little slack in his duties, standing off while eggs cooked in a pan, a blond Eloesian.

"Signore!" Giufrio said. "Where can I find the kitchen maestro?"

And the blond Eloesian began babbling in his tongue, and Giufrio remembered his lessons from the pedagogue in Villa Regis.

"Down the hallway," he was saying, "to the left."

And Giufrio walked at an easy pace down the hallway, and at an easy pace, turned to his left.

~

The kitchen maestro, Giufrio saw, was sitting at a table. Coins were spread out on the table, and he was counting them, arranging them by silver, copper and gold. The kitchen maestro was wearing a blackish-green vest and gray trousers—*Noted.* Who knew what would help in Giufrio's investigation?

The kitchen maestro looked up, and Giufrio saw a head of white hair, a grayish complexion, harsh features. And when the kitchen maestro opened his mouth, Giufrio — for a reason he could not tell — expected a forked tongue to flick out from those massive chompers of his.

"Can I help you?" the kitchen maestro said.

"Pardon me, signore," Giufrio said. He reminded himself to keep his chess moves to himself. "I do not think we have met. I am Giufrio, Marshal of the Guard..."

The question was implied by his silence. But the kitchen maestro either did not understand, or did not take the bait.

So Giufrio said, "Can I have your name?"

"Alsumo," the kitchen maestro said. His voice was harsh and gravelly.

"Alsumo," Giufrio said.

It was not an Imperial name, though its source Giufrio could not place.

"I am sure you have heard, Alsumo," Giufrio continued, "the emperor's wife has died. The food tasters did not do their job."

"You haven't heard," said Alsumo dryly, "the physicians marked the cause as natural. Case closed."

"So you're saying the food tasters tasted the songbirds before the emperor's wife ate them?" Giufrio said.

"What else would I mean?" said Alsumo. "Would you please step out? I have an important task in this palace..."

Giufrio stepped out. He knew either Alsumo was lying, or the food tasters were.

He wondered, who did the kitchen maestro answer to?

Chapter Four:
The True Empire

Spyke watched Tyra Jade enter the doors of the wolf kennel. At first she walked, and then she sprinted, as the doors closed, and Spyke caught a glimpse of balls and bones and toys, and wolves of a similar girth and size as Tyra, though not of her color.

Yet the doors shut, and Spyke left a happy Tyra behind.

Spyke had a few hours to kill before vespers. But there was little for him to do. They needed to find Reev, and then they needed to retrieve their animals and depart. For he knew as long as they lingered, the chances of discovery would grow, and as soon as they were discovered, the mission was over.

For there was a traitor to the Empire in their midst.

The crumbling apartment blocks, the shops and market squares of Emporia stretched around Spyke. And Spyke realized he had not been in this part of the city before, though he had spent the bulk of his adult life here.

Peremmum, across the sea, was where he had been born. It was where his family had first traveled from Khandara. It was where they had become Imperials to start with.

Peremmum was where the emperor Khandaraeus would trace his origins to, and though he and Spyke were distant relations, second cousins, they had never met. But Peremmum was where he and his family had become Imperials. Spyke's family had lingered a little while longer in that eastern city than the one currently enthroned.

Fortunato wished to regroup at vespers. Then where would they check for Reev? Military prisons? Temples of Amara, sanctuaries for the poor? Or perhaps, they'd hope Reev would be drawn to the lights of Imperial Square, and meet them there. It was anyone's guess.

But Fortunato would not rest until this mission had resumed, until again they were journeying for *Naron Da.* That was the whole of Fortunato's purpose, what he had dedicated his life to.

The afternoon was growing late.

Spyke was amid the slum apartments, the trash and debris, and the gardens where users of Haroon spice congregated, of the west side. Spyke had his trusty Dohorensi board. He was not afraid to use it.

And amid the crowd, of a lesser quality than the assorted masses of Imperial Square, there was commotion, and a flash of gray and red. Imperial soldiers in shining breastplates, in red half-capes and steel helms with red horsehair crests, were pushing their way through the street, and they were looking directly at Spyke.

"Vitto Khandulis," said one, using Spyke's legal name, which no one who loved him used. "The ward legate of the Metropolitan would like to have a word with you."

The eyes of the government were everywhere in Imperial City. Spyke's presence had been noted. And Spyke would not resist, because he could not.

"Of course," Spyke answered.

~

The long shadows of the afternoon were growing, and Fortunato had a feeling, though he had not been to Imperial Square before, that this was the dullest part of the day, that the morning crowds had dispersed, and that the city would take on a new yet lively character at night. Lively — not necessarily safe. Fortunato, of all the party most at home in Imperial City, and surely the most hunted, would have to guide the party to safety.

He imagined Reev, lost amid these dark streets, a target because of the innocence and naivete he would surely exude. He would be a target, and Fortunato would have to find him before the mission failed, if it had not already.

Yet as Fortunato stood and stirred amid the crowds — innumerable yet obviously less than before — he heard noise, and the scattered "oohs" and "ahs" of a spectacle taking place.

In a corner of Imperial Square, not far yet distant, there was a stage set up, and people gathered.

"What play will we perform, Rufo, this New Year's Day?" said a woman, comely, with two keen dark eyes and hair dyed poorly, blond with clear strands of brown left untouched. Her beauty was one of the streets, rough yet striking.

Wrinn had turned to look, and Xan was following in his wake.

"Say, I don't know, Sylvia," said a man opposite her, on the stage, handsome — also a rough beauty of the streets, dark, with scars along his face and on his arm, and on his bare forearms tattoos he had left uncovered. "I remember a tale from the old book, you know, the one my mother used to make me read, the one where the queen Varae is sent to die."

"Queen Varae?" said Sylvia the actress in a teasing tone, playing off his charismatic energy. "Who's that?"

"Queen Varae?" Rufo said. "Say Sylvia, how about I just say the lines, and then you take it from there…"

~

The brick homes of the Metropolitan were ones Spyke recognized, though ones he had seen at a distance. They were Imperial City's oldest district, kept pristine out of religious respect, and they were clearly of great antiquity.

For Imperial City, Spyke knew, was the largest city in Varda now, but it had not already been this way. The Imperials were considered the natives of the peninsula, but they had not always been native to it.

As he was led through the streets, which few walked, he wondered just what he would say, how guileful his tongue could be. He wondered how he would escape this. And he wondered, he supposed, what he would do.

The buildings lost their antiquity as soon as Spyke and the soldiers leading him took a turn down a crooked street.

Now they were no longer humble brick homes but, beyond a wall, grim buildings of tuff concrete. There were more soldiers, some standing at street corners, others who were departing in civilian clothes. And Spyke had been here before, a barracks of the urban cohort in Imperial City, the only legion that was allowed to operate within city bounds.

Spyke wondered what he would say, what he could do, to engineer a happy ending for Fortunato and Reev Nax, called the Prince of the Dawn. But fate had brought him here, to the center of world power, and what could be done, now?

The soldier ahead of Spyke led him through the door of a concrete building, and he was in a sparely decorated hallway, bare of ornament. Through another door was a room, in the room a desk, at the desk a candle burning. Behind the desk was the ward legate of the Metropolitan.

Vitto Khandulis, called Spyke, took a seat opposite the ward legate.

The ward legate of the Metropolitan was wrinkled and gray. There was a wart on his nose he hadn't bothered a surgeon to remove. He was gruff, but Spyke had a thought that in his day, he had been young and vigorous, and perhaps had ventured into the savannahs and rolling grassland of Khandara, or hewed down barbarians in the cold forests of the north.

Barbarian... that was what some of the most prideful and insular Imperials still called Spyke.

There were papers on the desk. The ward legate of the Metropolitan began to speak.

"Spyke," he said. "I shall use the name you prefer. I do this because we in the Imperial Army believe you are a loyal citizen and would do nothing to defame the Empire or the emperor. We believe whatever actions you took, licit or illicit, that contravened the laws of our nation are abjured by your blood, being a second cousin to His Excellency Khandaraeus, and seeing the good behavior of Khandara over the centuries."

Spyke looked at the ward legate blankly.

"Let me introduce myself," said the ward legate, "I am Caro Hudnato, and I do not believe I made my name clear in our correspondence via letter. I apologize, as it is custom. I was recently made ward legate by the honorable Thuban... I am sure you have heard of him."

Spyke had not, but he would pretend he did.

"We in the army and in the government more broadly have been undertaking an investigation of a certain traitor named Fortunato of Ríva, as I am sure you are aware," said Hudnato. "We are aware he has arrived in Imperial City, but we have made the decision not to arrest him. We wish to have all the information we can before we press charges and bring him to trial.

"And we are aware, Spyke, of your illicit actions in the Gallian War..."

Spyke gulped. He would call himself an above average liar, but he supposed they had gathered enough evidence that lying was futility.

"And we were wondering, Spyke, considering the threat that poses to your pay, to the retention of your rank, and if blood was shed, your freedom... if you would be interested in becoming a cooperating witness against Fortunato of Ríva when the magistrate acts and brings charges?"

What could Spyke say? What could Spyke do? Could he make

a statement of intent, and then pray to the gods they'd find Reev before the charges were brought?

Then, they would flee across the sea, hopefully out of the Empire's reach. But there was no place in Varda outside the Empire's reach.

"But there is something else, Spyke, something that might cause you to make the right decision," said Hudnato. "Fortunato of Ríva is fighting on behalf of a Telantine."

Spyke stirred in his seat.

"Do you know what the Telantines did to your kind?"

~

Reev had not left the room all day. Astarthe had brought him breakfast. She had brought him lunch. And now, she was bringing him dinner.

Astarthe set a tray before him. She had a tray of her own.

Steaming beef, whose hot spices Reev could smell, was before him, causing his stomach to growl. Mashed tubers, laden with hot gravy, tantalized the eye. Vegetables covered in salt and pepper, boiled and laden with a savory brown sauce, shimmered in the afternoon light.

And there was, of course, the wine. Watered down, thin, it was better than nothing — a goblet in its place on the tray.

But despite the food, what dominated Reev's mind were all the questions he had, the questions growing in number each hour he spent in the Imperial Palace.

"My necklace," said Reev.

"Don't speak of it," Astarthe said, "unless you wish to die."

"Why?"

"As I said," Astarthe began, "the True Empire shames the current one. And if you bear it, those who remember will try to kill you."

"Let me take it and leave," Reev said, "I will place it in my pocket. I was shipwrecked — "

"Quiet," Astarthe said. "I know you have no cause to trust me. But I am your ally. For I do not hate the True Empire. I am a rarity in these parts."

"Then let me leave…"

"I will not aid you in that," said Astarthe, "until you answer my questions."

"Like what?" Reev said.

"Like why you bear the coin of the True Empire," Astarthe said, "a vanished kingdom, a vanished people. Its very memory spurs those who hate it into rage."

Would Reev tell her? Would Reev tell her that the Telantines endured? Would Reev tell her he was descended of such blood?

Reev supposed he did not trust her, after all. Perhaps, someday, he would learn to.

"I cannot tell you," Reev said. "But I'd like for you to tell me about this True Empire, and what you know. For I know little of it, though I bear its coin."

"What do you wish to know?" Astarthe said. "For we are all in its shadow. All about you bears traces of it. For it ruled the world and it dominated it. It ruled in peace and justice."

"And what happened to it?" Reev said.

"Don't you know?" Astarthe said. "It began in victory. Its last days were greater than its first. And then it vanished from Varda."

"I know so little," said Reev, "perhaps you could start at the beginning?"

"It began," said Astarthe, "with the vanquishing of the Sons of Nachash."

"The Sons of Nachash?" Reev said.

~

The actors had quit their play.

The story had been a bloody one, ending with the actress Sylvia, playing Queen Varae, dying by poison. For all their rough looks and rough beauty, the rough stage and rough crowds, the actors Sylvia and Rufo were skilled, for they had transfixed the three warriors of the light before them, though Fortunato's attention had occasionally drifted to Reev and the perilous moment they found themselves in.

Wrinn and Xan, however, had not ceased their applause.

And Fortunato saw, on the sundial beside the Temple of Justice, it was past vespers.

They were late.

They were late, but Spyke was not there, not where he promised he would be. The steps in front of the Imperial Treasury were peppered with idlers, but among them, none were Spyke.

Yet the crowds in Imperial Square were lessening in quality. There were a few scowling faces now eyeing Fortunato's coinpurse.

And despite Spyke's absence and what may have befallen him, in this city wherein the two of them were traitors, he remembered none of them were as important as the success of the mission, the treading of their enemy Seymus underfoot, and the coming dawn.

"Let's get a room at an inn," Fortunato said to Wrinn and Xan. "We'll find Spyke later."

Chapter Five:
So Lonely

During New Year's Eve and in the ensuing days, Giufrio made a note of everyone's comings and goings, of every conversation taking place in the light of the sun and in the dark of the night. He instructed every member of the Imperial Guard to eavesdrop and note everything that seemed out of place.

Giufrio was convinced that an assassination had taken place, but the physicians had ruled inexplicably that Flavia, the emperor's wife, had died a natural death. He now suspected the physicians, for their conclusion seemed unlikely, if not impossible.

It was the seventh day of Albos, and outside there was a raging storm. In the banquet hall, the emperor sat with his feet on the stool as a dinner of roast quail was served to the partygoers. Giufrio had gotten their early, and had picked for himself a seat next to the emperor. He would be the emperor's eyes and ears, for the emperor could not see. And the Imperial Guard was charged with the protection of his life, the protection of his life and that of his family.

The Imperial Guard had failed.

This was personal.

Banqueters began to arrive, on this day, not more than the seventh of Albos. It was no holiday and no feast day. Yet Appenina the Younger, and Servillio, and Corvo arrived and took their seats, together with their families.

Then the door opened again, and another strode out, Valeria Verra now wearing a tight-fitting crimson dress.

The tables all were occupied, and Valeria made a huff.

But then Giufrio saw the chamberlain, newly appointed, one he knew as Aniabo, take her by the hand and call out in a loud voice, "Your Excellency the Emperor, all the tables are taken, and the seats occupied… we have one last guest, one you invited."

The emperor sat at the purple table, and seemingly did not hear. He sat in his seat, his feet propped up, and muttered senselessly.

Giufrio called out to him, "Your Excellency, Valeria Verra wishes to sit with you, and the chamberlain is insistent…"

Valeria Verra stared daggers at Giufrio, and the chamberlain gave him a sheepish look, as the emperor made a noise that sounded like assent, and Valeria Verra took it as an invitation, and sat at the purple table reserved for the emperor and his wife.

The emperor stirred.

He had not seemed grieved. But what went on in his court seemed not to concern him. His interest was in food most of all, and he showed little interest in governing. Giufrio had not been at the funeral at the request of the Maestro of Undertakers, Insilaco, and so perhaps the emperor showed more emotion then, but Giufrio doubted it.

Wherever he went, whether venturing from one room to another, took a crew of able bodied men. Physicians had tried to treat his sugar sickness with horseback riding, but the state of his health no longer made it possible.

And Giufrio sat, pretending to eat, pretending to drink, as Valeria Verra chatted.

And he noted who was absent from the banqueting hall, for one Astarthe and her consort, and for another, most notable, Valeria Verra's clumsy son, Verrus.

And he had thought, the crowded banqueting hall could have been arranged. And the suspect was obvious, but Giufrio would only deal in facts he could prove — for he could not overrule the emperor, and the emperor, for his blindness and his lack of awareness, seemed to be warming to Valeria Verra as she sat with him.

"Oh, what a tragedy it was that Flavia died," Valeria Verra said. "Death is so difficult. And I shall never forget how perfect the two of you were together. She looked at you so longingly. It touched my heart."

Giufrio knew that wasn't true, though the emperor, being blind, would not know.

Valeria Verra was beginning to cry, and it seemed to Giufrio that she could produce tears on command. Yet who was he, to assume she was a cold, heartless snake.

The emperor can only be convinced with facts.

"Oh, Flavia, what a loss for the world," Valeria Verra said. "She was a budding artist, wasn't she? She would collect seashells and make ornaments from them. I would have paid a libra for one of them."

Giufrio could not tell what the emperor was thinking, but he noticed he was inching closer to her. The emperor had largely left the governing of the Empire to the Imperial Council. The Imperial Council had come to like its newfound powers of control. And the emperor got to live as he wished, eating sumptuous meats and sugary pastries and spicy sauces, when he wasn't engaged in torrid affairs.

But looking at him, Giufrio wasn't sure how those torrid affairs were possible.

Perhaps, it was a topic best not explored.

"Seashell ornaments," Valeria Verra, "such charming work. And Yule ornaments made from odds and ends around the palace. She was such a novel thinker. Always dreaming up new ways to innovate with her art."

Valeria Verra was the consummate actress, and tears were falling down her cheeks.

"I've been lonely, too," Valeria Verra said. "I don't know if you heard, my husband Bartis passed on. The house in Nichaeus is so empty."

Giufrio could see Khandaraeus's fingers reaching feebly for Valeria Verra's arm, and it took all Giufrio's strength not to gag.

"My room is so lonely, here," Valeria Verra said.

What she was doing was so obvious, it shocked the conscience. And it took all Giufrio's summoned skepticism not to level his accusations already. But the emperor was a creature of basest passion. It seemed he did not care about the lack of dignity. His fingers were now strumming her hand.

"It seems," said Valeria Verra softly, and her tone was one of a succubus, "you are lonely too…"

Chapter Six:
When A World Was Born

Fortunato, Wrinn and Xan had checked every temple of Amara in the central city, and inquired at the barracks at the Metropolitan. None had seen any sign of Reev, and now, Spyke had disappeared, too.

Fortunato wondered if Spyke had gotten himself into trouble, having committed a bit of light treason in Gallia. Fortunato thought the Imperial government would recognize Spyke's face, but only participants in the Gallian War would know Fortunato's.

And so Fortunato and Wrinn had continued to operate, and Xan had continued to pray loudly, as the search for Reev seemed futile. And Fortunato wondered in the end if Xan's words contained truth, if Reev had washed into the sea, and the mission was over.

Fortunato, however, would not give up until he knew.

And for now, Fortunato of Ríva seemed an unknown in Imperial City, and the traitor general who had fought against his own country walked unmolested in the streets of the city he had fought against.

Yet for Fortunato and for Reev, time was running out.

In the chilly Albos air, as far away he could hear the crashing of the waves against Imperial Harbor's breakwater, Fortunato searched Imperial Square, yet again, in vain, and had a thought that perhaps Reev was not in Imperial City at all, that the barrel had swept him further across the shore, and he was in some flyspeck town on the Imperial coast.

But Fortunato had an unshakeable feeling that the one he searched for was close.

~

What Astarthe had told him was not the full story. Astarthe had provided a frame, and it seemed she was unwilling to paint the whole picture.

As Reev looked down on the swarming crowds of Imperial Square, from his high vantage point in his Imperial Palace bedroom, he tried to piece together what she had told him, that Telantis had ruled the world in peace and justice, and that its founding had come with "the vanquishing of the Sons of Nachash."

Astarthe had said that, like the Telantines were a people, the Sons and Daughters of Nachash were a people too, and that the Telantines and the Sons of Nachash were natural enemies, opposed by their very natures. It was with the vanquishing of the Sons of Nachash that Telantis was born.

It was all a little hard to fathom.

He did not have a clear image of the Sons of Nachash in his mind. When he thought of the Telantines, he thought of himself, or the idealized imagined memory of his mother.

What did the Sons of Nachash look like, they who were opposed to him due to his blood?

He did not know. He only knew he had to get out of the palace. But he would not leave without his amulet. And Astarthe refused to give it to him, holding him hostage until she told him what he knew, why he had worn the coin of Telantis about his neck.

He wore the coin because he was a Telantine, but he would not tell Astarthe that, yet.

There was a knock on the door, and Reev looked back. When the dark door opened, and the one standing there was not Astarthe, Reev repressed a sharp gasp.

He was tall, wearing a thin breastplate, with iron kneepads over tight fitting woolen trousers. About his shoulder was a red half cape. His attire was not that of a soldier, but of something else. And in his hand was a purple nightstick of iron, as tall as a walking stick, at the tip the portrait of a god, depicted as an old man with a beard — was it Alabaster?

The tall, muscular figure before Reev had a head of brown hair that was puffed up in places, hazel eyes, and a disarming confidence that could not help but put Reev at ease.

But Reev remembered where he was, and that ease evaporated.

"My signore," he said, "sorry to have startled you. I am Giufrio Vallo, Marshal of the Guard. I'm sure you know, the palace is a bit unsettled as of late. I am charged with His Excellency's personal security. Surely, it would not trouble you too much to answer a few questions."

Reev stirred. He didn't know what to do. He didn't know how to act in this place, where he did not belong.

So he kept silent as Giufrio approached, and Reev eyed his purple nightstick, which could surely split skulls and crack bones, but which Reev thought, acted foremost as a symbol of the authority that had been delegated to him.

"Astarthe, Her Eminence, wife of Appian, claims you are her consort," Giufrio said. "She claims you are a prince from Gad."

Reev nodded his head.

"But there have been no princes in Gad for some seven hundred years," Giufrio said, "and I am not sure if the Getic barbarians ever used the title 'prince' among themselves."

Reev did not know what to say. He did not like to lie, and he was not good at it. Whenever he tried to lie, people seemed to be able to tell. "I am a prince of another kind," said Reev. "And I am from Gad. From Noricum, in fact."

"Your accent makes it seem that way," said Giufrio.

Reev had spent his formative years in the town of Norwood. Nothing he said was untrue. Norwood, least of the towns of Noricum, was his hometown.

"You are not the only one of Noricum in the palace," said

Giufrio. "Great men have come from there. The emperor Numa, in fact."

Reev did not know much about Emperor Numa, nor did he know much about the Imperial coastlands where he now found himself. All he wanted was to complete his mission, to leave the Imperial Palace with the amulet his grandfather had left to him, and speed on his way to *Naron Da*. All he wanted was to crush Seymus underfoot.

"Your name is Reev Nax," said Giufrio, "this, I have gathered. I have learned other things, too. For one of my tasks is to investigate. And some have claimed Astarthe's story is false, that you did not arrive with Her Eminence the day before New Year's Eve, but that you arrived in the palace another way."

Reev looked at Giufrio blankly. And he had a feeling, one that had no basis in observed truth or circumstance, that Giufrio was trustworthy, and that amid a brood of vipers, he was no serpent.

"You're telling me the truth," said Giufrio, "correct?"

"Listen to Astarthe," Reev said. "She has no reason to lie."

"Something else," Giufrio began teasingly, "some said you were wearing a necklace when you got here. What happened to it?"

"I never had a necklace," Reev said, and his conscience was struck, and he was about to retract his lie, when amid the silence the sound of shouting broke out, deafening noise, and weeping and wailing.

Reev followed Giufrio's fleeing form, to retract the lie perhaps, and he was out in the open, amid the palace's richness and art-lined corridors, and at last in a room colored purple, a balcony looking out to sea, and standing amid the carpet and rugs the form of Valeria Verra and a crowd that included Astarthe, screaming.

Reev was amid the crowd, then, a prince from the town of Noricum in Gad, or so he had said, as Giufrio tried to restore order, and at last lifted up his purple nightstick, and the panicked crowds fell silent.

"What happened?" Giufrio said. "Tell me."

Valeria Verra was weeping. "Khando took a fall."

And Giufrio rushed over, then turned to the crowd, as Reev remembered, Khando was the emperor's son, and that the fall from such a height was a drop of many fathoms, which none could survive.

~

"We've checked the temples to Amara that house the homeless," said Fortunato. "We've checked the barracks in the Metropolitan. We've scoured the Suburro and the west side. What have we left out, Wrinn? Help me out."

Amid the crowds, Wrinn had a slumped look, defeated.

"Fortunato," Xan said, "I don't think Reev is in Imperial City."

But Wrinn answered and said, "He is here."

The dull afternoon colors were fading to red and bronze.

Spyke was missing... where had he gone?

And for the better part of two weeks, they had engaged in this fruitless search, during these days of Albos. Amid a winter wind, the crowds seemed to be stirring.

And Fortunato knew what was happening before the voices of Imperial Square's favorite actors were buzzing in his ears like a stinging gnat.

"Say Rufo," said Sylvia, "I'm feeling a little something. A little dizzy."

"You'd best be careful," Rufo said. "The stage is pretty high, you might take a fall. Have you heard the one about the Good King Anastasios who took a tumble from a high tower and died, and his kingdom was taken from him?"

"Say," Sylvia said, "that sounds familiar. Can I play Queen Pythia?"

~

Reev had returned to the room in which Astarthe had been hiding him. He was pacing about, and he wondered if he should flee without his necklace.

But it was his grandfather's heirloom. It was one of the last items of Telantis that remained in Varda. And besides being his and his people's insignia, he had a feeling it would be wrong to leave without it, that the gods wanted him to keep it.

And so he remained as the Imperial Palace exploded into chaos for a second time, and as Reev worried he would be caught in the path of deadly ambitions and plots.

Reev would lay low for now, and try to navigate the storm, until Astarthe relented and gave him back his amulet, and sped him on his way.

As he sat, waiting for the arrival of his matron, the architectural flaw in his room began to work wonders once again.

"Oh, Verrus," said the voice of Valeria Verra, having put aside her fake tears, "the emperor seems to love me dearly."

There was a pause.

"A passionate night last night," said Valeria Verra, "the eve of such a tragedy. Oh, the burdens I bear for you, sweet Verrus."

"So you had a hand in all this," said the voice of Verrus, deep yet nasal.

"You have your father's hair," said Valeria Verra. "Why can't you have his craftiness and desire for power?"

"I'd like power," said Verrus. "But Father had black hair."

"It looked red to me…"

~

Like clockwork, night was setting in, and like clockwork, the crowds were growing rougher. Fortunato, so desperate now, was willing to try about anything, to fight in the streets on the chance he could beat the truth out of some ruffian, and learn that Reev was being held hostage in a Suburran slum.

But he had no reason to think that had been Reev's fate. And he had two others in his charge, Wrinn, barely a man, and Xan, whose former life had made him fragile.

"Another day, another failure," said Fortunato.

And Fortunato was tempted to have a drink for the first time they had departed on the doomed ship *Velatari*, and the mission to tread Seymus underfoot had run aground on a sandbar across Imperial Harbor. But he would not drink, for he would keep all his wits about him. He could not afford to have his mind at ease. For it should not be at ease.

They were walking through the doors of a new inn Fortunato had picked out. They stayed at a new inn each night, for Fortunato knew that rumors would swirl, and that eventually it would be known that the traitor general had come to Imperial City.

When that knowledge reached the emperor's ears, it was over.

When Wrinn stormed through the doors of "The Mad Philosopher," his tongue was dry, and what he had been descending from their rented room to do in the night to avoid Fortunato's disapproval, now, he could not wait another moment to do in the open.

With two copper coins from the coinpurse that belonged to the party as a whole, he strode up to the bar, and he ordered a tall glass of ale.

He did not care that Fortunato looked on. And he did not care that in the Empire, the choice was one most common to barbarians. For wine, watered down, was the Imperials' drink of choice, and Wrinn could no longer abide wine watered down. Nor could he bear waiting until the dark hours of the night until to do so. It had been that rough a day.

"A beer, coming up," said the barkeep.

And Wrinn's mouth watered as the liquid gold bubbled down from the tap, into a glass made just for him. His tongue delighted at the sight; his mind took pleasure in what was surely Fortunato's wrathful look behind him.

And he took a drink, and he drank richly.

At last… a pleasure granted him. He needed it badly.

He looked back and saw Fortunato and Xan at their table, and the angry look he had expected had not materialized.

But the ale, bubbling in the glass, now rolling down his throat, had been worth the price. Yet someone had sat next to him, someone not in their party, an Imperial a bit down on his luck, judging by his ragged unwashed tunic that had seen better days.

And Wrinn saw, he had a glass of ale, too.

"Elder," he was saying to Wrinn, using the Imperial term for "elf." "Crazy times we live in, huh?"

Wrinn looked at him blankly.

"You haven't heard?" the Imperial said. "The emperor's son, fallen from one of the palace towers… I saw his mangled body with my own two eyes. I think, someone pushed him…"

And something else came to Wrinn in that moment, a realization, as the night wore on.

~

"How are you holding up?" said Astarthe to Reev in the room where she had stowed him.

"Can I have my necklace, so that I can be on my way?" Reev said quietly.

"I will give it to you," Astarthe said, "if you will tell me why you bear it."

"And if I tell you why I bear it," Reev said, "will you speed me on my way? I have important business elsewhere."

"Business outside Imperial City?" Astarthe said. "You said you were shipwrecked. Where were you going?"

"And you said you had a vision of me in the harbor," Reev said. "Are you a seer? Can you then divine the truth?"

"Not quite a seer," Astarthe said. "Once, I was a budding sorceress. But when I married Appian, I gave up my powers. Perhaps, it was a flash of insight from my former life."

"Who is Appian?" Reev said.

Astarthe looked out the window, into the dark night. "My husband's presence is still felt here, rest his soul. The Governor of Khazidea. He has been dead many years. He was the Emperor Numa's best friend, and he led the Empire through many crises. He was worshipped as a god in the East, but he hated that and was never comfortable with it. In fact, the Imperial Council had to stop him from attempting to stamp that out."

"Your husband," Reev repeated her words, and then he looked out, too, into the night, the lights of Imperial City like stars bunched together.

"My husband," said Astarthe. "He was from the provinces. The Imperial elites considered him a bumpkin, but they could never seem to thwart him.

"A provincial, from a minor noble family. He was Imperial through and through, but in his romantic affections, he craved the exotic."

Reev looked at Astarthe, and saw that she was smiling, remembering her husband wistfully.

"The exotic… look at me," Astarthe said. "The Queen of Haroon, when that title existed. I bore him two daughters. I gave up my sorcery for him. I do not regret it. In my seventy-four years, he was my guiding star, my only love. And now he is gone."

"He seems to cast a long shadow over this place," said Reev.

"A long shadow," Astarthe said. "Not a strong enough phrase."

"May I have my amulet, Astarthe?" Reev said.

Astarthe's smile grew faint. "Not until you tell me why you bear it, Reev Nax."

~

"The actors," Wrinn said to Fortunato under the soft candlelight of the inn, "are telling us what goes on in the Imperial Palace."

When Wrinn said the words, Fortunato thought it unlikely, but then he pondered it, and questioned.

"Nonsense," Xan said.

"Perhaps," Fortunato said, "in a city where any word spoken against the inhabitants of the palace is punished with death, the truth manages to find its way out, in some hidden channel."

"And so the empress is dead by poison," Wrinn said.

"Speak quietly," Fortunato said.

"Her son is dead, too," Wrinn said at a whisper.

"But none of this will help us find Reev," Xan said. "Stay focused, Wrinn."

Fortunato looked about in the dim light. There were men entering with scars and scowls, and men entering with the reddish eyes that were the telltale sign of Haroon spice. The roughness of Imperial Square outside was beginning to filter into the Mad Philosopher.

~

At the witching hour, surely, Reev was stirred awake.

"The funeral is tomorrow," said the voice of Valeria Verra. "Be on your best behavior. Don't act suspicious."

"Shall I play my kithara?" said Verrus. "I have a more joyful occasion in mind, for that," said Valeria Verra.

Chapter Seven: Dark Avenger

The funeral took place underneath the light of the palace dome.

The Maestro of Undertakers had used the latest technology to dress up Khando, but the emperor's son was still mangled and all the chalk powder and alchemical compounds could not take away the look of hopeless terror on his face.

And so, under the palace dome, underneath the fresco of the Apotheosis of Claudio, the gathered members of Khandaraeus's court had gathered.

Well, Giufrio noted, except the emperor himself. The doors to the palace dome were too narrow for the cart to fit through, the cart that transported the emperor. And the emperor himself was tired and exhausted, and had denied the Maestro of Undertakers' idea to demolish part of the wall, or hold the funeral in a nontraditional room for the emperor's designated heir.

Giufrio observed the gathered faces, though he had determined it was not his bias that led him to the obvious culprit. And so he did not even glance at Valeria Verra, the object of his newfound enmity, but saw that Astarthe and her consort were present.

The priest of Imperium began his soliloquy. "Gathered friends," he said, "we come to mourn the departed, one on whom the authority of Imperium was poised to rest. But Imperium had other designs, one which shall in the end surely bear forth the cause of the Empire's power and might." It was Valeria Verra that had other designs. Giufrio wasn't looking at her.

He was having a hard time looking at the body, too.

Yet Giufrio swallowed his pride, threatening to break free. He continued to look, to gaze, to watch and observe. And he noted that Valeria Verra's clumsy son was nowhere in sight.

But the doors to the palace dome opened, and then he was.

The doors to the palace slammed shut, and judging by the look of concealed aggression on Verrus's face, it seemed he wanted the doors to slam.

He was holding a kithara. Giufrio wanted to run for the hills.

And Valeria Verra, he noted, in the span of a moment was staring daggers at her son.

"Hello, friends and family of Khando, of which I am one," said Verrus. "I know that *some* people think I shouldn't use my gifts, but my gifts were given to me, and it would be a shame if I just hid them in the dark, especially on such an occasion. I find the sound of the kithara to be quite healing.

He began to pluck the strings. "This is called, 'Be Gone, Death!' "

O Death, Eater of Worlds
Fashioned on the chthonian plain!
Whom shall stand against you
On the wine-dark sea I ride?

O Death, dark avenger
On the lightless seas you arrive
Avast! Be Gone! No more!
Else the world will fall to me

Verrus's fingers for once seemed to pluck the right notes, at the right time and the right frequency. His voice for once seemed to carry well, and a hint of passion to be in it.

And something else Giufrio thought, the thought of the boy taken to temple each feast-day at Villa Regis, that the words were true, but that they did not speak of the notoriously slothful and negligent Khando, nor Verrus, but that the world would fall to someone else.

Who then would the world fall to? And which world? Varda?

Valeria Verra huffed and stormed out of the room. Verrus's weak eyes followed after her, seemingly touched by regret.

There were muttered utterances of satisfaction among those gathered under the palace dome, under "The Apotheosis of Claudio."

~

Though the suspect was beyond doubt, and in Giufrio's mind Valeria Verra was already a murderer, Giufrio knew the emperor was the law embodied, and that to no law he was subject, and none under his protection would face the law's wrath.

And so that night, the night of the funeral, he watched with trepidation and disappointment the emperor Khandaraeus seemingly unbothered by the death of his son, having invited Valeria Verra to his table, and seemingly unable to keep his hands off her.

Giufrio wouldn't let it stop his pursuit of the truth.

No, he would use this disgusted feeling to dig even deeper.

His disgust would spur him on.

He would get to work in the morning.

The first crime, the first murder, had been of Flavia.

Flavia had been poisoned, and Giufrio had done his research, and thought it likely that a poison mushroom that grew outside the Hollow Hills had been used.

Food tasters were commoners, often criminals, and would have no motivation to slay Flavia, the emperor's wife, née Karbo.

Could Valeria Verra have managed to bribe a food taster? Not without making a stir.

Not without alerting the kitchen maestro, Alsumo.

So Alsumo had to be involved. Alsumo had to have switched the plates, or otherwise ordered the food tasters to stand down. So Alsumo and Valeria Verra were in league.

That raised questions of its own, for Valeria Verra had no official post in the palace. She had married into the Empire's elite, and to her, the palace had given an open invitation.

Perhaps, that was enough of an opening to work her dark magic.

And so, in the light of the dawn, Giufrio sped his way to a place he rather didn't like going, a place that was hostile to the palace and everyone in it, a place opposed to they that dwelled in the palace — even the Marshal of the Guard.

He walked across the Sky Bridge through the doors of the Council House, where the Imperial Council held court.

~

The powers of the Imperial Council had dwindled steadily, year after year and decade after decade. The reforms of Emperor Numa had gutted it, but enterprising councilors had managed to claw some of their power back.

It was still a shadow of what it once had been, however.

As he passed through the pristine marble halls, he saw scornful looks of the blue-caped Council Guard, and glares from the attendants, a sea that followed each of the thirty Imperial Councilors, who represented Imperial City's thirty wards.

The Maestro of Appointments was appointed by the Speaker of the Council. She was a dark-haired woman in a red gown, with dark eyes, and she seemed unhappy at once, as soon as Giufrio stepped into her chambers.

"What is this about?" she said. "Have you taken a wrong turn, Marshal of the Guard?"

"I am sure you have heard," Giufrio said, summoning all his charm, "of the deaths on the other wing of Imperial government. The emperor's wife, the emperor's son. A bit of a crisis, no?"

"Well, we in the Imperial Council don't like a circus," she said, "and we rather wouldn't like you to bring that mayhem here."

"Mayhem," Giufrio said. "For me, it's personal. And it's a crisis for the nation we both serve. I'm trying to get to the bottom of it before it drags the nation down with it.

"Tell me, Signora — "

"Fulvia."

" — Fulvia. Who appoints the kitchen maestro?"

"The Maestro of Wine and the Palace Larder. Akdaro."

Akdaro, another name that sounded of the same ken as "Alsumo."

"And who appoints the Maestro of Wine and the Palace Larder?"

"The Chamber of Wines and Sundries, a body of five appointed by the Maestro of Palatial and Ministerial Appointments."

"And who is that?"

"Thuban."

The name struck Giufrio as familiar.

"And who appointed Thuban?"

"The emperor himself."

So was there a conspiracy, then, in all?

Chapter Eight:
The Rabbit Trail

When the sun arose on what Fortunato thought was sure to be another fruitless day, he thought of Spyke, disappeared, and wondered if it mattered.

Spyke well could have died, yet Fortunato could not afford to add another fruitless search on top of this one.

"Where shall we look today?" Wrinn said from behind him.

"Perhaps, we should leave the city, and search the shore," said Xan.

Fortunato's gaze was looking upward, at the white buildings and the windows, at the colonnades and mansions all about him, and wondered where in this city Reev could be.

Wrinn had a sense — Reev was here.

And Fortunato trusted it.

~

Reev had prayed, and he still felt the gods did not wish to leave the Imperial Palace without the necklace.

He could tell Astarthe what he knew. But would he trust her? Could he tell someone in such a nest of vipers that Telantis lived?

Perhaps, even someone sympathetic to the True Empire wasn't ready for such truth. Perhaps, in someone who said they were sympathetic, it would spur her to betray him.

Could he risk it?

Yet he would not leave... he would not leave without his grandfather's amulet, the coin necklace of Telantis.

There was motion through his open door. There were two lanky figures garbed in cloaks.

Then there was a face, looking into his room.

The face startled Reev, wrinkled and gray, with long gray hair.

There had been one face, and then there were two.

The second face had the same sallow complexion at the first, but to that face was added a dark charisma, one that seemed to stir, rather than devotion, fear. His eyes were dull and brown, and to Reev they looked soupy.

"Signore," said the second man, and his speech had an accent Reev couldn't place, "what are you doing in Appian's old workroom?"

"They have painted it, Thuban," said the first man. "They have turned it into a bedchamber."

"Quiet, Alsumo," said Thuban.

And Thuban strode in, and he saw that Thuban's robe was darker than Alsumo's.

"You are Astarthe's consort, no?" said Thuban.

"I am," Reev said, and there was no lie in it, though he was nothing more than a young man Astarthe hooked by the arm, an accessory for Astarthe at grand parties and occasions.

"And you claim to be a prince," said Thuban.

"I do," said Reev.

The elves, after all, had called him the Prince of the Dawn.

"I am sorry, I and Alsumo are a bit suspicious," Thuban said. "We know unwelcome parties have come to Imperial City."

"Imperial City?" said Reev.

"A traitor general," Thuban said. "And another who accompanies him, whom we cannot find."

Fortunato. Reev's heart leapt in joy. Fortunato and the party were not far.

Reev tried not to react, tried not to show any sign of emotion.

Alsumo and Thuban exchanged glances and then slipped out of the room.

And Reev thought, and wondered, if he should find Astarthe's room and locate his coin amulet himself, then flee the palace.

But then he thought, how would he find Fortunato?

And another thought, darker, if he had come to Imperial City looking for Reev, and the Imperial government wished him imprisoned, was he already locked up in a jail?

And if not, why not?

"No, no," the voice of Alsumo said. They had ducked into Valeria Verra and Verrus's room, and the flaw in the architecture was amplifying their voices. "We shall not just kill any intruder into the palace. It would draw suspicion, when our victory is nigh..."

"You do not think he is the Telantine," said the voice of Thuban.

"It is unlikely," the voice of Alsumo said. "And our people were thwarted by Claudio, and then they were thwarted by Numa. If we kill everyone we might suspect, the Imperial Council will take notice and foil our plans..."

After Alsumo spoke, there was a long pause. Thuban's voice at last was heard, clearly audible through the flaw in the wall. "He is not a Telantine, anyway... He cannot be. The Telantines had shining faces, and by their very gaze could strike down you or I. We will let him alone... I agree."

~

Though the emperor was wooing Valeria Verra, or rather, was being wooed, Giufrio had continued his work, to investigate, to somehow thwart what now seemed inevitable. Wherever the emperor was, Valeria Verra was sure to be found. And the Imperial Council could not be bothered to care about what happening a short walk across the Sky Bridge.

What was happening was obvious to anyone with a small bit of sense, but in the Imperial Palace anyone who raised a fuss or spoke out of turn was likely to be beheaded in Imperial Square and dumped in the South River. After all, the emperor held everyone's life in his hands, and the emperor now seemed to love Valeria Verra.

Giufrio had begun asking around about Thuban to those who had earned his trust. He had learned from the records in the Conciliar Library that Thuban had been appointed last year, and that in addition to making appointments in the Imperial palace kitchen he had also appointed the ward legate of the Metropolitan, and was attempting to name a new leader for the urban cohort, the only legion allowed to operate within the bounds of Imperial City. Red tape had bogged him down in that effort, and the fact that Thuban's tentacles were quickly spreading throughout the breadth of the Imperial state put a fire in Giufrio.

Yet Giufrio had learned in the Council House that Khandaraeus had appointed Thuban himself, in Brenua of last year. Khandaraeus would not have arranged the murder of his wife and his son. So what indeed had occurred?

Giufrio took a look at those gathered at the dining hall. There were so many unanswered questions.

And it frustrated Giufrio to no end that the emperor was above the law. He was the law.

It was a shame.

It had not always been this way.

The doors to the dining hall opened and servants began to ferry out silver dishes and goblets of wine. A pungent smell filled the room. When Giufrio opened the covering to his silver dish, he saw a dinner he had seen once before, and never dared to eat.

Sea urchins in a sauce of fermented fish. It turned the stomach, but it would be impolite not to eat, and Giufrio had seen Khandaraeus shove this monstrosity down his gullet before.

It was time to be brave.

But then there was a sound, one only the most obnoxious people make, the ringing of a fork against a wine goblet. And when he saw who made it, Valeria Verra, Giufrio was not surprised.

Valeria Verra's face was powdered so thickly with chalk she looked like a pantomime in Imperial Square. Her gown was purple — a crime, Giufrio remembered, wearing purple when you weren't part of the emperor's family, considered treason… the penalty, death.

But Khandaraeus was the law.

Rats.

Yet Valeria Verra's obnoxious gesture had caused the dining hall to fall dead silent. All were looking at her. She was standing tall over everyone. "My good friends, these winter days have been so rough for His Excellency's Court. So many tragedies have befallen us all, and I for one can't wait to bid the month of Albos farewell. But I have exciting news to share with you, something that is sure to cheer your heart.

"His Excellency Khandaraeus and I are getting married on the third day of the month of Kaldsil, just days from now. The reception will be held on the Great Porch with officiating done by the Chief Priest of Imperium. Everyone here is invited."

Giufrio spat some of his wine back into the cup.

Someone cleared their throat loudly amid the dining hall.

"Entertainment will be done by my son Verrus," said Valeria Verra, softly, more sheepishly. Then her bold craftiness returned as before. "The reception will be held in the dining hall at vespers. And I suppose that means, you're looking at your new empress."

There were no cheers of celebration, nothing more than blank expressions and looks of hidden worry. It seemed everyone knew what was going on except the emperor.

The emperor didn't know much.

Giufrio would let this light a fire under him. He had to act quickly.

He didn't know if he was on the right track. But Flavia had been poisoned. And if Alsumo was responsible, Thuban had installed him.

Thuban…

How deep did the rabbit trail go?

Late in the night in the Conciliar Library, while the rest of Khandaraeus's court was meant to be sleeping, Giufrio brought a candle amid the countless rows of towering shelves, records of the ages stored.

He had learned in this time that Thuban's position, Maestro of Palatial and Ministerial Appointments, gave him sweeping control of the personnel of the Imperial Palace and much of the military. Giufrio had also learned that the former occupant of the position, Noria, had disappeared while sailing in the Imperial Sea.

Giufrio did not quite know how to connect Thuban and Valeria Verra, in fact, they seemed to have nothing to do with each other, Valeria Verra living at the time in the navy town of Nichaeus and Thuban living his whole life in the Imperial City ward of Celsus Heights.

Yet something else he saw, the appointment of Thuban was done under the recommendation of Dario Corvinus, the husband of Appenina the Younger, who as of now was in the Imperial Palace chambers with his wife. Dario had recommended the appointment of Thuban, as noted in the minutes of the Imperial Council, Brenua 11, 1154.

This all could not wait, for the monster was inching closer to her goal, the title of empress or perhaps something more. Dario Corvinus could afford a sleepless night.

The Empire depended on it.

~

In the end, Dario was not in bed, but playing cards in the parlor with Giufrio's second-in-command, Barcho.

On the table, both of them had wine glasses and stank of the stuff.

In wine, truth.

"Dario," Giufrio said. "Can I have a moment of your time?"

Dario's brown hair glistened in the light of the candle on the table. "Sure thing, Giufrio," Dario said.

In the privacy amid the busts of the Anthans Corridor, Giufrio leveled with Dario.

"Why did you recommend the appointment of Thuban to Khandaraeus?" Giufrio said.

And Dario in that moment seemed to remember what, to him at the time, had been forgettable. "Well, you know, the Corvinus family are in the shipwright business. The Imperial Bay Company was threatening to withhold its shipments of tar unless Jiacomo Thuban was appointed. I thought the Imperial Bay Company had their reasons. I didn't think much of it."

The Imperial Bay Company was the most powerful assemblage of merchants in the Imperial world, so much so that various emperors at times had tried to set shackles on it. They held monopolies on sugar and tar by law, and dominated the spice trade. They were so rich and so powerful, various members of the Imperial Council were said to be bought off. The Imperial Council had passed resolutions "condemning such slander," however.

"Khandaraeus made the appointment on my behalf," said Dario. "And tar's available and cheap. What is there to complain about?"

There was a lot to complain about, Giufrio now knew.

But he still couldn't connect Valeria Verra to Thuban. Valeria Verra's wealth did not come from the Imperial Bay Company, but instead from banking. The Verrus family gained its wealth from the

Venerable Brotherhood of Moneychangers.

"Asking a lot of questions, aren't you," said Dario, "and yet not doing the best of jobs." He had an offended look, like Giufrio suspected his hand in Flavia's murder. "That supposed 'consort' that Astarthe brought into the palace did not arrive with her. He was found clinging to a barrel in Imperial Harbor. A shipwreck was found not far-off, abandoned…"

Chapter Nine:
Foiled

Giufrio was empty-handed on the third day of Kaldsil.

The Imperial Bay Company had engineered the appointment of Thuban, and though Giufrio was certain there was a connection to Valeria Verra, he had not assembled the pieces before the dread day.

And so he watched members of the court, dressed up and smelling of ointments and perfume, walking toward the Great Porch as the wedding began. Giufrio shuddered inwardly, but tried to keep his cool. He was the last arrive, stepping in.

Beyond the porch, the glittering sea and the vista of Imperial Harbor, the faint horizon of Dualmis, stole the breath of the uninitiated, if the brightly colored tile and the twin statues of Emperor Claudio and Emperor Numa did not do so already.

Giufrio saw that Astarthe was there, but that her consort, who had a lot of explaining to do, was not. The priest of Imperium was waiting for the bride and bridegroom to arrive.

Verrus was standing off with his kithara, a nervous look in his eyes.

Giufrio took his seat in the back of the assembled court, the last to arrive, and as he did, there was the blaring sound of a double aulos.

Where the aulos-player stood, the doors were opened, and through the dimness of the palace interior Giufrio made out the sight of the cart used to transport the emperor. Yet the cart was budging against the frame of the door.

How had the planners of the wedding been so negligent?

The double aulos continued to blare, as engineers were summoned, and the whole of the door frame and the door removed, and an hour after the wedding was set to begin, the cart broke free of its roadblock, and emperor Khandaraeus was wheeled to his place.

The aulos player looked winded.

But now, he had a break.

For the bride now appeared, Valeria Verra, wearing an off-white gown, her black hair dressed up in flowers. She wore no veil, against all custom and tradition. She wanted everyone to see how beautiful she was, at all times, in all situations, at all places.

She was just that vain.

As she walked up the aisle, Giufrio laughed inwardly that a woman of such noblesse and beauty would be interested in a man like Khandaraeus for anything besides Khandaraeus's power.

And as she walked up the aisle, Verrus began to strum his kithara, and sing a song.

O Isdar, panting in the night
The shining one
Panting after the one she loves
The nubile queen
How many has she brought to her?
The shining one
Does Isdar now pant after him?
Bring her fertility to me

There were disgusted looks in the crowd, and Valeria Verra shot Verrus a glare that Giufrio thought could kill, but quickly recovered. She cleared her throat, and as the priest of Imperium began his soliloquy, a crane was ferried in from the dark corners of the room, and slowly lifted up Khandaraeus's massive body. Other servants ferried him a walker.

It seemed he wanted to stand at his own wedding, as was custom.

But his knees wobbled as he stood upright, and Giufrio cringed.

The priest of Imperium, dressed in a white robe, began to speak. "Soko Kattibo, called Khandaraeus, and Valeria Verra, have been brought together in the bonds of matrimony by the almighty Will of Imperium. And we know, the Will of Imperium only brings together men and women to further the Empire's power and might.

"And so I ask, Valeria Verra, do you take Soko Kattibo, called Khandaraeus, as your lawful wedded husband?"

Valeria Verra smiled and turned to the crowd. "I've been married three times, I'm not ashamed to say. I've been through it before, and I have to say, it takes a very special man to make me walk down this aisle again."

Giufrio wanted to vomit.

Valeria Verra's false smile grew, and a false twinkle appeared. Then came the beginnings of fake tears in her eyes. "You're special, Khandaraeus. So the answer to your question, Signor — "

The priest was looking at her in disbelief.

He wouldn't give her his name.

"The answer to your question, Signore Priest, is absolutely, positively yes."

Now, actual vomit was forming in the back of Giufrio's throat.

"And Soko Kattibo, called Khandaraeus, do you take Valeria Verra as your lawful wedded wife?" the priest said.

Khandaraeus opened his mouth, what came out was a squeak. And so he lifted his right arm, and his knees buckled. He was breathing heavily. He gave a thumbs up.

The priest of Imperium said, "I now pronounce you man and wife. You may now kiss the bride."

Valeria Verra, eyeing the crane and the cart, said, "How about we save that for later tonight?"

~

The feast was a dull affair. Valeria Verra continually eyed the room, examining, suspecting, making evaluations of who was there and who was not, and clearly dropping by tables, and attempting to eavesdrop. What she had engineered had finally come to fruition.

Or had it?

As Giufrio finished the last of his lamb brain, he had a terrible sinking feeling.

Chapter Ten: On a Barrel

Sylvia and Rufo were on the stage, and by now, Fortunato, Xan and Wrinn were eager listeners, having come to realize just what actors' jobs were in Imperial City.

Last afternoon, they had watched the story of the Famine of Sarxia — "a cut to the dole was coming," the crowds had remarked.

The afternoon before that, they had heard the story of Prothymus, the tragic hero who killed his father and married his mother. Fortunato didn't want to find out what that play meant, and took pains not to learn.

And now the stage was set up, though it was night.

It was night, and the crowds were rough, but Fortunato thought it would be irresponsible not to learn the way the gathered mob did.

Torches were set up on all four corners of the stage.

The faces of Sylvia and Rufo were wreathed in orange light.

It was Sylvia that began, this time.

"Say, Rufo," said Sylvia. "What will we talk about this time?"

"I don't know, Sylvia," Rufo said.

"How about barrels?" Sylvia said. "Barrels, and the people who cling to them…"

"I know all about people clinging to barrels," Rufo said. "In fact, someone clinging to one last night, at my house. Things were getting pretty hot and heavy…"

There was scattered laughter amid the crowd.

"Quiet, Rufo," said Sylvia. "I'm talking about the goddess Amara… clinging to a barrel, drifting toward the heavenly shore, transported to the realm of the gods."

"Is that how the story goes?" Rufo said.

"That's how *this* story goes," Sylvia answered.

~

Reev awoke to a blood-curdling scream. It was still dark outside his window, but Reev had a feeling that dawn was just about to make its presence known.

Through his doorway, Giufrio flashed by like a zephyr. And curiosity drove Reev after him, charging forth in his wake.

Reev followed Giufrio as Giufrio was joined by others, through doors and dark hallways, into the emperor's chambers, and at last his bedroom.

Amid purple majesty, there was red, everywhere — blood on the carpet, blood soaking the sheets, and blood all over the massive body of Khandaraeus. His wrists were slit, and in his right hand was a knife.

Valeria Verra was standing beside him, her gown spotted with blood. "Oh, I tried to stop him! I tried to stop him!" Tears were pouring down her cheeks. "He couldn't please me on his wedding night, and he decided he couldn't live another day…"

Giufrio then rushed to her and seized her by the hand, as if to tackle her.

"Lay off me, common-blood," Valeria Verra hissed, and no longer the mourning wife she was but the avatar of wrath.

A hand grasped Reev's, Astarthe — he turned and saw on her wizened face alarm, controlled panic.

In Reev's private bedchamber, Appian's former workroom, she said, "We shall go to safety. We shall flee this place and not be caught in the mayhem… we shall go where it is safest. Where is it safest?"

"Telantis," Reev said in jest.

But Astarthe's eyes were serious. "Yes, we shall go to Telantis," she said.

~

Reev was in the palace, that was what the party had determined, Fortunato, Wrinn, and Xan. In the light of the dawn, as they stepped out the doors of "The Happy She-Goat."

For who else had clung to a barrel in Imperial Harbor? And Sylvia and Rufo, using Amara in place of Reev, had said he had been transported to the realm of the gods, a dramatic stand-in for a grand place he did not belong.

Fortunato knew Reev did not belong here. He, and all of his party, belonged somewhere much better than that den of schemers.

Fortunato, Wrinn and Xan walked out into the midst of Imperial Square and crossed its breadth amid the growing crowds.

Across from the hippodrome, the palace's mismatched assembly of towers and additions, balconies and alcoves dominated the equivalent of three city blocks. From it, a Sky Bridge projected, connecting it to the towering Council House.

Whether by guile or by force, whether it took an army or overpowering force of will, Fortunato would enter in, and snatch the Sage from the nest of vipers wherein he was held prisoner.

He uttered a vow to the gods in the stillness of the morning.

Chapter Eleven:
He Walked On the Moon

The waves raged on the carrack as it traversed the rough waters of the Imperial Sea. Reev had said in jest they would take shelter in Telantis, and Astarthe had rushed him onto her private ship, and sailed out of Imperial Harbor, despite the danger of winter storms.

Reev felt safer amid the roiling waves and the howling winter wind than he did in the palace, where Valeria Verra and her son lurked.

They had been days out to shore, yet life aboard *The Northward Star* was not rough going. Astarthe's personal chef made them, each morning and each night, meals that put *Velatari's* ship's biscuit to shame. Grain and dried meat they cooked into stews in the ship's galley, amid the winter wind and frosty waves, for Astarthe and her platonic consort.

And Reev did not quite know where they were going, but he was glad to be as far away from Valeria Verra and her son as possible.

~

The skies were clear, and the waves were still, when their journey ended. They were amid islands of black silt, which circled around a spot of open sea.

Reev said, "Where are we?"

And Astarthe, garbed now in a yellow gown that fell to her knees, said, "You wanted Telantis. So I took you there. We are in the middle of the Imperial Sea."

Reev gazed at the islands, and the vastness of the waters.

It was risky to sail in winter and few did it, but here they were.

"The rim of a mountain that erupted into fire, and sank it and all the land around it into the sea," said Astarthe. "Some said the Telantines died, but I don't think so."

"What do you mean?" Reev said.

"I think," Astarthe said, "that time and space bent, and that the Telantines were spirited away, leaving only two bloodlines left, so that the sons of Telantis could vanquish the sons of Nachash in Varda, too."

In Varda, too, she had said.

The sun was shining bright.

And Reev said, "I am a Telantine."

Astarthe answered, "I know."

~

They turned around, and no longer faced winter weather. For many days the sailing was smooth. But as they broached the island of Dualmis and Imperial City, the seas had become rough again.

They were back in Imperial Harbor, and when they returned, they returned at dawn.

The skies were a fiery crimson, staggering in their intensity of red color and flame-orange clouds.

Before Reev and Astarthe reached the palace, tension was palpable in Imperial City, threatening to break free.

And rumor preceded them, that the emperor's will was read, that Valeria Verra's son Verrus was now to occupy the throne.

"A Telantine man walked on the moon," said Astarthe softly as they entered into Reev's private chamber. "You have nothing to fear from the Sons of Nachash."

Chapter Twelve: Amarothic

As soon as the will was read, the papers of coronation were delivered to the Imperial Council.

As soon as the Imperial Council received the papers, they summoned the prospective emperor, as was customary.

Giufrio followed the schemer through the halls, as the law demanded, and Valeria Verra was following them both.

~

The seats of the Imperial Council ringed the Council Chamber in a circle, set high above anyone they wished to question or impugn. Thirty faces looked down on Giufrio, Marshal of the Guard, Verrus, prospective emperor, and Valeria Verra, his mother.

They were faces of wrath.

The Speaker of the Council, Corvus Corbulo, had a seat high above the others. Like the other councilors, he wore a long white tunic with a purple sash. His hair was white, and he was clean shaven. His eyes were blue, and like the others, his eyes were of wrath.

"Greetings, Verrus, Valeria Verra, and the honorable Giufrio," said Speaker Corbulo. "I would like to congratulate first and foremost Verrus on being named emperor in His Excellency Khandaraeus's will.

"And I would like to give plaudits to him and his mother Verra on executing the most obvious coup imaginable. It is surely one for the record books, the way you engineered the poisoning of Flavia, the death of Khando, and the murder of Khandaraeus in the span of two months."

Valeria Verra howled and hissed. "Slander!" she cried.

But no one believed her, in the Council House nor in the building a short walk on the Sky Bridge away.

"I am tempted to give you an award," said Speaker Corbulo, "for your shameless plot. I will also note you are the consummate actress, and would put to shame any of the hacks who appear on Imperial Square's stages."

Valeria Verra's teeth were barred; she was like a wild animal, ready to tear her prey apart.

"The Imperial Council has been preparing for this moment as we watched your enemies disappear," Speaker Corbulo said, "as Giufrio's negligent hand allowed you to work your dark magic."

Negligent — at least they knew he wasn't in on the plot.

"In your estimation," Speaker Corbulo said, "you thought the reforms of Numa had rendered the Imperial Council powerless. But when all thirty of us are united, the Imperial Council retains great strength."

"I read the law!" Valeria Verra howled. "I studied it. You cannot deny the emperor's will. My son will be on the throne and you cannot stop it!"

"You speak the truth, but only part of it," Speaker Corbulo said. "Indeed, Verrus will be seated, but under the terms of an Amarothic emperorship.

Valeria Verra howled and hissed, and spittle fell on the marble floor, the marble floor on which was painted the Imperial eagle. "What is an Amarothic emperorship?"

"In the fourth century of the Empire, a civil war broke out between an emperor and the Imperial Council," said Corbulo. "The emperor, who was suspected to have committed bribery, refused to exit the White Throne. In the end, the war was settled, a treaty signed in the city of Amaroth... that his powers be restrained at all times, until he was cleared of the crime.

"What is bribery, compared to cold-blooded murder?"

If Valeria was standing an inch from Corbulo, Giufrio had a thought she would try to do to him what she did to Khandaraeus.

"The reforms of Numa overlooked the terms of an Amarothic emperorship. As long as the thirty Imperial Councilors are unanimous, the emperor will be bound to such terms. Each edict he makes, each regulation he issues, must have the support of a majority of the Imperial Council to be given the force of law."

Valeria Verra's face was a bright shade of red. But in Verrus's eyes was a gaze cold and calculating.

"If any councilor objects to such terms, let him speak," said Corbulo.

There was silence.

Valeria Verra screamed and fled through the doors.

"The Amarothic emperorship of Verrus begins on this day, the fourteenth day of the month of Kaldsil, year 1155 of the Empire," Speaker Corbulo said. "In any other era, you and your mother would be food for fishes in the South River."

~

Spyke returned on a cold Kaldsil day to the chambers of Caro Hudnato, ward legate of the Metropolitan.

He had spent the past days at his old haunt, at Fort Modestus in West Limes. He had come back, having read the books of history that Caro Hudnato had given him.

And he realized, if the Prince of the Dawn was descended from such a people, then let the dawn never come.

"Are you ready to play?" said Caro Hudnato.

"I will help you," Spyke said. "I cannot betray my ancestors. I will lead you to Fortunato of Ríva."

"He is not the one we want," said Caro Hudnato.

"I do not know where Reev Nax is," Spyke said.

"Let's wait, then," said Caro Hudnato, "until all of them are in our nets."

Chapter Thirteen: Blood in the Sand

Where to start, Fortunato wondered?

How to begin?

As he stood in Imperial Square, he saw the crowds were swarming, this fifteenth day of Kaldsil. He saw that the crowds were forming into unruly lines, and that all these gathered commoners were waiting for something.

Fortunato walked toward the front of the lines to observe, and Xan and Wrinn followed. He saw they were gathered before desks that had been ferried out, and that before the desks, men and women in the tunics and sashes of the Imperial government were handing out coins and clay tokens.

"The dole," Wrinn said softly behind him. "I heard that you can exchange one of those clay tokens for wine, or for seats at the Arena…"

The Imperial Arena, Fortunato thought. He recalled the Imperial court had a special box.

If Reev was held prisoner, witting or unwitting, was it possible that Fortunato might see a glimpse of him there?

Were they not so desperate that they should try everything?

And Fortunato found himself lingering in the line, and with him Xan and Wrinn. At last they were at the front of the line, and a pudgy-faced man snapped at him, "Which ward do you live in? And which councilor has pledged himself to you?"

"I'm from Ríva," Fortunato said.

"An Imperial citizen," said the man, "is so entitled to a dispersal from the treasury. By law, a citizen of the ward of the Metropolitan… twenty denara should get you through the month. Use these tokens to avail yourself of entertainment and stay out of trouble."

The party's coinpurse got a little fatter. And Fortunato walked south, followed by Xan and Wrinn, in the direction of the arena.

~

There were no buildings for a wide span around the titanic amphitheater.

Before the main entrance was a titanic bronze statue of Kharnus, god of wrestlers and athletes, with two weights in his hands.

The crowds about them were swarming for the afternoon's games.

And Fortunato almost stopped himself, at such a desperate ploy.

But were they not desperate?

Was there not a small chance, infinitesimal, that this could work, and Reev see them, and leap to them from the box's ledge, and disappear amid the furor of the raging crowds?

It was worth a try, Fortunato supposed.

For now, it was, at least.

He could hear Wrinn grumbling behind him.

"Reev," he was saying, "Reev is in danger…"

But in desperation, desperate attempts were, by definition, not foolish.

And he passed under the archways, amid the raging crowds and beside the food and wine vendors, without guilt.

They were seated a good distance from the Imperial box, but if Fortunato craned his neck, he could have a good look at its occupants.

Yet Wrinn was restless, and had not ceased his complaining,

that they were watching these games when Reev was in grave danger.

Fortunato was not a demigod; he could not storm the Imperial Palace and overcome the legions. They would have to try new things, and seemingly desperate gambits, to prevail.

The seats were filling up with people, countless seats circling around a pit of sand. And though Fortunato had been to the amphitheater in Ríva, he knew he had never seen anything so grand in his life. From all corners of Varda, the people of Imperial City were filling in the Imperial Arena. When Fortunato had heard in his youth that the Imperial Arena seated eighty thousand, he hadn't believed it… but now he did.

"My family in Kav wouldn't believe this," said Xan.

Xan, the former warlock, Fortunato remembered was of a princely family of Kav. Fortunato was sure the spires of the Xandrast family castle did well in terrifying the local peasants, but Fortunato could not imagine they would bring such awe as this.

Around the glittering amphitheater, a sea of people had gathered for the afternoon games. Fortunato did not know what to expect. Ríva had its own arena, but he had never been there, and Riva's amphitheater was not so grand as this.

A water organ began to play, piercing in its ghostly melody, and the swarming crowds of people looked up at the Imperial box.

Fortunato looked up and saw the emperor enter, and when he saw who wore the purple robes, it was not a swarthy man of Khandara but someone entirely new, pasty with a head of fiery red hair, thin and yet somehow fat, with blue eyes whose pupils were so black and empty they threatened to steal the soul.

Fortunato wanted to scream. They were only several yards away, the Imperial court, easily seen when Fortunato craned his neck.

He heard someone call out from the stands below, "Our new emperor, Verrus!"

Still craning his neck, Fortunato awaited what he had come for, a glimpse of the one they sought, one he would whose attention he hoped they could gain.

But behind him, instead, came a woman of stunning beauty, fair and black haired, and dressed all in black. Her midnight black eyes seemed as dark in the pupil as Verrus's, yet her effect was one of a night predator fascinating her prey.

"I think that's his mother Verra!" shouted a woman up above Fortunato.

And Fortunato wondered how a woman of such beauty could have given birth to a creature like Verrus.

Behind the emperor and his mother were an assemblage of men in fine tunics of red or blue, and women in silken pastel-colored gowns. But Fortunato, continuing to crane his neck, even as he heard the game music began, saw no sign of Reev.

Reev had not come to these gladiatorial games. Fortunato was not surprised. They were beneath him.

Fortunato at last turned back to the game, now underway before them. The gates had opened and two gladiators had stridden out.

One was garbed head to toe in armor, with a bowed helmet, holding in his hands a trident and a net.

Another was in the nude save for a shield, vambraces and pauldrons; he held a barbed spear in his hand.

"A Myrmidon against a Wilderman!" cried a young man in the seat below Fortunato. "My favorite!"

At once the heavy-armored Myrmidon charged the Wilderman, but the Wilderman stepped with ease away, and the Myrmidon almost tripped.

It became apparent to Fortunato that with the bowed helmet, the armored Myrmidon could scarcely see.

The Myrmidon turned around and gripped his trident again in his hands. Again he came charging. The Wilderman batted with his spear, and his spear grazed the trident. A masterful flick of the wrist, and the trident fell to the sand.

Three strikes fell in quick succession; the first scratched the armor, the second made a dent, and the third found its way through the weaknesses in the armor, and the Myrmidon was impaled straight through. Blood and intestines flew up into the air, and the bloodthirsty crowds began to cheer, all at one, deafeningly, seeming to shake the seats themselves.

There was no sign of Reev. "Wrinn, I think you're right," Fortunato said, but his voice was swallowed up in the noise of the crowd.

And Wrinn had stood to his feet, cheering, with a bloodthirst and fascination in his eyes that Fortunato had never seen before.

After the Myrmidon and the Wilderman came a match between the spear-and-shield wielding Thartan versus the sword-wielding Thenoan. Following that, the victorious Wilderman and the victorious Thenoan did battle.

The sand was now stained crimson, and the barbed spear was still sticking from the dead Thenoan, when the Wilderman took a bow, and the water organ began to play.

"Hail, Aidano, he's our man!" some of the audience around Fortunato began to stir up a chant, but the noise was swallowed up by applause.

After the individual battles came team battles, the Sharks of Nichaeus against the Harbor District Warlords. More blood was spilled, and the sand of the arena was growing redder and redder.

Soon, there was more red than yellow to be seen.

And Fortunato, realizing this was futility, that it would not end in the rescue of Reev, at last shouted loud enough to be heard, "Let's go!"

Xan seemed obliged, but Wrinn said, "No."

After the team battles came battles of the huntsmen, fighting beasts of Varda's dark corners. Then the water organ began to play again, and it was announced there would be a brief intermission before the night games.

"I want to go to the night games!" Wrinn insisted.

And Fortunato was insistently opposed.

~

Wrinn had never watched something that had so fascinated him, he realized. He had watched mortal combat from the safety of the stands. And he realized, exiting swiftly out of the Imperial Arena's expertly designed corridors, that he was no coward, he wished to participate.

He looked around in the courtyard surrounding the Kharnus statue. "I'll meet you back at the Pot of Gold," recalling the inn they had booked for the night.

And Fortunato, seeming to know, and Xan, seeming to suspect, gave him brash smiles, and vanished into the swelling crowds, the mass of people exiting Imperial Arena.

And Wrinn began to inquire, from person to person, about how a person such as he could participate in these games. Some gruffly dismissed him, but others pointed to an office on this or that street, in some scummy area of town.

It was growing late, and the night games were threatening to begin. He was about to risk going to that office in that scummy part of town, where he wondered if a man now lay in wait, when through the crowd a man approached, a man with a scar-pocked face and a harelip.

"Elder," he said, "I overheard you wish to participate in the games. Few wish to throw their life away. But a gladiator can make a pretty denara. And I can see by your staff and your knife you are a warrior. I will sponsor you, if old Scauro can have a cut. Fifty denara, for every hundred you make."

"Thirty," Wrinn insisted.

"How about forty?" Scauro said.

And Wrinn wondered if he should have set his opening bid lower, if he could have gotten more.

Chapter Fourteen:
The Amulet

In the wake of Verrus's accession to emperor, Astarthe had insisted, and Reev had agreed, that he should lay low a few days and bide time before his departure. Astarthe had agreed with Reev that he was in danger, that he should flee with all due speed, but that the manner in which he left the palace was of paramount importance. And bit by bit, he had told her a few details of why he was in Imperial City and how he had ended up here, though not the whole part. Yet Astarthe, now, Reev would trust with the whole truth, and with his life. She loved the Telantines, and she hated the Sons of Nachash.

It was a cold day in Kaldsil when the door to Reev's bedchamber, Appian's former workroom, opened, and the Queen of Khazidea appeared, bright eyed and smiling. She strode in. "Verra and her son are busy," she said as she drew near. "They are observing construction in the Cloaca. They will not notice if you leave, now. Let's go get your amulet, Son of Telantis."

She seemed to recoil, that she had said such a thing too loud. But she turned and Reev followed her, through the nesting web of corridors and antechambers, to a place Reev had never been before — Astarthe's suite.

~

The walls were painted blue, with cloud motifs and amid the clouds the painted forms of cupids with their bows. There were lanterns in every room, spreading light everywhere one walked. There were couches and beds, and divans aplenty, and when they reached Astarthe's bedroom, there was a window overlooking the limitless urban horizon.

"Your amulet," Astarthe said, "I placed it in my keepsake box." She went to a dresser beside her bed and took from it a box of dark brown wood. She opened it, and she gasped, and swallowed a scream.

She looked to Reev, eyes wide like saucers, like a fish hooked from the sea.

"It's gone," she said.

It had been taken. And Reev trusted Astarthe. He believed her story.

"I'm sorry," Astarthe said. "I did not do this — "

"I believe you," Reev said.

And something else he realized.

"I will not leave without it," said Reev.

"Don't be so foolish," Astarthe said. "What is a coin, compared to your life?"

"One of the last things of Telantis that remain in this world," Reev said. "And I feel the gods wish me to have it. I will find it. Who has been in your room, Astarthe? Have you kept a careful account of your company?"

"My daughter," Astarthe said. "Her husband, Dario. But cleaners come at the start of each week, and I am not present. And I leave for feasts, but I always keep the suite locked."

Astarthe gazed deeply into Reev's eyes.

"Do not die for a coin, son of Telantis," said Astarthe. "Is your life not worth much more than its sigil?"

Reev felt a stirring in his heart, one that he believed would never go away. "I will not leave," Reev said, "until the amulet is back in my hands."

"And if all hope of Telantis falls," said Astarthe, "it will be for a coin you left behind. Why couldn't Telantis have raised a shrewder son?"

"I'm going to fight in the arena," said Wrinn amid the crowds of Imperial Square. "A man named Scauro is sponsoring me. The first game is next week…"

"This is folly, Wrinn," said Fortunato. "We are here for the Prince of the Dawn, for the treading of Seymus underfoot."

"And when I fight," Wrinn said, "they in the palace will take notice of me. Who knows what my participation will spark?"

But to Fortunato it seemed Wrinn was making excuses, that he had seen the adoring faces of the crowds, that he been overcome with the primal fascination that came with the spilling of blood and entrails. He had been a spectator and then he had wanted something more.

Such a path had brought many gladiators to their fate.

"Wrinn, you aren't doing this," Fortunato said. "That's an order."

And Wrinn said, "You aren't my master."

It was true. Fortunato could not stop him. But Fortunato would stick to what mattered. He — and the former warlock, Xan, he thought with a suppressed sigh — would not cease in their efforts to bring Reev back to safety. He and Xan would not relent until they and the Prince of the Dawn were back in the gods' graces, headed toward the "port on the Empire's southern coast," again traveling to where destiny lay, *Naron Da*.

"Good luck, Wrinn," Fortunato said. "You'll need it."

Wrinn looked away, not heeding Fortunato's warning. And Fortunato realized he could not stop him from becoming the arena's newest victim.

Chapter Fifteen:
Down the Rabbit Trail

Valeria Verra and her spawn, Verrus, were touring a construction in the Cloaca.

The improvement to the city sewers was something they would take credit for. Yet it was not Khandaraeus or the two hellions that had secured funding for the new pipes and mains, but instead their predecessor, Marcus Amaranthius.

The two hell-spawn would take credit, but Giufrio could not afford to care. They'd be gone all day, and Giufrio had a chance to run free, to plot, to plan, to make his next move.

For he had not gotten to the bottom of the truth before Valeria Verra and her son engineered their coup, but he had found the beginnings of a rabbit trail. And as he sped down the hallway, and as the hallway became the Sky Bridge, he knew that as things stood, he was not equipped to follow that trail to its conclusion.

It would take a bit of help from one he thought was a sympathetic ear, if a profane outburst had been any indication. Giufrio had played both sides, disguising his burning hatred for Valeria Verra and the misshapen creature she had forced onto the White Throne.

His feet swiftly carried him to the official chambers of one Speaker Corvus Corbulo.

A Council Guard stood at the door, his blue cape contrasting starkly with his fine blue raiment.

The Council Guard eyed him harshly, the Marshal of the Imperial Guard versus one who protected thirty doddering fools — natural enemies.

"My signore," he said, "Speaker Corbulo is a busy man."

"It has to do with the speaker," said Giufrio. "We in the

Marshal Guard have become aware of an imminent threat to his life."

The Council Guard stepped aside.

Lies and more lies.

It was part of the job.

~

Speaker Corbulo was at his desk, on his desk a mound of papers that threatened to become a desk itself. There was a jar of ink, and in it a quill. And when Speaker Corbulo fixed his scowling, wrinkled face on Giufrio, his scowl turned into a grimace.

Not happy to see Giufrio, as expected.

"What are you bothering me with, now, Giufrio?" said Speaker Corbulo. "We are currently dealing with an influx of rokahn in Upper Zarubain, a threatened rebellion in Galiope… disturbances in Khazidea — and, of course, an Amarothic emperorship in which we thirty must consent to each edict."

"It's that emperorship I'm here for," said Giufrio. "The emperorship we both agree isn't on the up and up. I heard your accusations, and I agree with them. I began to investigate, but not before Valeria Verra dropped the mask and left a trail of bodies, all before I could react."

Speaker Corbulo's hateful glare softened. It seemed, for a moment, he wished he had not been so hostile to Giufrio from the beginning. He said, "The truth, what good would it do us? For Valeria Verra's spawn now sits on the White Throne, and calls himself the emperor. It was Numa, curse his name, that gutted our powers. What then, can we do, to Valeria Verra's spawn, who now rules? We cannot remove him, not even by unanimous vote, like we could in the past. We must suffer under this Amarothic emperorship in perpetuity, until a dagger strikes Verrus in the heart, or Alabaster calls a lightning bolt down upon him."

"But there are thirty councilors," said Giufrio. "Those are a lot of men to keep in mind, men of great ego and many passions, who may have divergent opinions. Perhaps, if the truth was known, it would help to corral them, so that the Amarothic emperorship never becomes a true one."

Speaker Corbulo's glare had vanished. He was gazing into Giufrio's eyes. "For once," he said, "an inhabitant of the Imperial Palace makes a cogent point. For corralling those twenty-nine councilors is a task fit for Helemon, who carried the world of Varda on his back. And though there's no sign of cracking, no Amarothic emperorship has lasted in perpetuity."

"But perhaps, this one can," Giufrio said, "if we get to the truth."

After Giufrio explained what he knew, about the appointment of Thuban and his connection to the Imperial Bay Company, Speaker Corbulo looked rattled.

"Giufrio," he said, "I think you're onto something. But you will be contending with powerful forces, if you continue in your pursuit of the truth. The truth… it may cost you your life. Are you up for it?"

"The truth is all I want," Giufrio said.

Speaker Corbulo gazed deeper into Giufrio's eyes, then seemed to look beyond them. "The Imperial Council has little power, now. But not everyone in the Empire knows this. Some will see a sigil of our authority, and think they are in danger if they disobey."

"How do you mean?" Giufrio said.

~

In the dark hours of the night, when Valeria Verra and Verrus slept, while the watchful eye of the emperor was gone, the Imperial Councilors — elderly men, all — met in secret.

"A vote," said Speaker Corbulo, "to grant unto Giufrio Vallo a

Writ of Mandamus, that he bears the authority of the Imperial Council against any who would stand in the way of his investigation."

The vote in the end, was twenty to ten. Even in the pursuit of truth, these thirty doddering fools could not cobble together a united front.

But Giufrio had a Writ of Mandamus, and in secret, it was delivered to him the next morning.

Chapter Sixteen: The Blast

Inside Wrinn could smell the dust of the arena, and beyond the gate, he could see the light of the morning sun.

Against the angry hectoring of his sponsor Scauro, he had decided to bear none of the gladiatorial uniforms, not the Getan, not the Thartan, not the Myrmidon, but instead the white shift, the quarterstaff, and the elvish longknife of the *dó kentari*, and nothing more.

And yet, as he heard the beginnings of the audience's cheers, a lump had formed in his throat.

Was he nervous?

The gate ground open, and the water organ began to play. Wrinn heard the shouting of Scauro from behind, "Get out there, Wrinn! What are you waiting for?"

And Wrinn took a step in the bright sunlight, and as his sandals crunched against the sand, he looked about him and saw the countless people in the stands. Throngs and throngs were sitting in their seats, a multitude from all over Varda, a sea of humanity. They began to cheer, and their cheering seemed to deafen Wrinn, and shake the earth at his feet.

His opponent was rushing at him, a Getan wielding two sabers in his hands and an iron breastplate. Wrinn rushed forth, and the cheering and adulation of the crowds spurred him on. He remembered his life as a pit fighter in the Northern World, and he thought, there was nothing like this.

The Getan came whirling at him, slashing with his sabers in wild strokes, but Wrinn remembered his training and ducked away, and was easily out of the path. His white shift did not hinder his mobility as he sprang back and forth. He struck with his quarterstaff and the Getan fumbled.

The Getan came charging again, and Wrinn speared him with the quarterstaff's blunt edge. A tooth fell loose, and blood spurted, and the audience's deafening roar became an earth-shaking thunder.

The Getan slashed with his saber again, and nicked Wrinn's wrist. A bit of blood began to drip, as Wrinn found his center, and drawing back and then stepping to the side, opened a wide berth between them, and broadened the battlefield.

The sun was shining up above.

He called on every god that could hear him.

He looked to the Imperial box, and saw inscrutable figures. He could not tell if Reev was among them.

"For Reev!" he called out, and charged the Getan, assailing him with a flurry of strikes and swipes, bludgeons and parries. By the time his storm of blows ended, the Getan had lost his grip on one of his sabers, and was staggering backward.

The crowd's noise had lessened, forming a relative tense silence.

The Getan roared and came charging. He slashed with the saber that remained and cut a piece of white fabric from Wrinn's shift. He slashed again, and Wrinn allowed him space to charge, allowed the Getan's attempt to dominate his movements. Another strike, and Wrinn parried.

Then, once after the other, Wrinn bludgeoned the Getan three times, first knocking loose three teeth, then crushing his forehead, then spearing him in the breastplate, and causing him to fall back a step.

Remembering what the crowds loved, he charged ahead, and taking his longknife in his hand, slit the Getan's throat.

Blood spurted, and the crowd shook the earth, from a deafening roar, to a ground-shaking thunder, to a world-quaking blast, a thousand, ten thousand, eighty thousand men and women at once, shouting at the top of their lungs.

The water organ began to play, and attendants rushed out, as some shouted, "Wrinn Finnis, victor!"

~

Wrinn entered the gladiators' chambers, sweating through his shift and covered in blood.

"Good work! Good work!" howled the voice of Scauro.

"We've made ten denara this day," he continued on.

"*I* made ten denara," Wrinn insisted.

"Yes, yes," Scauro said, "you are correct, my good signore. You are, after all, Scauro's shining star, and soon a star of the arena. Scauro will guide you through the coming pressures and look out, always, for your good."

Scauro did not have Wrinn's best interest in mind, he had to remember. But he walked amid the dingy darkness, seeing the other gladiators boxing the air and getting ready for their matches. He stripped to his loins and sat in a grimy chair, as Scauro wrapped a towel around his shoulders.

"I shall get you water, and bread, and anything you like!" Scauro said.

"Can you get me access to the Imperial Palace?" Wrinn said.

"To woo Valeria Verra? You and so many others," Scauro said. "Perhaps, someday…"

Chapter Seventeen:
The Quest

Reev's amulet was missing, the amulet his grandfather had left to him. One of the last things of Telantis that remained in the world, perhaps the only, had been stolen from Astarthe's place of safekeeping. And in the afternoons, or in the mornings, whenever there was a quiet moment, they plotted and strategized, and tried to uncover how it had been taken from its place, and above all who had taken it.

Reev had heard whisperings from various cretins in the palace that they were looking for a Telantine. The fact that Reev had not been arrested told him they did not yet believe it was him they were looking for.

But Reev was keeping a wary eye, one Primrane morning, as he sat in his private chamber.

He remembered, it had once been Governor Appian's workroom.

As he thought of who would have taken it, and why, one name and one face continued to come to mind, the Marshal of the Guard, Giufrio. Like Astarthe, Giufrio had been one he had inexplicably trusted. In a nest of snakes and vipers, his calm confidence and warm eyes had made him stand apart.

Could he, in the course of his work as Marshal of the Guard, pried in on Astarthe's belongings, and — having seized upon the wooden case — removed the coin necklace of Telantis, trying to trap Reev in a lie? Giufrio was the only person Reev had heard mention the amulet, the only one who had ever spoken of it since the day Reev clung to the barrel and emerged from those fateful waters.

As every day, the door opened, and Astarthe was there. Reev

said, "Have you seen Giufrio?"

Astarthe gave him a kind smile. "Let's go find him."

~

When they reached Giufrio's official chamber, another was there in his stead.

He was swarthy, black haired, but dressed in the same attire as Giufrio, an iron breastplate, a red half-cape.

"Signor Barcho," said Astarthe, "we're looking for Giufrio."

Barcho looked at Astarthe, then eyed Reev, and on Reev, his eyes lingered. "Astarthe," Barcho said, "and your consort. Giufrio isn't here. His grandmother in Latera has taken ill and he is on an extended leave. He won't be back. Maybe, for months."

Reev, knowing there was little hope, now, of finding the amulet, searched the room for his eyes, but only saw a desk, scattered papers, a shelf, and hanging on the wall a sword.

"He's not here, Reev," said Astarthe. "Sorry."

"Reev?" Barcho said. "What sort of name is Reev?"

~

They ventured out to the Great Porch quietly, not daring to express their worries.

For Reev knew his first name was unusual, and so too was his surname, Nax. Both were family names, surely of Telantine origin. And so Reev had left a small clue for what hunted him, a breadcrumb for the ravens to swirl about and gobble up.

Yet Reev was no less avowed, no less certain, that he would not leave until the amulet of Telantis was in his hands.

He would not leave the Imperial Palace without it.

Beside them were the statues of Emperor Claudio and Emperor Numa.

And as Reev and Astarthe stood there, fighting fear before vista of the glittering blue Imperial Sea and the urban sprawl of Harbor District, the doors opened again.

Reev did not hear them close.

But when he looked back, they had closed indeed, and a man was standing before them.

It was a face that was familiar, with tawny hair and blue eyes, one — if Reev was a betting man — he would have gambled nine out of ten times that he had seen him before. Yet who he was, and where they had met amid the sprawl of the palace, Reev did not know.

Yet the man's blue eyes keenly sparkled, and it seemed he had seen Reev before as well.

"A word of advice, Reev Nax," he said, and he circled about Reev and Astarthe. At last, he laid his hand on the head of the statue of Emperor Claudio, and faced them. "Don't go around, speaking rashly and boldly. You don't have an army to fight them like he did, not yet."

"Them?" Astarthe said.

"Find a name," said the man. "Something Getan. Stick to it.

"On the other hand, don't. Because Barcho knows your name, now, and he won't forget it. Can't go around sporting two names, because like I said, you don't have an army at your side... not yet."

"What are you talking about?" Astarthe continued.

And Reev, mystified, only listened to the man's words, for it was clear he knew something Reev did not.

"A final word," said the man. "Valeria Verra and Verrus have not noticed you. When they do, the game's about to be up. You have to play the game with what you're given.

"Reev Nax... what sort of name is it? You're Getan, or so you have claimed, so perhaps it's a name from some forgotten tribe. That could play in with the title of 'prince' you've boasted about. Cover up two lies, with one stroke."

"Neither of them are lies, signore," said Reev.

The man's eyes twinkled. He walked up to the edge of the Great Porch and looked down. "Do you see that? The crowds are parting. Valeria Verra and her son are about home. That's your signal. Get back to your room… don't linger."

Reev, mystified, turned around, and left the man behind, wondering just how much he knew, and wondering where Reev had met him before.

One thing he was certain of, they had not spoken before now.

Chapter Eighteen:
The Trail Deepens

Giufrio felt an uncharacteristic knot in his stomach as he walked through the Harbor District, toward the offices of the Imperial Bay Company. He had the Writ of Mandamus from the Imperial Council, enough to frighten the ignorant, enough for those who remembered a time when the Imperial Council and not the emperor reigned supreme.

It had not been that long ago.

Giufrio knew how to bluff; he knew how to play the game. He knew how to get a feel for people and he knew how to influence them. When the time came, he knew how to scare them.

The blue nightstick he carried around helped.

But amid the swarming crowds, the concrete warehouses, the filth and debris scattered about, that uncharacteristic knot of nervousness had not left him.

The Imperial Bay Company awaited.

~

The offices were on a high point overlooking the blue waters of the Imperial Harbor. The face of the building was concrete, with stripped-down pillars that gave the building no architectural support. There were signs that the building had once been beautiful, but the reliefs that once ran along the top of the walls had been sanded off, and the fluting that once marked the columns had weathered away, and was gone.

The Imperial Bay Company was an entity of immense wealth, and Giufrio thought that such a place would care for beauty.

But he guessed beauty wasn't of interest to them, only the

almighty denara.

He passed through a glass door and entered.

There was a woman sitting at the desk in front. She had a bothered look. Her skin was sallow, and her hair was bunched up tightly in a bun.

"Signore," she said, "we don't let any street visitors into the Imperial Bay Company offices."

"Do I look like a street visitor?" Giufrio said.

He was wearing his civilian clothes — nice clothes, but civilian — so he lifted up his blue nightstick.

The woman eyed the nightstick, and seemed to shrink back a bit in her chair. "You are — "

"An investigator, sent by the Imperial Council. Giufrio."

"If this is about taxes, all our taxes are calculated by Flavius Baris and Sons, on Way Street, in Celsus Heights." The woman was now looking at Giufrio with a hidden nervousness, one it was clear she was trying to hide, but one which she could not hide from Giufrio, an expert.

"It's not about taxes, signora," said Giufrio. "It's about something bigger."

"We've been faithful to the law," said the woman, and now she was failing to hide her nerves. Even a non-expert could see it, now. "Everything we've done has been according to Imperial Council rule and regulation."

"I'm not saying you're wrong," Giufrio said. "But I have a lot of questions. And you don't strike me as the one who's in charge. I'd like to talk to him — or her — now."

The woman nodded nervously and jittered as she stood up. She fled through a door, and Giufrio noted that though the Imperial Bay Company offices were pristinely clean, and composed of the highest quality cement, and its walls were faced with the whitest of whitewashed plaster, that there were no ornaments, no art prints, no portraits on the wall, no beauty. All the money of the Empire passed through these offices, and yet the people working in them had no reverence for beauty.

Giufrio, sensing an opening, passed through the door. An opportunity to take charge.

He found the Majordomo of the Imperial Bay Company in his private chamber, and the secretary from before was sitting demurely in a chair in his office.

On his mahogany desk was emblazoned in gold letters, "SERAPPO XARUS, ESQUIRE."

Giufrio's mind kept going back to the names "Alsumo" and "Insalaco," and the strange way they rolled off the tongue. Then he remembered, Serappo was not an uncommon name in the east.

"What is this about, Giufrio?" Where the secretary was a timid mouse, Serappo had a bold look. He was tall, with a round belly, and flaking skin around his cheeks. His brown eyes had a faint strength to their gaze, but at least he met Giufrio's head on.

"If it's about taxes, send your inquiries to 3 Way Street, Celsus Heights."

"It's not about taxes, Serappo," Giufrio said. He lifted his nightstick. "It's about this. Law. Order.

"It's about Thuban, and I want to hear from your own lips why you had him appointed in the Imperial Palace. I know why, but I want to know who told you to suggest him."

"There are seven majordomos of the Imperial Bay Company," said Serappo. "I am the chief one. But do you want to hear a little known trade secret? It's not us who gives the orders.

"Sure, we take trips to Sur or to Shush or to Seshán whenever there's trouble with the flow of the pepper and cardamom and ginger you people so crave, but it's not us giving the orders. As for the appointment of Thuban, it was made by a decision of our shareholders.

"If Thuban's doing a terrible job, I'm sorry, but it's not on my shoulders. I don't own the company. I just solve problems."

Giufrio knew Serappo would say what he would to get his company and his own self out of trouble. But what he said was plausible. "Who are your shareholders?" said Giufrio.

"There are hundreds of them," snapped Serrapo. "Do you want me to make a list?"

"I do," Giufrio said.

"Get out of here," Serappo snarled.

But Giufrio pulled the Writ of Mandamus from the folds of his cloak. "I don't think so. The Imperial Council says make that list, and make it right now."

Serappo went white.

And he'd do as Giufrio asked.

~

A white-faced Serappo eventually came to the office's front doors with a parchment scroll.

"Here it is, Giufrio," Serappo said. "Checked and double checked, every last one."

It was amazing what the threat of the law did to certain people. But if Serappo knew how toothless the Imperial Council really was, he wouldn't be acting like a frightened animal.

"Thank you, Serappo," Giufrio said. "If I have any questions, I'll be back."

~

Giufrio had told the Imperial court his grandmother in Latera was sick, his grandmother who did not live in Latera and had been dead for seven years.

It was a way to avoid the eye of the targets of the investigation, Valeria Verra and Verrus.

And so, he had booked a room at a dingy inn a block from Imperial Square, the best room in a house of dim-lit, poor rooms.

He settled in, and lit a candle in the fireplace. He began to read.

He noted that, though it was true in some literal sense that there were hundreds of shareholders, the vast majority of shares in the Imperial Bay Company were held by three names.

One, Jiacomo Kerius, owned twenty-four out of four-hundred and fifty-seven total — another, Marco Kerius, owned seventy-five shares.

But the largest owner by far was Huardo Lornodoris, owning two-hundred and thirty-six shares… an outright majority.

The rest of the names owned one or at most three of the shares, and some of the names were holding companies, legal entities that cobbled together enough funds to buy such an expensive piece of commercial property.

So the shareholders had demanded that Thuban be appointed, and such a demand could not have come without the consent of one Huardo Lornodoris, who owned most of the Imperial Bay Company.

The name Huardo Lornodoris was not one unknown. The Lornodoris family was among the richest in the Empire, and in prior days had been represented on many seats of the Imperial Council. It was the most blueblooded of bluebloods, one of the Empire's founding families.

And not for the first time, Giufrio wondered if he was on a rabbit trail to nowhere.

Yet he wouldn't give up now.

Huardo Lornodoris, a member of one of the most ancient Imperial families, had wanted Thuban, and perhaps Verrus on the throne.

Yet such a man would know very well that the Imperial Council had no power. The Writ of Mandamus wouldn't work on him.

Giufrio stared into the fireplace in his room and gazed into the flame, plotting, planning, thinking.

Chapter Nineteen:
A Day at the Races

Where was Fortunato to go, and where was he to look?

He and Xan had cased the Imperial Palace the past few days, getting as close and taking as much a risk of arrest as was reasonable. Fortunato knew Xan had in his possession the Skeleton Key, an item of magical power that would unlock any door in Varda. But the Imperial Palace was clear of traffic for many fathoms around, closed off by a gate, and guarded at all times by a small army of guards.

Fortunato wondered if Reev was being kept prisoner, but the actors Sylvia and Rufo seemed to indicate he had been taken to a place of great honor.

Why, then, had he not slipped away?

Perhaps, he was a prisoner amid luxury. Perhaps, though he was living richly, he was ultimately a hostage.

As Fortunato and Xan stood amid the swarming masses of Imperial Square, there was the sound of scattered shouting — "The races! The races! I can't wait!" And he could see the swarming crowds were moving in the direction of the hippodrome, the racing arena that had not yet opened to the public during Fortunato and the party's sojourn in Imperial City.

~

They had to pay triple the price, but Fortunato found seats next to the Imperial box. Members of the court would be present, easily visible, and perhaps Fortunato's foolhardy plan would pay off, this time.

The crowds in Imperial Arena, Fortunato realized as he and

Xan stumbled into their seats, were packed in one place, but here, they stretched around for what looked like a city mile around the racecourse.

Eighty thousand souls could fit in the seats of Imperial Arena, but Fortunato had a thought that triple such a number could fit within the hippodrome.

Xan eyed the Imperial box, still empty. "Perhaps," he said, "we should climb up there. It's not too great a leap. We'll tell them we're foreign dignitaries and those fools won't know the difference."

But Fortunato was not so stupid. He was bold, perhaps reckless, but not stupid.

As they sat in their seats, men came by hawking stewed chicken for a copper coin apiece. Then came wine sellers, as the sea of people took their seats around the vast stadium.

"Say," Xan shouted to a man and his wife sitting just below him, "the Imperial box is empty, and the race is about to start."

The woman looked up. "It's empty," she said, "because those lucky *lupas* can see the race from where they rule over us."

Fortunato looked back, and saw, beyond the rising seats, the glittering white towers and turrets of the palace.

~

Reev lingered on the balcony outside the feasting hall, no longer accompanied by Astarthe. Amid the urban sprawl, in the daylight, he could make out the hippodrome, just beyond Imperial Square, and from where he stood, he could see the crowds massing into their seats. He would be able to watch the entire games from where he stood.

And, perhaps, he would.

Yet behind him, through a glass door, there was noise.

Reev saw through the glass door the faces of Verrus and Valeria Verra and something drove him to the edge of the balcony. He scrambled, not thinking, only reacting, and at last found himself under a table, between two potted ferns.

Valeria Verra and Verrus have not noticed you. When they do, the game's about to be up, the man in the Great Porch had said.

And the door opened, and Valeria Verra and Verrus did not notice him. They had not seen him, and Reev's thundering heart began to ease its pace.

Valeria Verra stood there, and Verrus. Valeria Verra had a wine glass filled with water in her hand.

"Oh, these dreadful Imperials," said Valeria Verra, "they love their blood sports."

Were they not Imperials?

"And they love their wine," Valeria Verra said. "When I put water in a glass, sometimes it tricks them, my son. But it's poison to your blood, Verrus, so don't drink it."

Verrus said, "You know I don't like the taste."

"Look!" said Valeria Verra. "It's about to begin."

~

Fortunato turned back to the stadium, and the racing grounds, brilliant yellow sand against a gray stone backdrop. As he watched, a woman sprinted out waving a white flag, and disappeared through one of the doors far below.

Gates opened, and chariots burst out, quadrigas pulled by four horses, five chariots in number.

They raced ahead, and the crowds began to cheer, and Fortunato, having resigned himself to failure yet again, began to cheer along with them.

"Who do you want to win?" Xan said.

There was a red chariot just ahead of the others, there was a green, there was white, and amber, and blue.

"Blue," Fortunato said, perhaps only because it was lagging

behind, in last place, as the chariots made a turn around the circular arena, and Fortunato watched with bated breath as they just barely managed not to crash into each other.

Green was ahead, but white was speeding along.

~

"The Imperials are so silly, Mother," said Verrus from the balcony, as Reev listened. "They've attributed grand notions to the charioteers. The blue, they say, represents the power of the people. The red, the glory of the aristocracy. The amber, the foreigners. The green, the priests."

"And what does the white represent?" Valeria Verra said.

"I do not know," said Verrus.

Valeria Verra's eyes, Reev noted, were now following the amber charioteer with eager interest.

Reev tried to eye them from his hiding place. He saw that neither of them were wearing his necklace.

~

The blue charioteer was speeding around a turn, along the ovular racetrack. The amber was trying with all due speed to gain on him.

The amber charioteer began to swiftly turn, with all the force of his four horses. But the blue charioteer made a swift pivot, and broke free of the amber charioteer just as the amber chariot crashed into the dividing wall, the *spina*.

An explosion of wood and horses enveloped the amber charioteer, and a cloud of sand kicked up, obscuring sight. The audience began to cheer wildly, at the thought of the maimed charioteer perhaps, but maybe Fortunato was cynical.

The white charioteer was now in second place, and gaining on the blue.

Green and red were now far behind.

~

"The Imperials and their silly superstitions," Valeria Verra said. "You know, Verrus, a strong Empire is not in and of itself good for us."

"What is in and of itself good for us?" said Verrus.

Valeria Verra seemed to pause. The words seemed to escape her, as Reev watched from his hiding place.

But as Reev fixed his attention on the hippodrome, and saw the white charioteer narrowly pass the blue charioteer at the finish line, words seemed to at last form on Valeria Verra's lips.

"Don't worry about the Amarothic emperorship," said Valeria Verra. "Mama monster is on it."

"Don't call yourself that," Verrus said. "You know I don't like it."

"But mama monster loves it," Valeria Verra said.

And Verrus eyed her quietly.

~

Blue had not won, but it had been second place. If Fortunato had placed a bet, like so many others, maybe he would have made a little money. These prize seats had eaten into the party's coinpurse, and there had been little to show for it.

"Maybe," Fortunato said, "these desperate gambits should be a bit more focused."

But how would they get into the palace, the most secure location in Varda? How could they possibly enter in?

Perhaps, someone else had an idea.

Perhaps, Wrinn.

Chapter Twenty:
The Feint

Wrinn stood in the sand of the arena, and the crowds loved him.

He could hear them chanting his name.

Before him stood a dead gladiator dressed in the attire of a Khazidee, chainmail and a thick khopesh. His blood had turned the yellow sand around him red for yards around.

"Wrinn! Wrinn!" amid the noise, a vocalization was forming.

Wrinn would try not to let it get to his head.

Oh, who was he kidding?

He began to strut about the corpse of the Khazidee, and he looked to the massing crowds. He beckoned with his hands, for more, more noise, more enthusiasm, more something. And as the deafening roar of the crowds grew, the water organ began to play, and the gates opened.

It wasn't part of the plan.

But two dark shapes were now emerging, foes he and his sponsor Scauro hadn't signed up for.

They were dogs, Wrinn saw, dogs with sets of tangled fangs and wet muzzles. On their sides and their backs were what looked like crystal markings that glowed bluish-white in the Imperial City sun.

Their eyes gleamed with a spark Wrinn thought he had seen in Gastreel the Green Wizard's magic-working before. And then they were gone.

Wrinn looked about him, searching for the dogs, as he felt the sensation of teeth sinking into his thigh.

Wrinn screamed out in pain, as some in the audience gasped and some cheered, and he whipped around, and saw the dogs had vanished from view, then reappeared right behind him.

There was something more than canine mischief to these dogs.

He struck one with his quarterstaff and it whimpered and whined. He speared the other with his quarterstaff's blunt edge, and it vanished again.

He laid savage blows into the dog that remained, until it turned its tail and sprinted away. "Wrinn, victor!" shouted an arena attendant, as other attendants rushed out to collect the bodies, and herd the mystical dogs away.

~

Wrinn sat in the pit, fuming.

"They saw how many you've lain low," Scauro said, "and they didn't want you too prideful. So they sent those swamp dogs out to rattle you a little bit, and make sure you don't get too big a head."

"They made me look a fool."

Scauro knelt down, and began to apply a bandage to Wrinn's still bleeding thigh.

"They'd better start paying me more," Wrinn said, "or I'll quit."

"Like Hell you will," Scauro said.

And Wrinn realized, Scauro was right. He had been a pit fighter in the north, but this felt like his true calling.

This was all he wanted… to be a star of the arena, and nothing more.

Chapter Twenty-One:
A Little Closer

How did one investigate a man as powerful as Huardo Lornodoris?

And was there a conspiracy after all?

Could Thuban's appointment be incidental, and Valeria Verra won him over, and promised him some gift when her son became emperor?

There could be no conspiracy, but for the bad feeling in Giufrio's gut, one he had learned to trust.

That feeling had led him here, to the quiet avenues and broad thoroughfares of Celsus Heights, where the towering concrete apartment blocks and the urban squalor were nowhere to be seen.

No, there were clean streets, and shops that closed just after dark, and taverns that didn't let in any of the riffraff.

Celsus Heights had a policy of no riffraff. It was a perfect place for a man such as Huardo Lornodoris, a perfect place for a chameleon to hide. And who was there to unravel the mask?

~

The first night he spent in Celsus Heights, he found the dingiest tavern he could, one which was cleaner and finer-furnished than any tavern in Imperial Square. It was there he began asking around.

"Who is Huardo Lornodoris?" he started with, and as he learned more, he said, "What can you tell me about the mansion on 7 Port Street?"

"It belonged to his father, and his father before him," a woman said softly in the dim candlelight.

"Who was his father before him?" Giufrio said.

"No idea," the woman said. "But I know, he was a rich man. And the pedigree of all these people are recorded in books. They want everyone to know their illustrious history."

Books... where did one find books?

And Giufrio knew, the bluebloods wanted to know everyone how blueblooded they were. They wanted everyone to know their ancestry could be traced back to the conquest of Anthania, and the unification.

Who really was Huardo Lornodoris, after all?

~

Books were to be found in a library, if Giufrio, no bookworm, could guess.

And though there was no comparison to the Conciliar Library and its stadium-sized collection of shelves, perhaps something that had to do with Huardo Lornodoris would be found in Celsus Heights.

After all, his father, and his father's father, had set up shop here.

He scoured a library near Huardo's residence, a pristine building on Myrtle Street. There were pedigrees of the Malchus family and pedigrees of the Jado families, but nothing of the sort to do with Huardo Lornodoris.

And he scoured the libraries, one at a time, searching for the elusive pedigree, wondering if it would all lead him nowhere, but knowing that such a risk came with the job of investigator.

He was reaching the last of them, days into his journey, when a curious tome on a shelf sparkled in the light.

On its spine was a title, *The History of Celsus Heights*.

And Giufrio knew he had time to spare. The pedigree of Huardo Lornodoris seemed nowhere to be found.

But he had noticed strange things about Celsus Heights, how Lornodoris and his close relations all seemed to live there.

And hadn't the secretary at the Imperial Bay Company said their tax work was conducted here?

In a strange place, in a ward of the city Giufrio had never been before, perhaps it was best to learn all.

He took the tome with him and found a seat by the light of the window.

Celsus Heights, it said, was founded by shipping magnate Celsus, who at one time controlled one third of shipping across the Imperial Sea. He was known for his unscrupulous business practices, and his impoverished tenants later spread a rumor that he was a Strig — "a kind of undead."

That was one way to get back at him.

Celsus Heights, founded in the 775th year of the Empire, was going strong.

After Celsus's death, the town continued to attract investment. It became the home of conciliar families and the home of various noblemen across the Empire. It was then that

Giufrio flipped the page. A large section had been torn out.

The remainder of the pages narrated beginning in the year 1101, that was this century. So from the year 842, until 1101, the pages were missing.

Giufrio eyed the author.

Alessandro Sopis, it said.

Two-hundred and fifty-nine years were erased from his work.

If Giufrio was a historian, he wouldn't be happy.

Moreover, the pages had not been crudely torn out, but removed expertly.

Giufrio flipped to the front, and saw that the book had been copied by "The Newmarket Manufactory" in the year 1138. That wasn't so long ago.

Giufrio took the book, and headed to the desk where the librarian still stood.

Outside the windows, the colors of dusk painted all in orange.

"My good signora," Giufrio said, "I cannot help but notice… there are pages missing from this book."

"That's strange," the librarian said, and she stood up. "We keep a watchful eye on our books, and do not allow them to be lent to those we do not trust."

"Pardon," Giufrio said, "are there other libraries that sell copies of this book?"

"I can look that up for you," the librarian said.

And she was such a kind woman, no Writ of Mandamus was required.

She departed into the library's inner chambers and returned with a list. "A library in Villa Regis carries it."

Giufrio's hometown.

"A library in the Strand, and two libraries in Meridia. All libraries in Imperial City are connected, you see. We talk to each other.

"We're a cabal, of sorts."

"Don't talk of yourself that way, signora," Giufrio said.

Giufrio thanked her for her time, and, taking the list, walked off into the cool dusk.

~

The next day, he started with his home ward first.

And as soon as he passed from Maxima to Villa Regis, he felt a little disappointment.

For the apartment blocks had not been kept up to his liking, and the homes seemed to be growing dilapidated. What's more, rougher characters seemed to have moved into town. It was not the Villa Regis of his youth.

But the library still stood, and he entered in through the pillared walkway. He scoured the shelves, and following the prescribed order, he located *The History of Celsus Heights* on the shelf.

Again he read, again he came to the year 842.

After Celsus's death, the town continued to attract investment. It became the home of conciliar families and the home of various noblemen across the Empire. It was then that

And again, the pages had been cut out with perfect precision, leaving a gap between the years 842 and 1101, where the book began again.

He went then to Meridia, and its two libraries, and found the same pages removed from the book. He ventured across the city to the Strand, and in its library, located a copy, tucked away in the basement. It, too, had been dissected, its pages removed with precision.

And Giufrio realized that this book had been altered by the order of some governmental or other powerful body, that there were no copies that remained to be seen that had the whole of the history of Celsus Heights.

Was he on the wrong trail? Everything of the Imperial Bay Company, Thuban and all the others, seemed to have something to do with Celsus Heights.

And why would each copy in circulation be altered?

Was there a copy that remained, in full?

Again, Giufrio's gut sense told him that the altering of the book, Thuban and the Imperial Bay Company all had something to do with each other.

His gut had not failed him yet.

But where could he go, and how could he locate a book that so many people wanted buried?

Perhaps, Giufrio should start with the author.

And so he asked around, first to the book sellers around Imperial Square, and then to the book buyers in Emporia, about the historian Alessandro Sopis.

Some were angry, some didn't know, but as Primrane moved into Tidusca, and the weather warmed, and the flowers of the trees in city parks were in bloom, Giufrio finally got an answer.

"They drove him out," said the book buyer in Newmarket.

"Who?" Giufrio said.

"The publishers," she said. "They made sure he never worked again. He took refuge in the city of Thénai."

Thénai was the chief city of the east, across the sea.

"He still lives there as far as I know," said the book buyer. "An apartment on Laurel Street."

Chapter Twenty-Two: The Secret

While Astarthe asked around, Reev had begun to grow restless as his determination to find the necklace grew. So restless was he, he was ready to take risks.

And he remembered Astarthe's words, that a Son of Telantis had nothing to fear from the Sons of Nachash.

Reev was a Son of Telantis.

And he had a thought, that his necklace was in the Imperial bedchamber. Where Valeria Verra and Verrus slept, they would keep their jewelry.

And Reev had seen Valeria Verra don new brooches and new pearl necklaces each day she walked through the palace. Reev believed that Valeria Verra, a murderess, was in all likelihood a thief, too, and that even before she had become the mother of the emperor, she had felt she was owed a run of the place.

Reev had not seen Valeria Verra or Verrus all afternoon, and a strange boldness filled him. He strode out into the hallway, past Imperial Guards, following a path he had been once before, when he witnessed the death of Khandaraeus.

He had reached the door, and the door was unguarded. What he did risked punishment if he was caught — death, maybe. Buf if he succeeded, he would find his amulet, and speed away from the palace to find Fortunato.

Then, their mission could resume. They could begin anew their journey to *Naron Da*.

He opened the door and entered, and not long after it had shut, he heard the footsteps of an Imperial Guard, returning to his post. How ever would he leave now?

He would find a way.

~

He opened tables and desks amid purple walls and purple carpets, and he saw that Valeria Verra and her son had removed all the portraits and artworks from the wall.

All was purple, the color of royalty and Imperial majesty, yet now seemingly bare, stripped of all its life and soul.

But the tables and desks he opened were filled with various odds and ends, jewelry that was not the amulet, under one shelf a distaff shaped into the form of a snake… a thimble made of silver, and in the corner of one room, a spinning wheel.

He remembered — the bedroom.

And he hurried to the bedroom, retaining his boldness, retaining the spirit that had driven him here.

He saw purple bedsheets that not long ago had been stained with blood, a bed that once the rightful emperor had slept in.

And then he saw the jewelry case, and swiftly ran to it.

There were pearl necklaces and emerald brooches, diamond earrings and sapphire rings. There were necklaces of gold and silver, and necklaces of electrum. There was an anklet, a bracelet studded with fiery rubies — a fortune, if Reev had a mind to steal.

And there was the sound of a door opening and slamming shut.

For a moment, Reev's boldness threatened to spill into panic, and he rushed into the doors of the bedroom closet, and hid himself among clothes.

"Verrus," he heard a voice, a voice he had come to hate. "Have you been rifling through my things again?"

"No," snarled the voice of Verrus.

"There's been a new cleaning crew," said Valeria Verra. "They aren't of the same quality as before."

"Well," said Verrus. "Clean it up, yourself."

"Quiet, you. A *qizim* does not clean."

"You are not a *qizim*."

"I am, and so are you," said Valeria Verra. "Don't you forget it."

Reev wondered how he would ever get out of this predicament. Would he wait until morning?

He remembered the words of the man in the Great Porch.

Valeria Verra and Verrus have not noticed you. When they do, the game's about to be up.

And so he remained perfectly still. He tried to breathe silently.

"What are we having for dinner?" said Verrus.

"I have something special planned," said Valeria Verra.

There was a sigh.

"I am having dinner brought here," Valeria Verra said. "It's something special planned for us. Because I have something important to tell you."

"Oh, dear," Verrus said.

"Don't talk like that," Valeria Verra said. "It's important."

There were footsteps in the bedroom, and through the slits in the closet Reev could see Valeria Verra in a loose sleeping garment. She was lying down on the Imperial bed.

Did mother and son sleep that way? Reev shuddered. He would try to think the best, even of Valeria Verra and Verrus.

On second thought, it was impossible to think anything good of them.

But eventually Valeria Verra and Verrus were sitting on the bed, and as they stirred, the door to the Imperial suite opened. The smell of cooked food wafted in, sizzling meats and savory sauces.

"Your father's favorite meal," Valeria Verra said.

The door to the bedchamber opened and there was a meal on two trays, a steaming roasted chicken and mashed tubers doused in salt. On the trays were two wineglasses filled with water.

"You're wrong, Mother," Verrus said. "Father had far better taste than this."

"Leave us," said Verra, and the two men carrying the trays departed through the doorway. The door was shut.

"It's a humble Getan meal," Verra said. "A roast bird, and something to stick to your gut. Good for a long day on the farm."

"Father didn't live on a farm," snapped Verrus. He was almost shouting. "He was a banker. And he would not so much as look at the province of Gad on a map."

"That's what I'm trying to tell you," said Verra. "Don't you understand? You're in denial, Verrus."

"What are you saying?" Verrus began to howl, and through the slits in the closet Reev watched as Verrus picked up the roast chicken and threw it at the purple bedchamber wall.

"Don't be angry," Verra said. "Everything I did, I did for you. For Appian had all your political acumen and stratagems, and he passed it down to you."

"What?" Verrus howled, as the truth dawned on him. His blue eyes were fiery with inchoate rage. "My father is Lucio Verrus!"

"Your father is Appian," said Verra. "He is your true father, and Lucio was none the wiser.

"Embrace it, Verrus! The Governor of Khazidea. I had no love for him… I saw his cunning and his political wisdom. I wanted it in you, now ruler of the Empire."

"You *lupa*!" howled Verrus, and he tossed the mashed tubers onto the carpet.

"Quiet, Verrus," Valeria Verra seemed unbothered. "Everything I did, I did for our kind… a safe place for us, a place for our kind to breed, to eat…"

"Shut it!" Verrus screamed, and his once-pasty face was now a bright cherry red. He grabbed Verra's tray and threw it in the midst of the bedchamber. Then he struck her.

"Don't touch me, Verrus!" said Valeria Verra. "I am a loyal

qizim. Do you think I would risk my firstborn son having Lucio Verrus as his father? Lucio Verrus, uninterested in politics, only interested in money, no acumen or grand strategy, no desire for power?"

"You *lupa!*" Verrus howled, and now Valeria Verra was standing upright, beside the bed. Verrus was charging her, and they were inches from the closet door. Reev was now easily visible through the slits in the closet.

And something drove him, an energy, a powerful force — he tore open the closet door and fled, to howls from Valeria Verra: "Look, Verrus! It is your father's ghost, sent to reprimand you! Get a hold of yourself!"

He could hear them fighting as he fled away. The guard posted at the emperor's suite did not chase him.

~

Hours later, wondering if Valeria Verra really thought he was a ghost, Reev hid away in his private bedchamber, the former workroom of Verrus's true father.

Lying in bed, he couldn't sleep, when he heard the door next to him unmistakably sweeping open and then slamming shut.

He could hear something like a feral growl.

He slipped into sleep, and then stirred awake again, again to a door.

"You told him," said a voice Reev had heard once before, the voice of Thuban.

"Yes," Valeria Verra said, her voice cold and emotionless. "He didn't take it well. He has said I will not be sleeping in the Imperial suite anymore. His eyes — his eyes…"

"The eyes of a *qizim* king," said Thuban. "You did what needed to be done. Our victory is at hand. And now — we must find the Telantine, and we must kill him."

Chapter Twenty-Three: The Leader

The Imperial Sea was navigable only from Tidusca to Anthanos, and most sailors only risked a voyage between Brenua and Brightleaf. Only five months were the true height of the sailing season, and in those five months, commerce untold spread from port of call to port of call.

From Khazidea — Giufrio thought aboard the ship he had booked, *Alabaster's Spear* — came the grain tankers with their vast stores of wheat. From Gad came lumber and fruit. From Eloesus came books and slaves. And from Anthania and Imperial City, now hundreds of miles behind them, came precious little. Imperial City was the great vacuum. It consumed; it did not create.

They had been at sea a few weeks, and the cerulean waves were the color of the sky. They were about to Giufrio's destination. They were about to Thénai.

~

When Giufrio stepped off the ship, he thanked the gods — as was his custom — that no storm had swept upon them, that he had not met a terrible fate in the briny depths.

When he stepped off the ship, he thanked the gods, and he saw, he was in another world.

The Long Walls which once protected Thénai from Kersepoli and Kersepoli from Thénai had been demolished on Imperial order, for in this now-united province the quarrelsome city-states had endured centuries of concord. The rebellions of the prior century had been squashed, and the destruction that the east had endured during the same time period had been mostly abated. Appian, he recalled, had secured vast funding for the rebuilding of the east, and some citizens of Thénai called the city Thenoa Appiana in his honor.

But even now, Giufrio saw, walking down the road, that despite the Imperial funds the east was different, and closer to the southrons. For as he walked down the newly-paved cobblestone road toward the city proper, he saw a fire temple on a hilltop and a nude statue that marked a path to a sacred temple of Isdar.

As the behemoth that was the city of Thénai approached, Giufrio smelled pipe smoke, a rare scent in the west. And he saw that along the road there were countless tombs and mausoleums, as was customary in this part of the world.

And then he saw the walls, staggering in height, flanked by twin statues — one, Amara in war dress, the other Alabaster bearing his lightning spear.

The smell of tanneries, smoke and effluent hit Giufrio hard after so many weeks at sea. And when he passed through the gates, he was in a city of wonders.

How many had passed through these streets, he wondered. All about him was the smell of spices, and all about him were easterners in their long tunics going about their business, southron men in turbans and southron women in veils. There were pillared temples and pillared taverns, colonnades and peristyles. In view, everywhere, was the High City, a mountainous outcrop on which was the Temple of Amara, partially ruined and faded yellow with time.

On Laurel Street, amid palms and myrtles, Giufrio inquired of the author Alessandro Sopis. He received mostly dark glares. One at last said, "Why do you speak of such things?" The eastern woman seemed afraid to even hear his name spoken aloud.

And Giufrio had a thought that there was one place where lips were loosed, where anxieties were eased, where the travails and troubles of life were washed away by the water of life, by liquid gold and blood-red wine.

"You must not be a local," said the Silver Fleece's bartender, an eastern man with a head of curly dark hair, "to speak his name aloud, so boldly."

"I am an Alessandro Sopis fanatic," Giufrio said. Was it not true?

"I came to find him here," Giufrio continued. "I thought he lived on Laurel Street."

"The Politarch of Public Good drove him out," the bartender said, "threatened to arrest him."

"Why?" Giufrio said.

"Why?" The bartender seemed impatient, but Giufrio was coming to realize he was afraid. "I cannot tell you why. But you seem a genuine man. Those of your disposition meet here on the last day of each week. They call themselves the Society of the Argent Fist.

"And you seem a good man, genuine. The passphrase is 'Imperia.' "

Giufrio nodded. "I shall be there."

~

The Writ of Mandamus had come with indispensable funds, and even here in the east, he could go to a banker's table and ask for whatever money he required. By law the Imperial Council still controlled the coinpurse. Though the emperor had the final say, what Giufrio spent would be so little in comparison to the Imperial budget as not to be noticed.

And so he spent the next days at an inn, listening for troubles, listening for rumors, any hint that might speed him along. There was talk of trouble in the south, and amid everything tension, no one wishing to say anything that would draw the ire of the Thenái government, and the ultimate Imperial government that controlled it.

A secret society was the only place one could speak, in such a milieu.

And though Giufrio was an agent of the Imperial government in some small sense, he could feel its opposition all about him. The truth tellers met on the last day of the week, in the Silver Fleece Tavern, and they called themselves the Argent Fist.

The Argent Fist had rented a room in a hidden corner of the inn. A woman stood outside the door, wearing a blonde wig and a red gown, her brown eyes with a glint that seemed to say to Giufrio, "I am someone you can trust."

Giufrio strode up to her. "Imperia," he said, and there seemed to be a hint of distrust in her eyes, but the passphrase — it seemed — unlocked all doors and barriers. Giufrio was now amid those who sought the truth.

They had gathered with wine glasses, the Society of the Argent Fist, amid a brightly-colored orange room. About them were paintings of the hero Theron in his lion-skin, the hero Helemon upholding the world of Varda on his back, and depictions of the Fharese-Eloesian War of ancient days.

The truth tellers were mostly young, fresh faced, and Giufrio's appearance did not stifle their laughter and their clear love for each other. In a city and a world where everyone watched their back, the truth was a potent salve.

And Giufrio was here to listen.

He took a seat at the far end of the table.

The truth tellers in the room seemed to gravitate toward one man in particular, brown of hair with green eyes. Between sips of wine they vied for his attention, and at last he spoke.

"The philosopher Nepodamos told us to be hospitable to our guests," he said, "for we do not know if we entertain a man of great stature, or great moral virtue. We do not know if he has great insights to share. And I see that we have a stranger here for this week's meeting. Let us welcome him."

Giufrio waved lightly.

The smiling faces made him feel at home. He felt disarmed, trusting.

"What brings you to the Society of the Argent Fist?" said the leader.

"I am here about Alessandro Sopis," Giufrio said.

The warm looks changed to ones of fear, but the leader gestured lightly with his hands. "He is new," he said. "He doesn't know the state of things in the east. Yet the fact he speaks so boldly, makes me think he is a true Imperial and not a false one."

The leader gazed into Giufrio's eyes, and he found himself disarmed even further.

"We call Alessandro Sopis the archon, and use no other name," the leader said. "The Politarch of Public Good is dumb and dull, and awful to look at, but she's locked up and killed three of us for getting too close to the truth."

And Giufrio realized, he was among people he was learning to love, though he was the Marshal of the Guard, an official in a government that had been persecuting them.

"Tell me why you're here about the archon," said the leader.

"The archon wrote a great book," Giufrio said. "Can I say the title?"

"Yes," said the leader.

"*The History of Celsus Heights,*" Giufrio said.

"Where so many started to learn the truth," the leader said. "And now, you know, the truth is being hidden."

"There were pages missing from every book in Imperial City," Giufrio said. "The same pages were gone in each book."

"Yes," said the leader. "Cheers, to someone who has taken his first step."

They took a sip of wine in unison.

"And now you question, now you wonder... why are the pages gone?" the leader said. "I'll tell you — "

"Giufrio."

"Giufrio," said the leader, "that the answer to that will lead you to why three of our brothers have been killed in the past year. It turns out when the Imperial Bay Company wants a book gone from the shelves, they'll find a way to make sure the truth is never learned."

Now, Giufrio knew he was on the right path.

"But I saw it coming," said the leader. "I had a copy of all the archon's books. And when the Politarch of Public Good came knocking, I told them I had lost them in a shipwreck. The fat toad believed it."

"Pardon," Giufrio said, "may I take a look?"

"I don't trust anyone unless they've drunk a full cup of this stuff," the leader said.

And Giufrio ordered wine, and as he drank it, he realized he had never felt so at ease, never so happy to be in other people's company.

The leader had a small apartment outside the Lion's Gate,

Thénai's traditional entry place.

The apartment was clean and well-manicured, spotless, and gleaming.

And through a door, and past a hidden panel in the wall, beyond the security of a locked box, were stacks of books.

The History of Celsus Heights was among them, and Giufrio could tell by the way the cover didn't sag that all the pages were complete.

He started where he had left off.

After Celsus's death, the town continued to attract investment. It became the home of conciliar families and the home of various noblemen across the Empire. It was then that new visitors arrived to the wealthy community. The patriarch of the new arrivals was one known as Jacra Thuban and his wife, Umu Thuban, whose first port of call was in the city of Thénai. The people, called the Qab of Thuban, were not native to Eloesus, either, but claimed in former times to hail from a town called the Rawsh of Thuban, and their land they called only the Ash-Land. They were fleeing persecution in the east, from which they were rescued by the intervention of the Imperial government in the year 841.

From the time of their arrival toward the close of the 10th century, the Qab of Thuban became traders and merchants. They would buy items in Imperial Square and then resell them at a higher price. There was a rumor they would file off the edges of gold and silver coins and then return them to circulation, but when the rumor threatened to turn into a riot, the Imperial government stepped in and thoroughly quashed it.

Giufrio continued to read, overcome by intense interest. He noted a passage toward the middle of the book:

Membership in the Qab of Thuban is passed down from mother to daughter, and from mother to son.

And Giufrio knew that the Jiacomo Thuban currently in control of the government was not the Thuban of the book, but that Thuban was a surname, and a family, to which he belonged.

He continued to read.

As the 800s turned into the 900s, the Qab of Thuban had accrued great wealth, and any discontent by the people was thoroughly quashed. The merchants of the Qab of Thuban began to intermarry into the Imperial elite, especially the Lornodoris family and the Kerius family.

And so he had it... why Huardo Lornodoris, the majority owner of the Imperial Bay Company, wanted Thuban in a position of power. He had used the Imperial Bay Company to threaten a boycott of tar, and the threat of that boycott to install one of his relatives.

Yet there was still no relation to Valeria Verra.

And even without Valeria Verra in the picture, Giufrio had a gut sense.

There was something more to all this.

Something much more.

"Thank you," Giufrio said to the leader. "My eyes have been

opened. But mostly, I wonder why the Imperial Bay Company was so keen on destroying these pages."

And Giufrio had another gut sense, a gut sense about where he could get all of the unvarnished truth.

"Where is the archon, now?" Giufrio said.

In the privacy of his apartment, the leader boldly said, "Alessandro Sopis spread a rumor about his death. Many believe it. But now he is hiding in a monastery. He is hiding from the Qab of Thuban. The priests are protecting him."

"You trust me," Giufrio said to the leader. "Trust that if I learn the whole truth, I can help you. What monastery is Alessandro Sopis in? Where has he taken the brown robes?"

"Cloud Temple Monastery," the leader said, "in Paladium."

Chapter Twenty-Four: The Contest of the Muses

The day was scorching, the day was hot, when Fortunato heard something that caught his ear.

"At today's Contest of the Muses, the Imperial court will be in attendance!" he heard a woman shout to her friend, amid the swarming crowds of Imperial Square.

The Contest of the Muses was a musical competition, held at the storied Odeon Theater in the Maxima District. And something else Fortunato knew, that there was only one sequestered section for the well-to-do, and the seats were available to anyone who would pay an exorbitant price.

He had given up on visiting amphitheaters and race courses to see a glimpse of Reev, but this... there seemed a possible strategy to it.

"What do you say, Xan?" Fortunato said after he had explained the idea.

"Why not?" Xan said.

And then he added, "I have a good feeling about it."

~

For a ticket price that emptied all but two copper coins from his coin purse, Fortunato booked seats at the golden box in the Odeon.

The theater unlike others in Imperial City was indoors, and the attire demanded was of a higher quality than the dirty grease-spotted tunics Fortunato saw everywhere about him. Even in the seats where the riffraff sat below, in a manner of speaking, there was no loud talk, only silence, as the audience took their seats.

As Fortunato sat, he could see the judges taking their place —
he saw, a famed kitharode, Gallus, a singer he had seen on
advertisements, Flora, and a harpist, Fortunato remembered, called
Timolo.

And as he sat, and the audience settled into their seats, and Xan
took the seat next to him, he saw to his no small wonder that all his
mad gambits were about to pay off. For amid the darkness of the
golden box, a dark-eyed beauty passed through the open door, one
whose name Fortunato knew… Valeria Verra. The emperor's
mother.

She took a seat next to him and eyed him quietly.

There had been many other open seats.

Fortunato guessed he still had his charm.

She smiled at him. "A pleasure," she said softly, but before
Fortunato could respond, the red curtains of the Odeon began to
roll open. The audience swallowed any word he might have said in
applause.

Onto the stage strode a man, fair, his brown hair coming to tall
tufts at the end, his brown eyes gleaming. The torc he wore about
his neck marked him as a Wilderman. In his hand was a fiddle. At
once he began to play the fiddle and sing.

O bright Tyrus! Now shining as a youth, a bright zephyr
I vow to remember
Laying enemies low, his brilliant hair in brilliant sun
I vow to remember

Old and yet young, and something strikes him
But light grows great
I vow and surely remember
And then the world will fall to him

The man's voice was pure, his devotion to what he called Tyrus was heartfelt. And Fortunato wondered if the world he spoke of was Varda.

Gallus, the kitharode judge, began to clap. "A faithful rendition by Brennus of Potter's Brook of 'Tyrus War-Maker on the Antipean Shore.' Well done, and I congratulate you on the effort."

"Your voice is pure," said the female judge, Flora. "Your love pulses through every note."

"I think I know someone who's going to the next round," said the harpist judge, Timolo.

Brennus of Potter's Brook departed, and another entered, one everyone knew.

"Our emperor, Verrus," said Flora. "He has instructed, and I read, to treat him just as another contestant, and to 'let his music amaze you.' "

Fortunato realized Valeria Verra's hand was touching his thigh.

Verrus, red-haired and terrible-eyed, began to strum his kithara. His hands strummed the kithara with perfect skill, but without the passion that no one could teach.

His voice was also perfectly trained, yet passionless and dead.

O wine like ink, it flows
Pythio! O Pythia!
O wine so red, it grows
Pythio! O Pythia!
Flowing red down mountains
Pythio! O Pythia!
Ever a gift so great?
Pythio! O Pythia!
To hea'ns our praises go
Pythio! O Pythia!

The audience was silent. Verrus cleared his throat. "It was called, 'Ode to Wine.' "

The judges also fell silent. At last, Flora spoke.

"Well, Verrus," she began, "I can tell you've practiced... It was — it was — ehrm — how should I say this..."

"Workmanlike," said Gallus, "like a workman. A skilled workman."

Verrus glared at them, fuming. He seemed able to understand the judge's, and the audience's, and Fortunato's reaction.

He was awful.

"The kithara was out of tune!" said Verrus. "Let me tune it."

He began to crank and pluck the strings.

"Here! Let me start again!" said Verrus. "This one's called 'Strychus and Nysimachë.' "

From the golden plain of Harkeon
I bring to you a Nautilan tale
A tale of rich hues and dark colors
Yes, one to stir joys and sorrows both
The tale? Strychus and Nysimachë!

A woman screamed in the audience.

Yes, please gather round and settle in
For the tale though interesting is long

A man fainted. An infant began to cry. A woman sitting in the back began to wail, a man to weep — as if he had been sentenced to die.

Time will fly by you as a sea-bird
As I sing feats of the Cnidan coast

A man sprinted for the exits. A woman joined him. Fortunato could feel a rawness in the back of his throat.

Valeria Verra howled "Mama monster loves you, Verrus!" and that settled that, not even Reev's rescue was worth the price of being Valeria Verra's paramour.

Hecatomb hecatombos! Take heed...
Hecatomb hecatombos! Enjoy...

Fortunato could feel his heart racing, as men and women raced for the exits, as he worried if he left right away, he'd be caught in the stampede. The judges were looking this way and that, not sure what to do.

The story begins, as all good tales
With a prologue that sets the stage...
A prologue to paint scenes without ink
But I shall not rush this wondrous tale...

Fortunato no longer cared for his safety, or about Valeria Verra leading him to the Imperial Palace. He only needed to flee. He vaulted over the golden box, into the crowd that was now stampeding out of the Odeon, for fear of hearing just one more of Verrus's notes.

He fled, and Xan was behind him.

Hecatomb hecatombos! Take heed...
Hecatomb hecatombos! Enjoy...

The fresh air kissed Fortunato's cheeks, the fresh air and the sunlight. He would no longer have to hear Verrus's music. And in that moment, that sweet moment, it seemed worth the cost of abandoning his quest.

Chapter Twenty-Five: Star Power

The gates opened, and Wrinn had a craving for more.

He had a craving for more applause, more battle, more blood in the sand.

And he watched as, to his surprise, the arena promoters were finally trying to find his match.

For now, not just one walked out, but two, one dressed in the bulky armor of the Myrmidon, another dressed in the spear-and-shield bearing Thartan.

And Wrinn thought not of his life, not of his safety, but pleasing those in the crowds, those gathered in the seats for the afternoon games, those who now loved him.

He beckoned with his hand and the cheering grew louder, as the Thartan and the Myrmidon began their charge. He swept with his quarterstaff and met the spearing of the Myrmidon's trident head on. His quarterstaff, carved of red yew from the forests of Doncalion, did not break or splinter at the blow. And when he caught it, his admirers among the audience howled out his name — his elven ears could distinguish it amid the roar.

The Thartan struck, and Wrinn pivoted out of the way, taking the trident with him. Using his quarterstaff, he flung the trident yards into the distance, struck the Thartan in the head and speared the Myrmidon — but the Myrmidon was covered head to toe in iron plates.

Curses!

The audience howled and cheered as the Thartan charged. Wrinn dove away and the Thartan tripped; he took his longknife and pierced the Thartan, straight through, in the neck — as the crowds roared, an earth-shaking thunder, a world-quaking blast.

But the Myrmidon was now on him, and tackled him to the ground.

He had wrapped his gauntleted hands around Wrinn's neck. "Why?" he heard the Myrmidon grunting. "Why, Wrinn Finnis, do the crowds love you best?"

~

Wrinn had dispatched the Myrmidon, and he had dispatched the Thartan. The sand had grown redder, and Wrinn's fame had grown more undeniable.

Now, he was sitting in the relative relaxation of the pit, as Scauro tended to his wounds.

"Good work," said Scauro. "You scared me out there."

"They sent two after me," Wrinn said. "What are they thinking?"

"The promoters like a good show," Scauro said. "They want the audience on the tip of their toes. And soon you'll be a right star..."

"How much money have I made today?" Wrinn said.

"Fifteen denara," Scauro said. "A right star, Wrinn... a right star, you'll soon be..."

Chapter Twenty-Six: Dinner at Verrus's

At dinner, Valeria Verra acted every bit like she thought Reev had been a ghost, an apparition of Verrus's true father, an apparition of the husband of the one who sat across the table from him now, who was stroking his hand.

He had told bits and pieces of the truth to Astarthe, former Queen of Khazidea, to whom now he was the platonic consort.

But Valeria Verra had not acted the part of suspicious empress mother. She was now acting the part of empress mother scorned.

Her son, Verrus, dressed in purple, sat at the purple table alone.

Valeria Verra was sitting at a table far off and eyeing him constantly.

Reev had not told Astarthe what he had witnessed. He was not yet ready to break her heart.

For Valeria Verra had confessed before Reev that Appian was the father of Verrus, and Valeria Verra seemed to give the impression that it was a dark secret, not widely known.

How would Astarthe feel, to know she had some relation to such spawn?

Astarthe was eyeing Reev, and her brown eyes glinted, as the doors to the kitchen opened and food was served — a dish, steaming, was placed on their table by a scullion.

Astarthe opened the dish and her lips puckered. "Flamingo tongue," she said with a grimace. She placed the cover back on. "Perhaps, you are a more adventurous eater than I. I've tried it once before. Only one person in the palace likes it."

"Who?" Reev said.

Astarthe's eyes inched in the direction of Valeria Verra, and in the language of friends, it was clear it was who she meant.

But Valeria Verra, sitting at the table alone, was not touching her dish.

She opened the cover and puckered.

As the diners began to eat, Verrus was looking at his mother.

"Won't you eat it, Mother?" Verrus said. "Your favorite!"

"I'm not hungry," said Valeria Verra. "I had a late lunch."

It was untrue. Reev had seen her eat lunch with the rest of them.

And Verrus, it seemed, was keenly intent on his mother eating the flamingo tongue.

"Eat it!" Verrus said. "Eat it, Mother!"

"No," Valeria Verra said coldly, "I will not, ever."

"Shall I force it down your throat, mother?" Verrus said.

"I'd like to see you try," Valeria Verra said.

Her words seemed to drive something in Verrus, and he stood up and stormed over. "Eat it!" said Verrus.

"Did you put something in it, Verrus?" Valeria Verra said.

Verrus drew back, and began to weep softly. The feasters of the dining hall were all looking at the spectacle in stunned silence.

"Perhaps," said Astarthe, "we should eat this in private."

~

They took the dinner to Astarthe's suite, and the flamingo tongues, on a bed of groats, were more palatable than Reev imagined.

"I feel," Astarthe said, "there is something you're not telling me. Something you're leaving unsaid..."

"You know me all too well," Reev said. "I told you — "

"You told me you were in the Imperial closet," said Astarthe. "You told me you witnessed a fight."

"I did not tell you everything," Reev said.

He hesitated even now, but he and Astarthe, now fast friends, he her platonic consort, should be truthful — so he thought.

"Valeria Verra told Verrus that Appian is his father," Reev said.

Astarthe did not take in a sharp gasp of air, nor did her eyes widen in surprise. No, her eyes softened and then looked away, seemingly transported to another place, another time.

"I had a thought," she said. "Long ago... so, so long ago..."

She had indeed been transported.

"For as a youth I played the part of Khazidean queen. The Fertile Queen must be fertile. But when I married Appian, I never so much as looked at another man, until I met you."

Yet Reev and Astarthe's relationship was platonic.

"But Appian... he betrayed me twice. Once, in Khazidea, with a woman like me. Then, when he was invited to Valeria Verra and Lucio Verrus's wedding. For then Valeria Verra fell upon him, and he was whisked away in a moment. He apologized to me constantly. He said... he said... it was not about basest passion to her, or so it seemed to him. She wanted something — his life, his essence. And he apologized continuously throughout our marriage, to his dying day."

"Did you forgive him?" Reev said.

"I did," Astarthe said, "but when I looked at Verrus — I had a quiet thought, one I tried to repress. For Appian would be so ashamed. I hope he has found his rest... I suppose it is all true about Verrus and my husband."

Now sadness seemed to dawn in her eyes. She looked up sharply. "We shall get you to your room. Big things are afoot. We leave for Porto tomorrow."

"Porto?" Reev said.

"A resort city on the northern tip of the Island of Dualmis. In late Brenua it is our custom for the court to move there. And when the heat is too intolerable even there, in Sextil... we make our move for the mountains, in Paradise Gardens."

But Reev had a feeling he would not go so far, that he would be gone from these people soon.

~

Reev stirred awake in his private chamber. It had to be the witching hour.

He could hear Thuban's voice, even now, in the middle of the night.

"You know, Valeria, we switched out your plates," Thuban said. "He intended to give you the black mushroom-laced dish, but we have been taking care of you."

There was silence a while.

"You aren't going to Porto," Thuban said.

"I am," said Valeria Verra. "And I know the son I raised. I know what he intends. But I did it for the *qizim* everywhere. If he kills me, it was worth the cost."

"So selfless are you, Valeria," Thuban said. "Not a *qizim* trait."

"I will not die, if I can help it," Valeria Verra said.

Chapter Twenty-Seven: Truthward

When Giufrio stepped off the ship into the harbor of Sanctum, he thought he saw a city under siege.

The vestals and monks walking about the harbor did not acknowledge him, but hurried about, on their way, doing their business hastily.

Outsiders, in Sanctum, the city of priests, it seemed were unwelcome. But Giufrio wished them no ill. He had only the highest love for the priests and the Pontifex.

Yet he wondered what the source of their fear was.

And he remembered there were no taverns where he could gather intelligence, on just how to find this mysterious "Cloud Temple Monastery" that Alessandro Sopis was hiding in. There were no real civilians here, only monks and vestals and servants of the Magisterium. The libraries they had were not open to the public. And though Giufrio did not want to use it, he wondered if the Writ of Mandamus was his best bet.

Where was Cloud Temple Monastery? Where could Giufrio begin?

He began inquiring amid the white temples and white-faced monasteries, of any priests who would venture to give him their time.

And they gave him his time, but the information they were willing to divulge was lacking.

"Cloud Temple Monastery?" they would mutter. "Why are you asking this?"

And at last, having asked every monk and vestal on a street

called Straight Street, there was commotion around him — amid the monks in their habits and the vestals in their white veils, a man pushing through in a brown friar's robe. He said, "Signor Giufrio, you called yourself," he said. "The Pontifex would like to speak to you."

The Pontifex, the chief of the priests of the Empire and the wider world, wanted an audience with lowly Giufrio. And lowly Giufrio would grant his request.

~

The Pontifex was the chief of a council of priests and representatives of the priestly orders called the White Synod.

Giufrio walked amid the grand arches and vaulted ceilings, following the friar who called himself Niko. He passed statues and statuaries, amid marble tiles and marble grandeurs, reliquaries and frescoes to dazzle the eye. And then he passed through a vast corridor, and through that corridor a door — beyond the door, a humble chamber overlooking the ocean and the glittering white city of Sanctum.

There, the Pontifex stood in his miter and long white robe.

"Giufrio," he said. "Marshal of the Guard. And one I trust, for I saw you are a devoted member of the Temple of Hieronus in Villa Regis."

"I haven't been there in years," Giufrio said. "The palace work has enveloped me."

"Honesty," the Pontifex said. "I was right to trust you. And I question, why do you ask of Cloud Temple Monastery? Be as honest as you were before."

"I — "

Giufrio paused. If there was anyone to trust in the world, it would be the Pontifex.

"I hear someone is being hidden there," said Giufrio.

"Someone you are after?" said the Pontifex.

"Far from it," said Giufrio. "For I feel I am beginning to discover a grand conspiracy, one I have only begun to unravel."

"You are an agent of the Imperial state," the Pontifex said.

"The Imperial Council," Giufrio said. He pulled the Writ of Mandamus from his cloak pocket. "They compel you to obey."

"The boy who went to temple in Villa Regis will compel us to do nothing," said the Pontifex.

"But he will ask, and plead," said Giufrio, "for he wants no harm to come to Alessandro Sopis, but only wishes to know what Alessandro Sopis knows."

The Pontifex smiled. "Well, Giufrio," he said. "I am inclined to trust you."

The smile vanished.

"One now sits on the Imperial throne," said the Pontifex. "And with his appointment, the skies in Imperial City turned a shade of crimson. He is currently bound to the terms of a weakened emperorship. He is emperor, now, in only name, and the Imperial Council restrains him at every turn."

"It can stay that way with your help," Giufrio said. "I'm doing this on behalf of the emperor's enemies."

The Pontifex nodded. "I will send you an escort to Cloud Temple Monastery. I will tell no one of this. In the Cloud Temple Monastery, the former emperor Claudian once took the brown robes. Claudian, whom the east falsely called a god."

The Pontifex was peering out to the sea, yet his mind and his eyes appeared to be elsewhere, in another place, another time.

"The truth," said the Pontifex, "will change your world."

Chapter Twenty-Eight: Doors and Gates

On a boat guarded by Imperial soldiers and Imperial marines, Astarthe and Reev her platonic consort rounded the island of Dualmis, and at last, found themselves at a natural harbor within the glittering sea.

There were mounting hills around the natural bay, and on the mounting hills brilliant white villas. There were men and women sailing in the bay on vessels designed for pleasure. As the boat drew near, Reev saw taverns along the shore, taverns in which men and women in the finest of clothing — clean tunics of white or yellow, brilliant embroidered gowns of red and pink and scarlet — sat with glasses of wine amid the constant sea breeze, which helped abate the constant heat.

And he had a thought — a sense — a remembrance of words said, now half forgotten, that Porto was a scene of debauchery too, that the most illicit entertainment could be found in this place, and were part of its draw.

As Reev stepped off the boat, with Astarthe's arm hooked in his, he wondered how he'd go about locating his necklace here, if it was in the possession of the Imperial Guard — yes, the Imperial Guard.

For not only did they protect the emperor and the emperor's court, they conducted investigations in a city without a city-wide town watch. Perhaps, they had been investigating Reev's sudden, mysterious arrival, and in the course of their investigation, found Reev's coin amulet and set it aside.

Barcho, the second-in-command of the Imperial Guard, passed by Reev and Astarthe. He had a mind to follow him. But he had to be careful; he had to be wise.

~

"Our former villa," Astarthe said as they broached a gate, and found themselves at a long walkway lined with cypresses and palmettos. "Appian and I, I mean."

And as Reev walked, arm in arm, with Astarthe, down the walkway, and as the gravel crunched against his shoes, and looked at the stable in which horses still roamed, he had an inexplicable feeling that the place he was venturing to was haunted.

Beside a fire, as Astarthe made a Khazidean bean-and-rice stew, doused generously with long peppers, Reev wondered at the marble statuaries, and at the paintings of simple pastoral scenes from Gad, Appian's home province.

"Where was Appian from?" Reev said.

"Gad," Astarthe said, "and how often did he say he missed it…"

"I mean, which town?" Reev said.

"Norriva," Astarthe said.

Reev took in a soft gasp. "That's not far from Norwood," he said. "Of course, in Norwood, they had taken to calling it 'Norbrook' in a proud Getan manner. Anything Imperial they attempted to erase."

"He was from a small town," Astarthe said. "His family was of small wealth, but of illustrious lineage. He and his best friend, Numa, saved the Empire. I witnessed it… I was part of it."

Reev wondered how many stories Astarthe had to share. She had been a sorceress once, but had given up her powers… she had married an Imperial war hero and become one to whom the Imperial court owed an open invitation. Both Appian and Astarthe had come from illustrious family lineages, unlike Reev.

Yet wasn't being of Telantine blood the most illustrious lineage of all?

"My necklace," said Reev as the stew bubbled and boiled, and its aroma filled the great hall, "I had a thought — the Imperial Guard has taken it."

"It's possible," said Astarthe. "They are always investigating things, always prying, always searching. And though I tried to keep the manner of your arrival hidden, I sent soldiers to fetch you from the water. They know; they remember transporting you to the palace."

Astarthe took bowls and began to ladel the stew into them.

Then, as she handed Reev his bowl, her eyes sparkled. "You know," she said, "the Imperial Guard is holed up in a villa three doors down, across from Verrus's. And Verrus is gone tonight — he is touring a construction in Porto. The Imperial Guard will be gone, too."

"We should try," Reev said. "We should see."

"Are you willing to take that risk?" Astarthe said.

"I am," Reev said.

~

The cicadas were singing, and the ocean's happy breeze was too far to offer much relief from the baking heat. Reev, in his tunic, was sweating as he followed Astarthe, as sunset turned to night.

Venturing, together, they headed down the gravel walkway, then turned down the road. Both of them were sweating and panting by the time Astarthe made a motion, and began to walk down the road.

Reev had a horrible sense, a pang of nervousness and fear, that he had drawn in Astarthe to this mission, one she wasn't equipped for.

Yet he did not stop her as they passed down the cypress-lined lane, to a vista of an empty stable, and a villa that had seen better days.

Reev watched as Astarthe walked up the path, and then to the front doors. She laid her hand around the knob and twisted, but the door wouldn't open.

"Locked," Astarthe mouthed.

And Reev felt that familiar fear rise in him as he followed her around the front door, to a side door.

The door on the side had been bolted shut.

And there was commotion — there was noise, shouted voices rising above the silence. Astarthe waved, and then began to sprint into the woods, as Reev caught a glimpse of the face of Barcho the lieutenant of the Imperial Guard, and then joined her.

They fled through the woods, and were back at Appian's villa. Amid the dying embers of the fire, they questioned whether Barcho had seen them.

Chapter Twenty-Nine:
The Challenge

The gates opened, and the arena promoters had sent an army.

Well, not quite an army, Wrinn noticed, but four gladiators dressed in the attire of a Khazidee — chainmail gowns and two-handed khopeshes.

It almost seemed unfair, it almost seemed unworth the risk, but the crowds' excitement and love for Wrinn had grown with each new obstacle placed in his path. How could he say no to giving them a good show?

The gladiators struck with their swords, and their swords whipped the air against Wrinn's artful dodges. Wrinn struck with his quarterstaff, but their chainmail gowns were finely woven, and the gladiators' chests were well-muscled.

The crowd's cheering was lower in volume, a tenseness that struck the beginnings of fear in Wrinn's heart.

But Wrinn was the consummate professional.

He battered a gladiator twice with his quarterstaff. He struck with his longknife, but again the blade failed to pierce the iron scales. Another storm of blows came then, khopeshes cutting through the air — his arm was nicked, and then blood began to spurt. There were howls of fear in the audience, gasps his elven ears could distinguish.

He realized, he could not take these four on at once.

So, he wouldn't.

The gladiators struck, and Wrinn leapt away, yards beyond them. Wrinn was unarmored and unencumbered, quick on his feet.

The gladiators charged, and Wrinn crossed a wide berth, opening up space. There were disappointed hisses in the crowd as the gladiators failed to catch him, and in the stands, it was dawning on the bloodthirsty audience that they never would.

Wrinn wanted a good show. But it wasn't a fair fight. Maybe, if the promoters gave him a fair fight, he'd be inclined to give them the show they wanted.

~

"It's not fair," Wrinn said in the darkness of the pit, "and if it's fair, I'll fight."

"Be careful what you wish for," Scauro said as he dressed his wounds.

Chapter Thirty: God of Frenzy

The Pontifex had given Giufrio an escort, a paladin whose warhammer was tied to his back in a great brace. The paladin rode on a towering white charger, and the Pontifex had given Giufrio a warhorse of his own.

They were venturing east by north-east along a causeway through the sweltering reeds and stagnant waters of the swamps. The paladin had said, if Giufrio took this road, and did not stray from it, it would bear him to the Cloud Temple Monastery's high steps.

They had been days through a landscape that did not change, wetlands as far as the eye could see. They had traveled speedily, and the Pontifex in addition to providing Giufrio an escort, had given them ample road-bread and salt pork, and most importantly his blessing.

Indeed, the paladin and he seemed of one mind, and though they did not speak specifically of Alessandro Sopis, they spoke in guarded words of the one who sat on the Imperial throne, one whom the priests had come to view as unworthy, as an enemy.

And why did they view him as an enemy? Giufrio had a feeling Alessandro would tell him why. After all, it was the priests who had been hiding him, the priests who had been acting against the interests of the Qab of Thuban, when the Imperial government acted as their protectors and benefactors.

Perhaps, they who thought of the gods and heavens above all were not inclined in the Qab of Thuban's favor. Such people could not be easily bought off, and would never bow to threats of intimidation.

Yet the monks militant, though masters of hand-to-hand

combat, could not contend with the Imperial Army. So the monks and vestals, the priests of Sanctum, had to be shrewd in everything they did.

In the baking heat, made sweltering by the water, the air and the land itself seemed to waver. They were far gone from Paladium, when down the lonely causeway, Giufrio saw they were not alone.

A crowd of men were riding in on horses from the opposite direction, and though the paladin rode on as always, Giufrio had a sense in his gut, one he learned to trust.

He removed his nightstick from its brace.

The crowd had slowed their riding, and now were blocking any path through the causeway.

They were a motley crew, one a Khazidee, one whom Giufrio guessed was a southron. And they did not have Giufrio and the paladin's good in mind.

The Khazidee seemed to be the chief of them. He had ridden to the front.

"What is this about?" said the paladin.

The Khazidee said, "We know who you accompany, Signor Paladin."

The paladin at last realized this crowd was hostile. And he removed his war-hammer from its brace, wielding the mighty weapon in both hands.

"We do not like the questions he is asking," the Khazidee said.

"Why don't you speak to me directly, coward?" said Giufrio.

And Giufrio wondered if this unruly crowd of men, nine he guessed in number, would end his life, and end all hope of the truth emerging to the public. He uttered a prayer under his breath.

"Turn around," the Khazidee said, "and you will have no trouble."

Giufrio was not an equestrian. He was an Imperial; he fought on foot. And so he dismounted, and bore his nightstick, gazing upon the crowd with all the authority that had been given him.

"You won't be able to stop the truth from emerging," Giufrio said. "It always has a way…"

"We will not retreat," said the paladin. "We were sent by the Magisterium. We do not fear mortal men."

"You will fear me," the Khazidee said, and in the span of a moment drew something from his pocket. The next thing Giufrio knew, he was enveloped in a cloud of poison gas.

What happened next Giufrio did not know, a storm of steel and moving bodies, shapes against a green canvas, as Giufrio exerted himself to his maximum capacity, and also did not breathe. Something struck him on the head, but he rolled with the blow, as he blocked and jabbed, struck and disarmed, pierced and bludgeoned, with his nightstick in a wild Breckonalian frenzy.

When the smoke began to clear, he could see horses fleeing, and he could see the Khazidee fleeing too.

He chased him like he was a common criminal in Imperial Square, except now, Giufrio was fueled by anger. He sprinted down the causeway and caught up to the Khazidee. He struck and his skull burst with a loud crack; blood and bits of brain flew everywhere, even landing near Giufrio's lip.

And remembering what the Qab of Thuban had done over the centuries, and what they had done to Alessandro Sopis, and what they had done to the east and the Imperial world as a whole, he did not relent his blows, until the Khazidee was motionless and bleeding, crushed and bruised — dead on the causeway, before marshy ground.

Giufrio at last allowed himself to cough.

He looked back, at his work, and saw what had taken place amid that wild Breckonalia.

The bodies of their attackers lay bleeding or twitching, crushed on the ground. The poison cloud, cast by a coward, had given Giufrio the cover to work his magic.

Yet the paladin, he saw, was on the ground of the causeway,

lying still, bleeding.

Giufrio repressed a scream and rushed up to him.

Giufrio could see he had been stabbed, and that a knife was still sticking in his back.

"Go," said the paladin. "Don't worry about me. I will be all right."

He would not be all right in this world.

"Don't wait. Gallop! There are surely others. This road will take you directly there, as I said…"

"Gods be with you," Giufrio said.

And he knew they would be. His warhorse lingered nearby.

But the paladin's words had seemed a command, a final command from a good man.

And Giufrio swept himself onto his horse, and obeyed the words, galloping through the aftermath of his Breckonalian frenzy, down the causeway, knowing surely there were others.

~

It was late afternoon when the first sign of what was coming emerged.

The outlines of mountains to strike awe in anyone, so massive they scraped the sky, mountains no Imperial had ever crossed before, stretched from one side of Giufrio's horizon to the other.

Even now they were a promise, but the promise struck terror in anyone who saw them for the first time. And Giufrio was seeing the Sky Mountains for the first time.

He uttered a prayer. He remembered the paladin's words.

Then, he galloped on.

Chapter Thirty-One: Porto

From the villa down to Porto, Reev walked with Astarthe's arm wrapped around his own.

The descending dirt road became a paved street, the paved street to avenues and squares, amid homes. And as they broached the outskirts of Porto, there were concrete buildings with red-shingled tiles, on them the words in Imperial, "Enter and Enjoy."

Into them, old gangly men were entering, and Reev shuddered at the thought of what they would have to endure, who received them.

"Porto," said Astarthe said, "a home of the rich, and those of perverted appetites. Almost anything can be found here for those of a twisted mind."

~

As they drew near the beach, there was a performer in the street easing the breadth of a sword down his throat. As he drew the sword back out into the air, a young man in a midriff shirt gyrated about the blade as beside him a boy blared a double aulos.

A woman patted on a drum a sensual beat as the young man gyrated with his hips and spun about the now extended sword, then twisted, singing softly, as he did, nonsense words. Others had gathered to leer at him and watch.

The young man removed his midriff shirt, then wriggled about the handle of the sword with such sinuous movements he seemed to have no bone in his body, as if he were a serpent coiled around a doctor's staff. The young man reached for his belt and as he did the crowds around him shouted in excitement.

Astarthe wrapped her arm around Reev tightly and sped him along. "Hurry! Hurry! I will try to protect my good boy from what is available in Porto..."

But Reev had a feeling, Porto would follow them.

On the sandy beach, the Imperial court were lying in the sun. Some wore swimming garments, but Barcho the lieutenant of the Imperial Guard, and Valeria Verra most notably, were garbed fully.

Verrus, wearing a swimming garment, his misshapen pasty body bare to the sun, had stepped up to the shore, and was dipping his toes into the water. He was a striking figure there, and Reev wondered what dark thoughts the emperor was having as he peered into the horizon.

"Porto!" someone was shouting from the street behind. "Where old men come to become young boys again and young men come to become girls! Our emperor is here, and he cannot resist..."

But Verrus did not seem taken with lust. His mind seemed focus on power and nothing more, on how to demolish the enemies standing in his way.

And Reev wondered what dark designs he would have if ever the terms of his emperorship were absolved. What would he do, with Valeria Verra in his ear? Reev still could not figure out what drove them, and what they ultimately wanted.

He did not want to be here, with them. He wanted his necklace, and then to be on his way.

But if he had not accompanied Astarthe to this sandy beach, he would no longer be hiding in plain sight. And hiding in plain sight was what he had done, even as "Thuban" and the cabal searched for the Telantine they knew had come with Fortunato.

As the waves crashed to shore, Verrus turned and eyed his mother Valeria Verra darkly. "Mother," he said. "Go on a walk with me..."

"I'm feeling a bit ill," Valeria Verra said. "I'm sorry, son, I can't."

Verrus looked at her with fury.

The tension between him and his mother had grown. It seemed he was caught between hate and love, the two strongest emotions. And Reev did not know on this day if hate or love would win, which emotion would prevail.

Valeria Verra had managed her life goal, to put her son on the White Throne, and — she had claimed — it was worth the cost of her life. But those were just words, and whatever evil designs Verrus had, Reev did not wish to witness.

"Shall we go for a walk?" Reev said softly to Astarthe.

"A walk?" Astarthe said. "In Porto?"

~

Reev did not wish to witness Porto's famed debauchery. But Valeria Verra and Verrus were in a contest again, and he didn't want to be caught in the aftermath.

And so, hand in hand, he and Astarthe went on a stroll.

Past a main square when a woman was dancing sensually, past a tavern where drunk men were staggering out not long after noon, Reev took note of what looked like a small house off the side of the street, and saw a pair of men stepping out, their eyes turned to shades of crimson.

"A drug den," Astarthe whispered. "Red eyes — that's what Haroon spice will do to you, long term. And make you dull and dull witted."

Reev wondered why people even bothered.

But amid all this, Reev felt he was in a relative safe haven, compared to the contest underway between Valeria Verra and Verrus.

And Reev knew he could escape them, and this, in Galiope. But

Galiope was far away, and he knew in his heart he would never return.

What had happened to Galiope? What had happened to Miss Glenda? What had happened to Ambrass, whom once, it seemed, was engaged with Fortunato in a bond of love?

The Imperials controlled Galiope, now. The Galiopeans were at the Imperials' mercy.

These people, Reev thought, as they passed by a street and saw a domed building with flashing green lanterns.

"The Temple of Bregedo," said Astarthe, "is nothing more than a gambling hall."

A woman was exiting the doors, weeping. Reev wondered how much money she had lost, spending so frivolously. He uttered a prayer for her as they passed along the way.

And Reev had seen just about enough of Porto. He wondered if Valeria Verra and Verrus had been separated, or if the contest had ended, and there was a victor. When there was a victor, maybe there would be a bit of peace, enough stillness and quiet to search for and find his necklace, and secretly depart.

They had made a turn and were facing wharfs and docks, and the waters of the natural bay. The midday sun was roasting, and the powerful ocean breeze was only a mild relief.

"Valeria Verra against Verrus," Reev said. "Who will win?"

"Valeria Verra finally got what she wanted," Astarthe said. "Her son is on the throne."

"And what will they do with their power now?" Reev said.

"I shudder to think," Astarthe said, "of what would happen if the Imperial Council fails, and all safeguards are removed…"

Chapter Thirty-Two:
The Greatest of All Time

The gates opened, and the sun shone down. The heat was baking in the Imperial Arena, as Wrinn expected the promoters again to send an army of gladiators, so as to find his match.

But instead, one strode out, a man garbed head to toe in full plate, wielding a massive sword in his right hand, and a tower shield in his left.

It was not a gladiator. It did not have the weaknesses of the Myrmidon, with his trident and his helmet that made vision difficult. It did not have the weaknesses of the Thartan, with his light armor. It was merely a man dressed for war, a killing machine.

And the promoters had agreed, one man versus one.

But this wasn't fair, either.

Yet he looked to the crowds and saw them massing, adoring faces now cheering his name. He had disappointed them once. He couldn't disappoint them now.

And so he waited as the armored man charged, and allowed him to think falsely that his *dó kentari* attire and quarterstaff made him helpless.

He allowed him to get close.

Then, remembering his training, he took a quick step, and struck with his quarterstaff as the man pitched back his sword to strike.

He crashed into the sand of the arena, falling face-first into the dust.

The stands erupted, an earth-shaking thunder, a world-quaking blast, a cacophony, a raging fire — a thousand, eighty thousand, shouting and cheering in unison.

The man had dropped his sword, and Wrinn had made it look

easy.

And despite his training, he wanted to rub it in. He dropped his quarterstaff, and picked up the man's sword — or tried to. The armored man had carried it in one hand, but it was so large, Wrinn struggled to carry it in two. As the man struggled to return to his feet, Wrinn pitched back the mighty sword and plunged it through his armored plates, all the way through his chest.

Blood spurted in a geyser, and the sand around the fallen gladiator turned red.

The water organ began to play, but the cheering was so loud, so manic, so world-shattering, that Wrinn could no longer hear it as soon as it began.

"Wrinn, victor" — the attendants rushing out said it, but Wrinn could only see them mouthing it.

He could hear nothing except the earthquake of the audience's cheers.

Wrinn stood staggered by the noise, the overpowering cacophony. He at last had fallen to his knees.

There was nothing, now, except the noise, nothing more than the audience before him.

~

"You're a right star, now," said Scauro in the dark cool of the pit. "You've earned your place with the greats."

Wrinn could not argue against it.

"Remember, old Scauro is the one who really has your best interest in mind," Scauro said. "A lot of people will approach you, now, and try to lead you down the wrong path. But Scauro never will, and he's proved it."

"How much money have we made?" Wrinn said.

"I don't want you to get too a big a head," Scauro said, "so I won't tell…"

"I'd like to have some of it," Wrinn said.

"In the bank, it collects interest," Scauro said. "Old Scauro gives you your allowance, doesn't he? He doesn't let you spend frivolously."

But Wrinn thought it was his right to spend frivolously after all he had risked, after all he had been through.

"Now, Wrinn," Scauro said, as he dabbed at Wrinn's dust-smeared forehead with a damp cloth and cut some hairs off his ear, "I have an opportunity for you I won't let you say no to."

"No unfair matches," Wrinn said.

"You won't have to risk life and limb at all," Scauro said. "Easy, free money. You'll have to go on a little stroll, however…"

Chapter Thirty-Three: At the Villa

It had been a scorching day, and now it was a scorching night. In Appian's former villa, Astarthe did not even dare make a fire to cook, but instead served Reev a salad made from chickpeas and garden greens.

Reev had avoided Porto in the days that ensued, and he and Astarthe had mostly holed up in the villa, and plotted, and planned.

Yet Reev was growing restless. "I think I'll go to Barcho's villa," he said. "I'll improvise. I'll find a way to search."

"But Verrus and his mother are at home," Astarthe said. "The Imperial Guard will be in that house, all of them."

Yet waiting until the Imperial Guard was gone seemed a poor proposition. Perhaps, waiting for a moment would be best, a moment when they were unguarded, a spare fleeting second where Reev could uncover his amulet, and then quickly find Fortunato and depart for *Naron Da*.

Leaving Astarthe would be difficult, however. She had become something dearer than a friend.

A guide… a beacon. No, a consort, full and true….

"You're brave," Astarthe said, "and when you get that fire in your eyes, I know I can't stop you. I'll stay behind. Finish your chickpeas first…"

~

The woods were dark outside Appian's villa. The skies were cloudy, and there were no moon or stars to be seen. Total darkness clothed Reev as he made his way down a path he had walked once before, now cutting through woods and the yards of other villas and not using the road.

The trees were dark shapes, and the villas were dark shapes. Reev knew he stepped to danger. But he knew he had a calling — to venture to *Naron Da*, to tread Seymus underfoot. And so he pushed past the trees, and pushed his fear away.

He had reached the villa.

There was an Imperial Guard standing at the door. Reev watched and waited. And then he remembered a door to the side, bolted shut. Would the bolts hold?

He passed around the villa, cloaked in darkness and unseen. He saw the door which Astarthe had tried and failed to enter. He walked up, tried the knob, and it was locked.

But around the villa, there was motion and the sound of shouting — people bearing torches, a crowd standing far off down the walk. The Imperial Guard, once standing at the front door, was walking toward the torch-bearing crowd.

And Reev seized the opportunity given to him.

The front door was open. He entered into the villa's winding chambers and corridors, a villa once in use but now a barracks for the soldiers that protected the emperor and his court. There were no paintings hanging on the wall, only whitewashed plaster. And where would they hide his amulet?

In the course of their investigation, if they had seized it, where would they hide it away?

He began to look through the rooms and saw in one a storehouse of swords and axes, gleaming weapons ready for the fight. He saw in another crates and boxes, which Reev did not have the equipment to unlatch.

The villa was a labyrinth, and there was little hope of him finding the amulet without help. He wondered — was there a way to ask, a way to inquire, a way to learn the information, without letting on that he was a Telantine?

There were muffled screams directly up above him, a wild cry — like someone needed help. Reev rushed down the hallway, up the stairs.

~

In a room on the second story, lamplight was flooding in from a room down the hall. Imperial Guards were posted at the door, and they saw him, and looked at him with no suspicion.

Reev, they thought, was a member of the court and nothing more, Astarthe's consort. Or so they thought.

The muffled cries were coming from the room.

Reev walked up and looked into the room, with so many lamps, it was as bright as daytime.

Barcho, the Lieutenant of the Guard and the current marshal in Giufrio's absence, was looming over the struggling form of a man.

The man had his hands and legs tied, and Barcho had a razor up to his neck. The man's arms and legs were bleeding.

"I said, who sent you?" Barcho screamed.

The man said something, muffled, delirious in pain.

He was garbed in dull grays and browns, and didn't seem like he belonged in Porto, an enclave of the rich.

"*Who sent you, scum?*" Barcho screamed, and this time sliced his shoulder with the razor.

The muffled cries turned to a scream, words formed, vowels and consonants: "Corvus Corbulo!"

~

When Reev departed from the villa, he saw the torch-bearing crowd included Verrus and a hysterical Valeria Verra, together with

Appenina the Younger and her husband Dario. Astarthe was now among them, having walked down the road. She took Reev by the arm and led him away, into the night darkness.

"A conspiracy," Astarthe said softly. "A conspiracy, to kill Verrus and attempt to install another emperor by the acclamation of the Guard."

They began walking through the woods, as cicadas sang, and the ocean breeze began to blow and to gust.

"Half the Imperial Guard was involved," Astarthe said. "They've fled, but they won't get far. And Corvus Corbulo — the worst will be saved for him."

Corvus Corbulo, Reev remembered, was the Speaker of the Council.

"Now, Valeria Verra has an opportunity," Astarthe said. "To install loyalists in the Imperial Guard — and a new council, not as hostile to her son. Corvus Corbulo tried to kill Verrus, but only made him stronger…"

And that, Reev thought, was a bad thing for the Empire, and for the world of Varda as a whole.

In the morning, reports swirled that the fleeing traitor guards had been captured to a man and had been put to death. Corvus Corbulo had fled for the Anthanian hills but had been captured. And the Imperial court could no longer afford to vacation in Porto but would return to Imperial City to restore law and order.

"Gods help us all," Astarthe said softly in the fresh morning air, and then buried her head in Reev's chest.

Chapter Thirty-Four: Just One Denara

It was Odens, and Imperial City was a furnace.

In the baking heat, the crowds in Imperial Square seemed to have lessened, but most simply continued their daily activities with a weary heart, under the burning sun.

Fortunato and Xan stood alone, plotting, planning, wondering, when they saw the crowds begin to gather in that familiar spot, around the stage.

Fortunato sighed. And yet he had been a diligent listener to the actors all this time, for hope of hearing something about Reev.

Sylvia and Rufo, the actors, appeared amid the lessened crowds. The sun burned down hot upon them.

And yet, as consummate professionals, they had not lost any of their heart or their cheeky grit. As they spoke in the baking sun, they had all their charisma and their magnetic draw.

"What shall we talk about today, Sylvia?" Rufo said.

"I have a surprise for you today, Rufo," Sylvia said.

"What's that, Sylvia?"

"Today's play is going to need some assistance from the Actors Guild, quite a few hands to make this thing work..." Sylvia gestured, and Fortunato saw a crowd behind them on the stage.

"Why do we need so many, Sylvia?" said Rufo.

Sylvia smiled. She flicked her dyed-blond hair back. "Today, Rufo, we're reenacting the seven thousand Thartans in the Pass of Meropis."

"Seven thousand Thartans!" Rufo bellowed in a manner worthy of a thespian.

"But first," Sylvia said, "a word from our sponsor..."

To the stage, one ascended Fortunato knew, one he couldn't

believe. Wrinn was standing there, and behind him a man in a cloak, whose face was scarred, with a prominent harelip.

Wrinn's sandy blond hair glistened in the scorching sun. It had been clearly styled and touched up with grease. Wrinn was holding in his hands a glass vial, in which was a bubbling blue liquid.

"After a hard day's work in the arena, fighting off all manner of Wildermen and Myrmidons, I turn to Regulo's Potions for anything that ails me," Wrinn declared. "Whether I have a body ache or a cut or a septic dribble that won't stop, or whether I just want a taste of something bubbly, I order one vial of Regulo's Miracle Concoction every night."

There was no way that was true, Fortunato knew.

"For just one denara per month, you can be like Wrinn Finnis and have Regulo's Miracle Concoction delivered to your door. Sign up at Regulo's Potions, 7 Wayward Street in Meridia."

Wrinn departed with the cloaked man. Sylvia and Rufo seemed uncertain what to do — and then they were looking away, peering beyond the crowds, in horror.

Fortunato looked where they were looking, to the gates of the palace, and saw the horror for himself.

A head had been mounted on a pike, the head of an old man, a head which was beginning to rot. As Imperial soldiers fixed it to a post, others came by with a wooden sign, and set it before the pike. The sign read:

CORVUS CORBULO
THE PENALTY FOR TREASON

There were whimpers of fear in the crowd, and the crowds quickly began to disperse. The actors began to inch away.

Fortunato wondered if they would continue with their play.

~

Far away from the pike, in a corner of Imperial Square, now quickly emptying, Fortunato and Xan talked softly.

"I think we should leave," Xan said. "Lay low a while…"

"But Reev is at the center of all this," Fortunato said.

Corvus Corbulo, he had gathered, was the Speaker of the Imperial Council. He had apparently attempted to kill the emperor.

What then, could they do? What could they possibly hope to do, waiting here? Fortunato had tried all manner of desperate gambits. What was there to do, besides marching through the doors and taking on all of the Imperial army at once?

~

In the soft candlelight of the tavern called the Suckling Pig, Rufo and Sylvia did not have their famed glamor. No, Fortunato thought, having happened for the first time on the same tavern as them, they seemed to belong amid the raging crowds of Imperial Square.

Not just Rufo had tattoos, but Sylvia too, and they were loudly complaining as they swilled their wine.

"Those *lupas* ruined a good show!" Sylvia said, and her voice was gruff and hoarse. "All we wanted is to put on a good show! That's all we wanted!"

"But also to educate!" Rufo shouted. Both of them had clearly had too much. They had started long before Fortunato.

"Yes, yes, we're educators, too!" Sylvia said. "About the seven thousand Thartans in the Pass of Meropis! That was valuable information that the people of the Empire could have learned."

"Seven thousand Thartans!" Rufo bellowed, and then he burped.

"And then those *lupas* put out a head on a pike, and it frightens the kids away! And we're empty handed! Why would they do this to us?" Sylvia's chalk makeup was growing smeared. Fortunato realized there were tears running down her cheeks. "We're educators, we're actors, we're teachers! We're all the people in this city have! They look to us, the poor, the hungry! And the *lupas* in charge ruin it! Why would they ruin it?"

The bartender shot them a look that seemed to say, "Get a hold of yourself!"

"It's not all glamor in this business!" said Sylvia. "It's hard work, and it's not good enough pay!"

The bartender looked ready to throw them out. The patrons of the tavern were looking at Sylvia and Rufo uncomfortably.

"Everyone says, look at you, Sylvia, you're so lucky, standing up there with all those doting eyes!" She brushed her dyed-blond hair. "No one sees the work that goes into this business! And they ruined it! Those *lupas* ruined it!"

The bartender was biting his tongue, hoping the actors would calm down, but Fortunato didn't think they had any intent on slowing down that swilling of their wine.

"It all started with the new emperor, if you ask me!" Sylvia said. "If I may be so bold…"

"Seven thousand Thartans!" Rufo bellowed.

Chapter Thirty-Five:
The Gate Beckons

It was a hot Odens morning when there was a knock on the villa door.

Reev rushed to answer, and saw Barcho standing there, the Lieutenant of the Guard.

He could sense Astarthe walking up behind him.

"Signore Consort," said Barcho, "a moment of your time?"

~

"We in the Imperial Guard are locking things down," said Barcho. "Making sure there was nothing we missed."

Reev nodded.

Barcho had taken a seat before the empty fireplace, and Reev and Astarthe were facing them in chairs of their own.

"I want, for the record, with all honor and justice as our witness, neither you nor Lady Astarthe have had any contact with Speaker Corvus Corbulo or the other three members of the Imperial Council who were conspirators…"

"Not at all," said Astarthe. "We have not said a word to any of the traitors, neither I nor my consort."

"As you know, there were traitors even among the Imperial Guard," said Barcho. "And yet…"

He fixed his eyes on Reev.

"There are mixed reports on the manner of your arrival, Signore Consort… Astarthe claims you accompanied her when you arrived at New Year's, but some say you arrived in a more mysterious manner… that you were connected to a shipwreck that came to shore, with one traitorous Fortunato of Ríva."

"Astarthe is an honest woman," Reev said. "Will you doubt her?"

Reev could feel his heart beginning to race. He was a terrible liar.

"I am sorry," Barcho said. "It's a tense time. And yet — I am afraid — you have not heard the last of this line of questioning. You will hear from me later…"

Barcho had departed, and Astarthe was beside herself.

"You must flee, Son of Telantis, and leave your amulet behind…"

"I will not," Reev said. "I am more determined than ever."

~

The next day, Sylvia and Rufo were nowhere to be seen on the stages, and the crowds milled around in confusion. Fortunato plotted and he planned, but the head on a pike before the Imperial Palace's gates seemed a warning not least to him.

What would they do, now?

Xan was appearing from amid the massing crowds.

"Fortunato," he said, "Signore, as these people say. I hear gathered word, some in the mob have taken Corbulo's side, and others Verrus's. I think it is our job to stay out of it."

"It is our task to rescue Reev," Fortunato said.

But now it seemed impossible.

"There's a rumor spreading that Corbulo wished to cut the dole, and Verrus wished to increase it," continued Xan, heedless of Fortunato's comment, "but some say Verrus wants to limit the distribution of tokens…"

That seemed to be the main concern of the Imperial City mobs, the mobs that councilors and emperors feared and wished to pacify.

The gathered mob was a difficult force to quell, and had great power, not just in its votes.

Fortunato's eyes inclined to the Imperial Palace. The head, it seemed, it was a message to him in particular.

Paranoia, perhaps. Thoughts of grandeur, maybe.

The head on a pike seemed to beckoning, *Really, Fortunato, are you man enough?*

He was.

~

Astarthe had packed her luggage as the Imperial court announced its plans, to make a frenzied return to Imperial City in the height of summer.

And as they bade goodbye to Appian's former villa, Reev had no small feeling of regret that peace could not have endured, and that he was now empty handed.

Fortunato, Wrinn, Xan — they were surely beside themselves. Yet his powerful feeling that he could not leave without the amulet was only growing stronger and more ironclad.

And he had a thought, that hiding in plain sight was better than hiding in Imperial City itself. For Valeria Verra and Thuban searched for the Telantine, to kill him, but they would never look among their own selves.

At least, they would not look yet. Barcho, however, had begun inching in that direction.

From the villa, down the road, they walked in the direction of Porto. Reev said a prayer for Fortunato, for Wrinn and Xan, under his breath, and his sense he should not leave without the amulet only grew stronger.

Could any but the gods create such a powerful feeling?

And yet, worry and fear crept in as he and Astarthe descended into Porto, as the road continued, and as they reached the bay and the Imperial court appeared in view. Verrus was standing there beside his mother, a crafty look in his eyes. And as Reev and Astarthe drew near, he saw they were walking into the midst of a conversation.

"Mother, I insist, you must ride in the boat with *me*," Verrus said.

"I will take my own boat," Valeria Verra said. "Another boat, entirely."

"Be careful what you wish for, Mother," Verrus said.

And the gleam in his eyes was not just crafty, it was diabolic.

Chapter Thirty-Six:
The Truth At Last

Wrinn was not immune to the news that had spread like fire throughout Imperial City.

There had been a conspiracy against the emperor, and as the conspiracy unraveled, the breadth of it was just beginning to make itself known.

"They are still arresting people," said Scauro in the cool damp of Imperial Arena's pit. "The Dux of the Brotherhood of Candlemakers... somehow, he was involved. They all really don't like Verrus."

"They don't," Wrinn said softly. And Wrinn thought that no one acted totally irrationally, that they must have seen something in Verrus that truly earned their enmity.

"The arena promoters have been asking questions," Scauro said. "Whatever happens, make sure it's clear, you love Verrus as the emperor."

Wrinn did not know Verrus from Solarias.

"You might perform for him," Scauro said, "after all..."

~

As tensions in the city grew, Fortunato had a thought growing, that he should storm the gate. It was insane, the height of folly, true madness amid true madness, but what could he do, and how could he get the mission back on track? The tension in the city was palpable, and he had witnessed fights amid the gathered mob, of people who had taken one side or another.

And where was Sylvia, and where was Rufo? Now, no actors even dared to broadcast the truth in the veil of drama.

Idling in Imperial Square, Fortunato looked ahead at the pike, at the gate, and wondered if it would break free with a quick charge. He imagined himself as some ancient hero, bursting in and slaying ten thousand men, rushing away with Reev and flying to *Naron Da* on the wings of an eagle. But he had to be realistic.

Yet as he stood, he listened, despite the tension threatening to spill into actual violence, the tenseness of words unsaid threatening to come to blows or sword-blows.

A woman was speaking: "The court has called an emergency session. They're returning to the city, from Porto!"

And was Reev among them? Could Reev be long dead? Could he be rotting in a jail somewhere? Was it possible?

~

From the harbor to the Imperial Palace, Reev and Astarthe walked with an armed escort. He passed through Harbor District, in the wake of Verrus and Barcho walking far ahead. They were passing beside the monuments and titanic temples that preceded Imperial Square. They were approaching the palace when Astarthe looked back, and then whispered in his ear. "Valeria Verra is not with us," Astarthe said.

Reev looked back too.

Then he realized, only one ship had docked with them in the harbor.

~

From the sweltering marsh, to a snowy loft in the sky, Giufrio had made his ascent. Far below, the air was sweltering and swarming with midges. Here, in the Sky Mountains, there was fresh snow. And ahead of Giufrio, between two mountainous ridges, was Cloud Temple Monastery.

Cloud Temple Monastery was massive, and it overlooked a high valley. It was faced with stone, and composed of several domed buildings, with storage houses for food and wine. An ancient paved path wound its way amid the titanic complex. Monks in brown habits were shoveling snow and ice from the paths as Giufrio on his warhorse pushed on.

Here was what the Imperial Bay Company so wished to squash, knowledge that one who hid here possessed. Alessandro Sopis was not far, now. And Giufrio wondered if the Imperial Bay Company had assumed they had driven Alessandro Sopis so far from public life, he was no longer enough of a threat to kill him.

Yet the truth would emerge. This, Giufrio vowed.

As he broached the courtyard, the doors to one of the out buildings opened, and a man strode out dressed in a brown habit.

His dark hair was cut in a tonsure, leaving the top of his head bald. Judging by the way he balled his fists, Giufrio guessed he was a master of hand to hand combat.

"Who intrudes upon the Cloud Temple Monastery, of the most reverend order of St. Traber?" the man said, presumably the abbot.

"One who wishes for your good," said Giufrio. "One sent by the Pontifex. One who wishes to hear the wisdom of Alessandro Sopis."

"I sense," the abbot said, "you were not intended to come alone."

"I was not," Giufrio said. "My pursuit of wisdom has had a cost. A paladin is dead. Bad characters killed him on the causeway across Paladium."

"Gods help us," said the abbot. "What the so-called *qizim* will do, to keep the truth from emerging. I shall show you to Alessandro Sopis, a man we dearly love."

~

Alessandro Sopis had his own set of rooms, a bedroom, a kitchen, a parlor and a study.

Alessandro Sopis was not as Giufrio expected, but Giufrio wasn't sure what he had expected in all. He was an easterner, clearly, with dark curly hair and an aquiline nose. He was sitting in his study when Giufrio found him, a quill in his hand and a paper on the desk, and some writing on it.

"Signore," said Alessandro Sopis. "An Imperial, I see. What is this about?"

"The truth," said Giufrio.

He pulled the Writ of Mandamus out of his cloak pocket.

"Also, this," Giufrio said. "The Imperial Council, with all its authority, compels you to obey."

Alessandro looked at Giufrio with a mocking smile. "I've been beaten in Isteros. I've been attacked in Imperiopoli. I've had my house and money seized by the Politarch of Public Good in Thénai. Do you think a man such as me will bow to the Imperial Council, or any government of mankind?"

"I don't," said Giufrio. "And I know it might not seem like it, Alessandro, but I'm on your side. For I noticed, certain pages were missing from your work, *The History of Celsus Heights,* in Imperial City. Every single book had the pages removed."

"The people you work for did that," said Alessandro Sopis, "at the behest of the Imperial Bay Company."

"I don't work for the Imperial Council," said Giufrio. "I serve the people. People like you. And I want to know the truth, because I don't know if you've heard, a new emperor has been appointed, and he has some connection to all this."

"A new emperor," Alessandro Sopis breathed. For a moment, there seemed to be a trace of fear in his eyes. "Marcus Amaranthius has been removed…"

"You're two emperors behind, in this monastery all alone," Giufrio said. "One sits on the throne now, named Verrus, and his appointment has something to do with the Imperial Bay Company."

"Gods help us," Alessandro Sopis said with a gasp.

"I want the truth, Alessandro," Giufrio said. "All of it. Because I'm not working for the emperor who just provoked that reaction in you, I'm working against him. And I'm an investigator, a professional. I know something's amiss when I see it.

"Why did the Imperial Bay Company want those pages removed?" Giufrio said. "They didn't quite seem so shocking to me."

"That's because I was only able to disclose a little of the truth," Alessandro Sopis said. "And in the end, what I did was too much for them."

"*Them?*" Giufrio said.

"There's another place, more private," Alessandro Sopis said.

~

Alessandro Sopis took a candle and together they ventured down into the cellar.

"I don't think anyone can hear me here," he said.

"Whatever makes you comfortable," Giufrio answered.

He lit more candles, and Giufrio could see a large empty space that seemed sound proofed, so as to cancel out all noise.

"I can't believe they finally did it," Alessandro Sopis said. "They have one of their own on the throne."

"Who?" Giufrio said. "The Qab of Thuban?"

"The Qab of Thuban aren't what they say they are," Alessandro Sopis said.

"What are they?" Giufrio said.

"For one, they aren't human," Alessandro Sopis said.

"What are you talking about?" Giufrio said.

Alessandro paused, and his voice lowered to almost a whisper.

"When the Qab of Thuban first arrived, people recognized them as belonging to a hostile species called the anguipeds. They couldn't blend in at first, but they came with ships and began — first at Thénai — to work their dark magic."

"This isn't in the book, Alessandro," Giufrio said.

"I only wrote what the publishers allowed," said Alessandro. "I dared not write the whole truth. For when the anguipeds were rescued from their persecution in Thénai, the Imperial government granted them special protections, seeing them as enterprising merchants and potential boons to the Imperial budget.

"They began to intermarry with the Imperial elite. In the first generation of intermarriage, the progeny loses their green and scaled complexion. In the second generation, their ears become rounded. In the third generation, they are indistinguishable except to experts, and as I'm sure you've learned, all the experts except me have been killed."

"And what do they want?" Giufrio said.

"The destruction of the Empire, and Varda itself," said Alessandro, "so that they can have a safe place to breed, and grow in numbers."

Giufrio believed Alessandro Sopis.

And he also realized other things, in that moment. For in the prior century, the Imperial Council and the government as a whole had taken actions that seemed inexplicable, not consistent with the nation's interests. The anguipeds in the government surely had a hand in it.

According to Alessandro Sopis, they had intermarried into the Lornodoris and Kerius families most extensively, names that had stuck out as villains in prior years.

And another fact was now evident, that the emperors Claudio and Numa had struggled mightily against these foes, but had not understood their true nature.

They had thought they were fighting traitors, when they had

been fighting anguipeds.

"My eyes are now opened," Giufrio said. "I thank you, Alessandro Sopis."

"You aren't mocking me, are you?" Alessandro Sopis said.

"No," Giufrio said. "Not at all. I believe I understand, now. And now, I believe we should all fear and resist the one now on the throne."

But still, there was no connection to Valeria Verra. More work was yet to be done before he could submit a report to the Imperial Council.

Chapter Thirty-Seven: Qizim?

The dinner, the night they returned, was like the calm before a great thunderstorm.

Everyone ate in silence, and Reev, fearing being noticed, uncharacteristically rattled, worried that Verrus at his purple table would take notice of him.

So he ate his roast pheasant in silence, and Astarthe was silent too as she ate. A cloud of suspicion and tension was over all. And the sense, a presage, a calm before something terrible, was only growing as the hour passed.

A conspiracy had been uncovered, and though the conspirators had been killed to a man, no one could say for certain just how deep the conspiracy had gone.

The doors of the dining hall swept open.

Valeria Verra stood there in a black gown, with murder in her eyes.

She was sopping wet.

"Mother!" Verrus said, and there was boundless terror in his gaze. "What's wrong?"

"You know very well what's wrong, *mugush*-spawn," Valeria Verra said.

Her hair was dripping; her dress was soaked. The murder in her eyes as she stared at her son became something more.

What was more hateful than murder?

"I took a boat," said Valeria Verra, and took slow steps toward her son. "We were far out to sea. Then the bottom of the boat fell in, and I was stranded, far out to shore."

Verrus was shrinking back in his seat. No longer the emperor he was, nor a man, but a mouse.

"And I swam, Verrus, I swam, all the way back into the harbor," Verra howled. "For a *qizim* does not just slither. She swims, better than a dolphinfish. And do you know what else *qizim* do, Verrus? If one of her young resists her, she eats him!"

Reev's stomach turned, and he no longer wished to eat the roast pheasant.

Astarthe began to get up from her chair, but Reev pressed his hand against her palm and she sat back down. He thought, if they left now, they'd be noticed.

Valeria Verra and Verrus have not noticed you. When they do, the game's about to be up.

That's what the man on the Great Porch had said.

You have to play the game with what you're given.

"You're delusional, Mother," Verrus squeaked. "The boat was seaworthy."

"You'll have to do better than that, Verrus, to kill a *qizim* mother," hissed Verra.

And she took a seat in view of her son, and her demeanor changed. She carried herself like a victor. "I'll have two servings, tonight," she said. "Verrus will watch his mother eat."

~

"What's all this talk of *qizim* and slithering and swimming?" said Reev.

The Great Porch offered a gentle breeze, a respite from the baking heat. The hand fans and the narrow windows simply weren't enough.

"I admit, I don't know Valeria Verra or Verrus very well," said Astarthe. "Before this New Year's, we only interacted on a few occasions over the decades. My husband Appian knew her a bit better. Her first husband, Lucio Verrus, co-signed the loans to rebuild the east. That is how my husband knew her…"

"I think there's something more to this than meets the eye..." Reev gazed, to the twin statues looking out to the city, Emperor Numa and Emperor Claudio, on the edge of the grand porch.

The doors opened, and Reev did not hear it close.

And a man was standing there. If Reev had seven denara, he would have bet six that he had seen the man walking about the palace somewhere. But whether he was a cook or a scullion or a member of the cleaning crew, he did not know.

He was not the same man who approached before, however, the one with tawny hair and blue eyes.

This man had dark hair and green eyes. He was dressed in a brown vest.

"Signore Reev," he said, "Barcho is on his way to question you. I recommend you hurry to your quarters and shut the door. If he thinks you're sleeping, he won't bother, and then I'd say there's about a seven out of nine chance he won't remember to question you in the morning."

"Where is my necklace, if you know all these things?" Reev ventured to say, but the dark-haired man smiled and exited as quickly as he had come.

Astarthe looked deep into Reev's eyes.

"I will obey him," Reev said. "I think he probably knows more than I..."

As Reev entered his private bedchamber, Appian's former workroom, he heard footsteps approach, a gait that he recognized as Barcho.

Barcho lingered a while, and then the footsteps echoed, the opposite direction he had come. The dark-haired man had been correct.

~

Reev stirred awake, and took in a sharp cold gasp. It was pitch black outside, surely the middle of the night, surely the witching hour.

"They will name a new Speaker of the Council tomorrow," Valeria Verra said in the adjoining room. "They are thinking of Mamerco Formusalis. He is not one of us, but he is pliable."

"Your son almost kills you," Thuban said. "You keep trying, with all your might, to give him power."

"Will I abandon the hope of our kind because of my life?" said Valeria Verra. "I have lied, I have cheated, I have stolen, I have killed... and now I will let my fear of the one I raised end all our hopes?"

"There is no hope for us, as long as a single Telantine lives," said Thuban.

"My son will hunt him down," Valeria Verra said. "My son will kill him."

"Your son's gift for politics and craftiness has amazed everyone in the Assembly of *Qizim*," said Thuban.

"My son... my son..." Valeria Verra paused, and there was an uneasy silence.

"Your son looks just like one of them," Thuban said.

"Except his eyes," Valeria gasped, and then she wailed, "His eyes! His terrible eyes!"

~

It was a little after dawn when there was a knock on Reev's door.

Reev remembered the warning from the dark-haired man, but, he supposed, if Barcho wanted to interrogate him, he couldn't stop him.

He hurriedly donned his tunic and trousers. He rushed to the door.

Astarthe was there, something hovering on the tip of her tongue.

"Reev," she said, "come with me. The Imperial Council is meeting today. Valeria Verra and Verrus are trying to end the Amarothic emperorship and give themselves a true one."

As they passed down the hall, she said, "There is a way to view the Imperial Council chambers, and the entry is in the palace."

Through a darkened door they walked, then descended down some stairs. They followed a dark tunnel under the Sky Bridge, lit sparsely with lamps, and Reev's heart shuddered as the floor creaked underneath his feet, at the thought of how far a drop it would be if the floor gave out. They took a turn, and then another, then one more. They had come to a dark chamber.

"The spy room," Astarthe said. "Once, the public could view the Imperial court's proceedings on certain days, but now only members of the emperor's court can do so. The laws were changed in the 10th century."

She finagled with something, and as light poured in, Reev saw she was opening wooden shutters. Beyond the shutters were an iron grill, and beyond the grill, a view of the Council Chambers.

A stone bench was in the middle of the spy room, and Astarthe sat down, followed by Reev.

The seats of the Imperial Councilors rung a circular marble space. There was a white chair and a yellow chair. Valeria Verra was sitting in the yellow chair, and Verrus was standing amid the circular floor.

"Speaker Formusalis, I was already saying — "

The man who interrupted Verrus had a thin, pasty look, wiry gray hair and weak eyes. "Your own mother accused you..."

Valeria Verra stood up from the yellow chair. "Your Honor, I was mistaken. There really was a flaw in the boat the designers didn't see. Please, correct Corbulo's mistake and end this Amarothic emperorship."

But Formusalis, despite his weak gaze, despite the fact he seemed a puppet, he was a puppet of the twenty-five other councilors around him, not Verrus.

There had been three conspirators in the Imperial Council, Reev remembered, beside Corbulo. Now, the number of Imperial Councilors was twenty-six, until new elections could be held.

"The manner of your son's appointment has still not been resolved," said Formusalis, "whether it was achieved through illegal means."

Valeria Verra did not hiss or howl, but sat back in the yellow chair with a crafty look in her eyes.

A councilor then spoke, one with white hair and blackish eyes. He was confident whereas Formusalis was timid. Reev saw a nameplate beside his seat: *Malchus*.

"I know you are eager to begin your emperorship," Malchus said, "but good governance takes time. And the Imperial Council will thoroughly complete its investigation before any status is changed. We all here agree that Speaker Corbulo's actions were abominable and beneath the dignity of his office."

"It was treason," said Verrus.

"Yes, it was," said Malchus. "But do not take our thorough investigation as a stalling tactic. We are only interested in the facts."

There was a pause.

"The emperor has made a motion to end the Amarothic emperorship," said Speaker Formusalis as if he were reading from a text. "I, however, counter, with a motion of continuance. Do any here object to the motion of continuance?"

There was a long silence, and no objections. Verrus did not curse or howl or hiss. He bit his lip. He was determined, and woe to Varda when he succeeded.

Chapter Thirty-Eight:
Past, Present, Future

Giufrio had learned a lot, he realized as he crossed into Sanctum's glittering harbor.

He had learned that the enemies of the Empire in recent centuries, perhaps a millennium, had not been at all what they seemed.

Monks and vestals hurried about their business, and Giufrio would say a prayer for them. But he had not left empty handed. He had gotten a little closer to the truth.

Yet one issue remained, one connecting piece... how to draw a line, from Valeria Verra to the anguipeds? Valeria Verra and Verrus were now entangled in the web of Imperial City politics.

But they were not from Imperial City. They had been guests in the palace when they engineered their coup.

And so, in the harbor, amid the priests and vestals, he inquired at the harbor office.

"My signora," he said, "when does the next ship leave for Nichaeus?"

"An hour from now," said the woman behind the desk. "If you deposit your money now, you'll be able to get aboard."

And so he would go, and venture, and risk life and limb, to make war on the anguipeds. Unlike Claudio and Numa, he would have a clear idea of who the enemy really was.

Before the day was done, Giufrio had left aboard a carrack, heading southwest through the sea.

~

Fortunato was pacing besides the Imperial Palace's gate. He did not know where to turn, who to turn to. It seemed to beckon, to dare him.

And he wished to push through, he wished to try his luck.

Yet as he stared at the gate, something else was filling him, a strange feeling, a feeling of longing and desire.

He found his eyes gazing to the Council House.

~

Reev had been in the spy room more often than he had not.

It was a dark place where he was not easily seen, where Barcho did not know to look for him, and where every day, there was a new chance to spot someone wearing his necklace, as the proceedings of the Imperial Council continued.

The Imperial Council had mostly dealt with the failed coup and its aftermath as the days proceeded, but one afternoon, there was a different sense in the air.

An Imperial soldier in a red-crested helm and a red-half cape strode into the central floor. He looked up at Speaker Formusalis and hailed him.

"Your Honor," said the soldier, "the Widow Queen of the Gypsies has been captured outside Haroon. She and her people were making their way through lands they do not belong and disturbing the locals. The governor wishes to put her to death and sell her people into bondage."

Formusalis twisted his lip. "Such affairs the Council cannot legally deal with, according to our rules and binding codes, without the presence of the emperor. Summon the emperor at once, and the Widow Queen you have captured."

Reev waited in the dark of the spy room for what seemed like hours, until at last there was motion, the door opening. Verrus entered in, and sat in his place, in the white seat.

Then the doors opened again, and soldiers strode out, and following them, one Reev knew.

Reev gasped, and his heart soared, at the sight of one he knew. It was Ambrass.

But then he remembered the danger she was in.

She was dressed in a light raiment, fresh-faced and beautiful. Her long dark hair flowed down her back.

"Your Excellency the emperor, Your Honor the Speaker of the Council, Your Eminencies everyone gathered here, I come to beg for my life, and the life of all my people," she said.

"And why should we let you continue to disturb the people of Khazidea?" said Formusalis. "Are their lives not as valuable as yours?"

Ambrass turned to Verrus, the one who really held her life in his hands.

"Your Excellency," she said, "our people do not wish you harm, only to be on our way. For we have been driven out of Galiope, and other towns before it, and wish to find our home, our true homeland, Vharat. We wish to coexist with the Empire and your glorious throne. We will do our best not to disturb the people of Khazidea, and all the Empire's possessions, as we make our way home."

"Why do they call you the Widow Queen?" said Verrus.

"My husband Gaius has passed on to see the gods," said Ambrass. "He is with our god, Kama, now."

"And why should I not have you killed," said Verrus, "and make a pretty denara off those wagons we have captured, not least your people. What can your people offer us?"

"Our god Kama can tell you your destiny," Ambrass said.

Verrus's cold eyes seemed to lighten, if it were possible. "Go on."

"I will agree to tell you your future, but only if you agree, you will let us pass," said Ambrass.

"This is nonsense!" shouted Formusalis.

"No," said Verrus, "I will be told my future. I agree."

Ambrass drew from her raiment the set of *tabbac* cards Reev had seen before, in the comfort of Glenda's inn. She strode before the lookers on, mouthed a silent invocation, and drew the top three cards from the deck.

"Past," she said, and flicked the card down on the marble floor.

The card came up, face up, a monstrous black figure with horns.

The Devil.

"Present," she said, and flicked another card down.

The shape of the world, blue water and green continents.

Varda.

"Future," she said, and a wind seemed to swirl, and the card landed face up between them.

Judgment.

Verrus howled and grumbled. "Foolish Widow Queen," he said. "I will have you killed anyway, and sell your people in the slave markets of Karthoon."

"No, you will not," said Speaker Formusalis. "An agreement has been made, and while the council is in session, it has the force of law. The Widow Queen will depart, and will have passage through Khazidea."

Verrus grumbled quietly as Ambrass gathered up her cards and departed through the doors.

~

As Fortunato stared at the gate, there was a pang in his heart; he had a sense he had missed something, that something dear was departing from him. As afternoon tilted toward night, Xan took him by the shoulder.

"Come, friend," said Xan, "let's have a drink."

And Fortunato agreed, and followed Xan, and left whatever he was missing behind him.

Chapter Thirty-Nine: The Truth Hurts

They were days out to sea. Aboard *The Jaine*, Giufrio was on the deck of the ship, as they passed by black-soiled uninhabited islands, ringing around a spot of open water. Above-head, there was a patter of rain, a harsh wind uncharacteristic, and as the vessel left the islands behind, Giufrio got a terrible sinking feeling, that gut sense that had never led him astray before.

~

It was days later when that gut feeling bore fruit. As they drew closer to Nichaeus, Valeria Verra's hometown, ships appeared on the horizon, black-sailed ships.

Pirates were hardly to be seen throughout the whole of the Imperial Sea, ever since the Empire had completed its conquest, but Giufrio had made powerful enemies. Would a powerful enemy allow pirates to sail the open seas again, just to neutralize its foe?

Giufrio had a thought it would.

And he had another thought… the truth would die with him.

As the black-sailed ships drew near, Giufrio put a hand on his nightstick and uttered a prayer.

An image flashed in his mind — a pot-bellied man in a panther-skin, wine dripping red down his fat cheeks.

And the black-sailed ships were gaining on them.

"Pirates!" howled the sailor at the ship's wheel. "I thought they were gone from the seas…"

The pirate ships were not so heavily burdened, and they were moving at a faster clip, on the back of the wind. They were quickly gaining on *The Jaine*.

As their massive prows drew near, Giufrio saw they were carved in the shapes of dragons, and that there were three ships in total.

The one now skipping next to *The Jaine* had corvuses.

In the span of a moment, the iron landing bridges fell, to the crunching of wood, and pirates fled onto the deck of *The Jaine*. They were dressed in a motley assortment of clothing, with bandanas covering their mouths, but their eyes, and the shapes of their faces, reminded Giufrio of Alsumo, the kitchen maestro, back in the Imperial Palace.

The captain of *The Jaine* drew his sword and rushed at the pirates. "What is this?" he howled.

But the chief of the pirates raised her hand and howled, "It is not about your merchandise, Captain Spurio."

Another image flashed in Giufrio's mind. The pot-bellied man was now astride a panther. His panther skin had been transformed.

"Not about our merchandise?" said Spurio. "What is this?"

"A passenger!" howled the pirate captain. "He has not told you what a wretch he is! For he wishes to bring our people to ruin! He wishes to thwart the grand design..."

Spurio looked to Giufrio.

"To arms! To arms!" Spurio howled, and the crew members of *The Jaine* drew swords and daggers.

"He is asking so many questions, and doesn't think of the consequences!" said the pirate captain. "Like what will happen, if the Telantines succeed!"

"Get off my ship!" said Captain Spurio.

And another image flashed in Giufrio's mind. The pot-bellied man on the panther was now offering him a glass of wine.

Drink.

"The world is not just yours," said Giufrio. "The anguipeds do not deserve a safe place, at the cost of another's destruction."

"Anguipeds! Look how he defames us!" said the pirate captain. "We are *qizim!*"

And Captain Spurio struck with his sword. The pirate captain narrowly blocked.

Another image flashed in Giufrio's mind, and he had drunken deeply of the pot-bellied man's wine.

Brecko... he was seeing Brecko, god of wine.

But Brecko was also the god of frenzy.

As battle consumed the deck of *The Jaine*, pirate against merchant, Giufrio joined in as his mind conjured up the sound of a frenzied hymn.

He struck the pirate captain with his nightstick and no blow had ever been so sweet. He struck the pirate captain again and the pirate captain's skull was crushed.

A bleeding body now lay on the floor.

Captain Spurio was pierced straight through by a pirate, as Giufrio gave in to the sound of the Breckonalia, piercing one pirate and bludgeoning another, jabbing a pirate off the deck and hearing a splash and then striking another to the sound of a desperate wail, blocking a blow and disarming a pirate in one motion.

Dance! he heard a voice, and he did a dance of battle to the tune of a frenzied hymn.

He utterly gave in to the Breckonalia, to the sound of frenzy, as a storm of blows consumed him, and he thought of nothing else.

Brecko! he heard a cry as he struck an anguiped pirate, and heard the crunch of crushed bone.

Wine! he heard a voice as he tackled a pirate to the ground and beat him mercilessly with his now dripping nightstick.

"Fury! Frenzy! Song!" he shouted, having given in, striding across the deck amid the frenzied dance, the sound of the frenzied hymn, the taste of imagined, intoxicating wine on his eager tongue.

And then he saw the aftermath.

The bodies of the pirates lay scattered about the deck of *The Jaine,* in physical positions that did not seem possible to Giufrio.

The bodies of the crew of *The Jaine* also lay about, their bodies cut or pierced with knives or swords.

And both *The Jaine* and the pirates' ship were taking on water. The poorly-designed landing bridge had damaged both vessels.

The cowardly anguiped pirates in the other two ships were now sailing away from the scene of the crime.

But Giufrio was still breathing.

And there was a lifeboat.

Chapter Forty:
The Frost Giant

The gates of the arena opened, and Wrinn strode out.

He looked back, and saw for the first time, the Imperial box was occupied.

Verrus was watching his show.

And so Wrinn beckoned with his hands, and the audience responded. Their cheers grew louder and louder.

He wanted the emperor to know how much the crowds loved him. After all, the emperor was paranoid.

~

Reev couldn't believe his eyes. His dearest friend, Wrinn, was standing amid the sands of the arena in the loose white garments and the quarterstaff and longknife of a *dó kentari.*

He was risking his life, and Reev couldn't help but think Wrinn was doing it for him.

Verrus, at the front of the Imperial box, was watching the gladiatorial games for the first time in many weeks. The crowds did not seem to love him.

They loved Wrinn, but they did not love Verrus.

~

Out of the gate opposite came another, and Wrinn saw again it was not a gladiator, but a man dressed for war.

A warrior, a soldier, a killer, strode out before the audience, garbed in full plate. And Wrinn remembered the intelligence that Scauro had disclosed, against all arena rules, that the man he was fighting was not a Getan from the province of Gad, but instead what was called a Geath, a barbarian among true barbarians.

The Geath's milky complexion and blond hair, his bright blue eyes, was clear to see in the sun. A frost giant he was, it seemed, and not a man — garbed in a horned helmet, and carrying a battle-axe in one hand that Wrinn didn't think he could carry in two.

The Geath tucked his shield in front of him and charged.

For the first time since Wrinn participated in the games, he felt true fear.

The Geath swung his battle-axe and roared, and Wrinn dodged just barely. Wrinn struck with his quarterstaff, but the Geath's wild swings had caused him to stagger too far back away.

He looked back at the Imperial box. Behind Verrus, he could see Reev — yes, Reev! — and there was a strange light in his eyes.

Wrinn felt a blow to his head, the blunt edge of the battle-axe knocking him to the dry dust and sand, and then the Geath's massive boot firmly stomp onto his chest.

There was no way Wrinn was moving.

The Geath leered above Wrinn.

He was looking to the Imperial box for a command, as was custom when the emperor was in attendance.

But Reev rushed forward ahead, in the front of the Imperial box, and twisted his thumb down.

The Geath grumbled in complaint at the command to spare Wrinn.

Some in the crowd booed, and some applauded. But Wrinn would live to fight another day.

~

"You've done bad, Wrinn," said Scauro in the pit. "You're losing star power by the moment."

Wrinn grumbled. But he had gained something; he knew Reev

was alive, and he knew he was amid the Imperial court, whether by force or by choice.

"We're going to have to up your game," said Scauro. "The promoters aren't going to like this at all…"

Chapter Forty-One: Yearning for Shore

The lifeboat had lingered for days on the open ocean. Giufrio had finished the last of the water yesterday, and the last of the road-bread two days before, when he sighted the coast. Before him was a green horizon, green growing trees and thick vines amid the scorching heat. And Giufrio was glad to see the shore, come whatever would, for another day and he'd be dead.

The anguipeds had drained him of all he had, or so they had hoped. He was thirsty; he was hungry. But he would not cease his fight, to wage war against them.

At last, he leapt out of the lifeboat, and swam through the sea, for shore.

~

There were cypresses and mangroves, vines and thick bushes all about Giufrio. Walking a foot through the forest took several blows of slashing with his nightstick. But he found a stream, bubbling through the thick mud and growth, and he cupped the water in his hands, and drank deeply of it.

To a man who had not drunk in a day, water was like the choicest of wine, the nectar that the gods were said to drink in heaven. He had his fill, and when he had had his fill, he drank some more.

And then he noticed something. All about him, in this thick forest, there was a rotten smell.

It smelled like a latrine.

And there was something else — silken packets in the mud, the remnants of Haroon spice use. He was not far from people, wherever he was.

Beyond the silk packets was more scattered trash, potsherds and scattered shattered amphorae, wine bottles caked in mud, oyster shells and discarded bones and bits of rotted food. The smell, of excrement, of the latrine, was growing more powerful with each step that Giufrio took. When he saw a dark shape rush through the trees, circling around him, spying for something to steal, he knew that it was a lemur, and that he had come to the Palladian Swamps.

In the delirium of thirst and hunger, he had not realized that he was in the Palladian Swamps, that he was just steps from Imperial City. Here the collected effluent was washed out of the sewers. It was a swamp created by the aftermath of a broken water main.

Here, Haroon spice users retreated to evade the law, and unsavory elements gathered in secret.

Giufrio spied a tent, and as he made his approach, headed due northeast, he saw culverts covered in graffiti, a ruined cement wall — and an assorted group of ruffians gathered. They were swarmed around someone.

A woman sat before a culvert, her eyes stricken with some strange madness, her brown hair falling in cascades down her back. She held these, the homeless and the down on their luck, enraptured. She had their devotion, and she had their attention.

"Heed the words of the urban prophet," she said, "whose words are written on culverts and sewer mains, and on the sides of apartment blocks.

"Heed the words of the urban prophet. The gods have not abandoned you, ye poor and needy, ye homeless and desperate. They have sent someone… and he is among you."

The crowds surrounding the urban prophet turned back to look at Giufrio.

The woman was mad, it seemed.

Or was she?

Giufrio strode in.

"He is hungry," said the urban prophet. "Get him something to eat."

A bedraggled woman in a dirty, torn brown gown walked up to Giufrio and handed him a hunk of bread.

"Thank you, signora," said Giufrio, and he ate, and he loved every bite.

"He is on a mission," said the urban prophet. "A mission from the gods. He cannot go to Imperial City, the great prostitute who lusts after strange flesh. There his and our enemies will lay their hands on him. He cannot go to where his enemies are, until he bears the sword of truth in his hand."

"Praises be!" a woman shouted in the crowd.

And perhaps it was the delirium of the long journey, perhaps being stranded so long at sea. But he was listening to this woman, amid this steaming artificial swamp, the result of a sewer main break centuries ago.

Should he really listen to this woman?

An image flashed in his mind — Brecko offering him wine, the wine of truth.

"I will drink," said Giufrio, loud enough for them to hear.

"Yes," said the urban prophet, "you will drink the wine of wrath, and pour out its fury on those who hunger for our flesh. You will become drunk and dazzled, and rain on them the fury that comes with truth. Hail, Brecko!"

And there was something to this woman, something more to her than her appearance would indicate.

"Go by the quiet road," said the urban prophet, "where your destiny lies. The cost has been great, but your reward will be greater. Flee the great prostitute, and go to the town where the truth lies.

There, be bold, and enter the gate."

"Hail the urban prophet!" shouted a man whose eyes were red, a Haroon spice user for certain. "Praises be!"

"Hail the urban prophet," said the crowd in unison. "Praises be…"

And Giufrio turned around, no longer going northeast but southwest, in the direction of Nichaeus, Valeria Verra's hometown.

"Hail the urban prophet," he said, to himself and no one else, "praises be…"

Chapter Forty-Two:
A Quick Dip

Fortunato cased the Imperial Palace for what seemed like the hundredth time, but there was no entrance, truly, except the front gate.

Yet he was not fool enough to try, not yet.

He was not yet a fool, but as his casing brought him back to Imperial Square, and the gate to the palace, and Corbulo's now-putrescent head, he was getting close to fool enough.

Xan called out. "Hey! Fortunato, I hear that the public baths are open, and that all classes mix. Might we catch Reev there?"

The public baths were free. Was it not worth a try?

~

They had come to the Baths of Tullio, a block away from Imperial Square. A line had formed at the front. Fortunato saw there was a drawing etched on the concrete, crude — the image of a gladiator with pointed ears, bearing what looked like a staff and knife.

Below it, in equally crude handwriting, were words: *"Wrinn, the elf who makes the Imperial girls sigh!"*

Fortunato didn't know what Wrinn had gotten himself into. But each game in the arena, he risked his life, and risked compromising his mission.

But perhaps, he had a higher end. Fortunato didn't know.

They passed through the doors, and the air was already steaming, thick with heat and moisture. As the Imperial men began to disrobe around them, Xan had a startled look, and not a little bit of fear.

"What did you think a bath was?" said Fortunato. "Will you dip into the waters in your heavy kirtle?"

"I thought, a loin cloth would be provided..." Xan was blushing.

Fortunato grinned and disrobed, then put his tunic, trousers, and undergarment in a cubby. He tried to make a mental note of which one.

And then he entered the Baths of Tullio.

~

Xan strode in, in the nude, not knowing what to expect. The Imperials around him were clean shaven and short-haired, as was fashionable here, but he stood out, a proud Kavan with a thick head of hair and a long beard.

His beard was thick, but he took good care of it.

Yet the Imperials seemed to look down on him as he passed through a set of doors, and saw a vast pool of water, as large as a stadium, from one side of his vision to the other, from which steam was emitting. There, men were soaking in the hot waters.

"Where are the women?" Xan said.

Fortunato answered from behind: "They go in the morning," he said. "The respectable ones do, at least..."

As Fortunato stepped into the hot waters, and sat down in the steaming warmth, Xan thought he was enjoying the baths for what they were, and not engaging in the mission — foolhardy as it was, unlikely a success as it might be, for hope that Reev was bathing here.

So Xan took a look around the hot baths, and saw that Reev was not numbered among the bathers. But the Baths of Tullio were vast, and so Xan thought he would go for a walk.

Beyond the marble-lined pool was a hallway, through a door, beside a sauna that seemed of the kind that Kavans used, where more men were gathered — none Reev.

And Xan continued, and found himself in another vast chamber, what looked like a tepid pool of lukewarm water, and he thought it was the intermediate room between hot and cold. He saw, beyond a glass wall, a room full of tables, on which were boards for chess and backgammon and wargames, where some men were playing — none, Reev.

"Hail, barbarian!" he heard a shout, and looked to his left.

A man was standing there, fair, with golden-brown hair.

"My handball partner left me. Will you play a couple rounds with me?" he said.

And Xan thought — there was some small chance he might know something, if not about Reev, then about the tense situation quickly building in Imperial City.

Through a door off the tepid pool was a handball court, and there they began to play, tossing a ball against the wood-faced wall. Xan rushed back and forth, playing handball, as the man slowly opened up, and began to talk.

The man was a vintner, a man of no small wealth. His store was in the west side, and he was concerned about the tensions building in the city, that some loved Verrus, and some loved the council.

"I've seen it come to blows, more than once," he said as he rushed across the room and hurled the ball at the wall.

Xan sprinted to his left and caught the ball in his hands.

"And why are you here, Ivan Xandrast?" the man said.

Did Xan dare tell?

No.

He would use his words carefully.

"I had hoped to see a glimpse of the Imperial court," Xan said. "For I heard the rich and the poor, the elite and the common, come here, to the baths, as one…"

"Not to the Baths of Tullio," said the man, as he caught Xan's barrage, and indicated he was ready to end the game of handball.

"The Baths of Tullio aren't secure enough for the Imperial court. When one of those *lupas* consorts with the common, they go to the Baths of Faustus in the Harbor District.

"My friend said he bedded Valeria Verra in Baths of Faustus washroom…"

Xan blushed. Perhaps, that was an item of information he did not want to know.

~

Xan wished to hurry, but Fortunato lingered in the tepid pool, and then he swam in the cold pool. By the time they were exiting the Baths of Tullio, Xan was fuming.

As an attendant scraped oil off Fortunato's body with a strigil, finally completing the process, Xan spoke.

"The Imperial court doesn't go to the Baths of Tullio," Xan said. "Only the Baths of Faustus."

"We will rescue Reev," said Fortunato. "This, I vow."

~

In the pit of the Imperial Arena, Wrinn had a bad feeling.

For the first time since he began, he was participating in the night games, with a lessened audience. Scauro had been right, his star power was fading.

"My star power is fading," said Wrinn aloud.

Scauro did not argue with him as he dabbed Wrinn's forehead

with a cloth. "Yes," he said, "but you can recover it, if you put a good show on tonight, no?"

Chapter Forty-Three: 6 Myrtle Ride

Mykono
Mykono
My-ko-no

As the singer in the tragic mask belted out the last note of "The Blessing of Mykono," Giufrio adjusted the collar of his tunic and took a deep breath.

The audience at the Royal Alabaster Theater in Nichaeus was preparing to leave. The stands surrounded an open-air stage in the center of the city.

As for Giufrio, unlike the gathered rich men and rich women, he had arrived at the outskirts of the city this morning, wet and covered in mud. He had marched to Nichaeus's city square, and marched to the Volusian Bank, and using his Writ of Mandamus, withdrawn twenty denara. He had purchased for himself the jet-black, collared tunic he was wearing now, a pair of fine black trousers of fustian, and topped it off with a silken undergarment. He had made his way to the Baths of Pergama, and cleansed himself in first the hot, then the warm, then the tepid, then the cold waters, and scraped every last inch of dirt from his pores. Then, taking his time, he had gone to the House of Sea-Nymphs on the outskirts of town, and availed himself of a beautiful blonde. A dinner at the tavern, a cup of wine to soothe his nerves, and a show at the Royal Alabaster Theater, and he was ready to work his magic — free of all inklings of lust, uncleanliness, hunger or raw nerves.

He was ready, and in the darkness, a man in a cloak was approaching.

"Signore Giufrio," he said, "your carriage is waiting."

~

As he approached the black carriage on the side of the street, the driver called out, "Where to, again?"

And Giufrio answered, remembering, "6 Myrtle Ride."

Here it was, the moment. A lesser man would be terrified.

But Giufrio was only determined.

The carriage passed through the city, rattling along the pavestones of the road. They passed by the naval offices and the naval barracks, as the pavestones gave way to dirt and gravel.

The carriage began to ascend, up a hill and then down, up a greater hill and then downwards, and finally, up to a rocky ridge overlooking the lights of the city below.

As they traversed the dirt road, in the dark, there were laurels and palm trees, and dry scrub brush where there were no paths into individual villas. The wheels of the carriage ground against the dirt and rocks, and eventually slowed to a stop. There was a path branching off the road, a gate and guards posted at it.

Giufrio was at Valeria Verra's house. The final piece of the puzzle remained.

He stepped out of the carriage and walked ahead, hearing the carriage pull forward, the sound of its wheels grind against dirt as it rattled away. The guards took notice of Giufrio as he approached, as he hailed them, and called out in a loud voice, "Greetings!"

The guards eyed him suspiciously and did not respond.

Just inches from them, Giufrio spoke. "The Imperial Council has given me this," he said, and pulled the Writ of Mandamus from the folds of his cloak. "A warrant to search Valeria Verra's house. You are compelled to obey."

The guards, two in number, bearing swords in sheaths at their sides, looked at him askance, skeptically.

"And what will they do?" said one, in the shifting shadows of the night. "An angry resolution? A sharply-written letter? I look forward to reading it. Have it delivered post-haste."

Giufrio looked at him, knowing there was little he could say.

He had been found out.

But he had come this far.

He wouldn't back out, now.

And so he departed, down the road, following through trees and bushes, noting that the house of Valeria Verra was surrounded by a pointed iron gate.

But in his training for the Imperial Guard, Giufrio had overcome more difficult obstacles.

And the guards had not followed him as he cased the perimeter.

He set his nightstick in its brace.

He uttered a prayer.

He gripped hold of the iron fence, and invoking a god — which god? — a man with a wild beard flashed in his mind, mouth dripping red with wine.

Brecko!

Invoking Brecko, he vaulted over the gate, and in one smooth motion, landed on two feet on the interior of Valeria Verra's yard.

There were more guards, but there were many doors.

All the doors could be, and probably were, locked.

But Giufrio would not abandon his quest. How could he?

As a guard doing a patrol passed by, he took his opportunity, rushing past a pool that had been emptied of water, and laid his hands on the first door in his perimeter. The knob twisted.

Unlocked.

And he entered into the house of Valeria Verra.

~

In the house, lit by moonlight and starlight, as Giufrio entered into the pristine though dark corridors, he had a feeling, one he couldn't shake.

This place was haunted.

This place, whose whitewashed walls were immaculately clean even when Valeria Verra was gone, whose carpets of fur or wool were expertly dyed, bore the memories of countless fights and ceaselessly struggles, of horrors untold that had never been made public.

That was Giufrio's gut sense, the gut sense that had never led him astray before.

He passed down the corridors, not sure of what he would find.

He saw a fire burning in the fireplace, and he realized the guards lived here.

He had been so bold. He would continue to be bold.

There was an unlit candle above the fireplace mantle.

He lit it.

And he saw, above the fireplace, a painting bordered in gold, a copy of a painting he had seen before, a grotesque humanoid being with horns and yellow fur, devouring people in his mouth, their legs visible as he shoved them down his throat.

What was this painting called?

He remembered: "Kronos Eating His Children."

What a sick mind was Valeria Verra, to portray it so prominently.

Beyond a glass window, a guard was just yards away.

He had not taken notice of Giufrio, the fool.

Giufrio felt some strange spirit guiding his steps as he walked down a corridor, past a bedroom which surely would bear him no fruit.

Beyond the bedroom was a study.

Yes, a study.

That was a good place to start.

There was a table with papers, a jar of ink and a quill resting in it. There was a reading chair, and there was a shelf that had more empty spaces than books.

Giufrio, setting the candle on the table, could see that all the books Valeria Verra had collected had to do with politics. There was a book of oratory by Cleon, a biography — *Ansolon and Hordo, Founders of Democracy*. There was a book, *Lives of Great Imperials and Easterners*. And then, a collection of books on the procedures of the Imperial Council.

Giufrio took one of the books of procedure and flipped it open.

It was heavily marked up.

The books declared how the procedures governed the creation of the law and the appointment of members to various positions. Valeria Verra had marked sections of the arcane legerdemain, and how a Speaker of the Council was appointed in varying situations. It was a lengthy tome, showing how much Valeria Verra knew, walking into her coup. She knew exactly, the ins and outs, of what was permissible and impermissible, how the emperor's will was to be respected and the Council's limitations.

The terms of an Amarothic emperorship, it seemed, had slipped by her.

But in the shifting light of the room, in the dull light of the candle, as Giufrio skimmed through *Procedures and Regulations of the Imperial Council, Volume VIII*, another tome caught his eye, tucked into the bottom of the bookshelf.

It read, on the spine, *The Pedigree of Valeria Verra.*

In the Empire, noble families went to great lengths to describe their family's pedigree.

And Giufrio set aside the thick tome he was reading, and took *The Pedigree of Valeria Verra* into his hands.

He opened to the front page.

The Pedigree of Valeria Verra
An Official Record

He saw, first, that Valeria Verra was the daughter of Sargo Verrus and Tima Lornodoris.

He remembered a passage in *The History of Celsus Heights:* "Membership in the Qab of Thuban is passed down from mother to daughter, and from mother to son."

And so he flipped past what he wasn't interested in, the pedigree of Sargo Verrus stretching down through the generations.

He flipped to where the ancestors of Tima Lornodoris were listed, and saw that she was the daughter of Ansolon Lornodoris the Fat and Mania Kerius.

Who was Mania Kerius?

The daughter of Postumus Kerius and Rawsha Thuban.

Rawsha Thuban was Valeria Verra's great-grandmother.

Valeria Verra was a member of the Qab of Thuban.

Valeria Verra was an anguiped.

~

As the gates opened to the Imperial Arena, a chandelier so large it seemed to Wrinn a wonder of the world was lifted down from what seemed to be the sky. So many candles glittered on its branches that the sand of the arena was illuminated, as if it were day.

Wrinn strode out to cheers, but his gait was not as confident. The Geath with the mighty battle axe, and his own defeat, had gotten to him.

Yet he steeled himself, and rushed forward. A gladiator was garbed in the attire of a Khazidee.

He rushed in, and there was a battle of blows, sword against khopesh — Wrinn made a twist, a tackling motion, but as he did, he saw that the Khazidee had already gone limp.

He saw there was a dart in his neck, a poison dart, and he was sinking in delirium.

And Wrinn had a thought — that the dart had been shot from the stands.

And he had an unshakeable suspicion, that the dart had not been intended for the heavily armored Khazidee, but for him.

"Nonsense!" said Scauro. "You're paranoid. You'll suit up and fight. Look — you have a victory, a new notch on your belt. Your star power will recover!"

But it had not been a victory. It had been an intervention by the Imperial promoters.

Was the poison dart, and the death, intended for him?

How could it not be?

~

In the spy room, Reev was alone, transfixed by the Imperial Council's minutiae.

A messenger had arrived, wearing an oiled cloak, and hailed Speaker Formusalis.

"Your Honor, a report of Khazidea," he said, "the wheat crop has been such a great yield, the farmers can scarcely believe it. There is not enough room in our granaries to store all the wheat during this year's harvest."

A hand grasped at Reev's shoulder. Astarthe was standing there, in the dark of the spy room.

"Reev," she said, "do you know it is late at night? Do you know you've missed dinner?"

But Reev wasn't hungry.

"Oh, Reev," he said, "I have a terrible feeling. I have a terrible feeling! I feel, something terrible is going to happen to us both…"

~

As Giufrio entered the house's main hall with *The Pedigree of Valeria Verra* in his pocket, he had an irrational feeling he couldn't shake.

He thought — he should venture through the door, heedless of the guards.

These guards, protecting an anguiped who wished to work her destruction on the Imperial people, and bring to death a nation so they could have a safe place to breed.

Why should he fear the guards? Why should he honor them, by giving them his fear? For in fear, there was respect, and he had no respect for them.

He marched through the front doors of the house, straight past a guard.

He did not hear the guard so much as mumble. He ventured to the front gate, and opened it, and to the guards it seemed he wasn't there.

What was happening?

It did not matter.

The Pedigree of Valeria Verra was in his pocket, and all the pieces of the puzzle had been assembled. He would tell the Imperial Council the truth, and they would hear it, and what they did with the truth would be on their own selves.

"Onward," he said, and felt himself carried forward, down the dirt path, down Myrtle Ride, to a bend in the road where the carriage was waiting.

Chapter Forty-Four: The Ancestors

From Nichaeus to Imperial City, a path connected the southernmost towns with the pulsing hub of commerce and humanity, a path called the Corbian Way.

Along its breadth were inns and towns that had grown up around crossroads, amid a wider urban sprawl, a super-city that dominated the southeast of the Anthanian peninsula.

It was down the Corbian Way that Giufrio walked, having left his rented carriage in Nichaeus behind. He walked confidently and boldly.

The anguipeds had sent their thugs throughout all of his travails. And now he was on the precipice, the precipice of revealing the truth to the Imperial Council, and then to Varda.

He was at the halfway point, and the midday sun was burning hot upon him. Dark shapes were approaching.

He knew it couldn't be so easy.

The men approaching, about thirty, had the look of soldiers, but they were not Imperial soldiers.

They wore breastplates, and green shirts underneath them. Their helmets were hooked and had green crests.

Did the Imperial government know a separate army was operating in the Anthanian peninsula?

Did they approve?

Perhaps a government long dominated by the anguipeds did.

Giufrio stopped his walk and stared them down.

He drew his nightstick from his brace and said a prayer.

The crowds cleared around the roads. It was Giufrio against thirty soldiers.

"What is this?" Giufrio wanted to say, but instead kept silent.

He'd let them talk first.

"Giufrio Vallo," said one of the soldiers, the chief of them, wearing a gold pin on his breastplate. "You are a fool for inquiring so deeply."

"And now I know the truth."

There was silence a few moments, but a wind began to blow.

"An army, not Imperial, operates broadly in the Anthanian peninsula," said Giufrio, "with the assent of a captured government. What would my ancestors think, if they knew?"

"Your ancestors are rotting in the ground," said the captain.

"My ancestors are in Heaven," Giufrio said, "and they guide my every move."

The captain looked disgusted.

"What is this?" Giufrio said. "You have uniforms."

"The Consulary Armies of the Imperial Bay Company operate with the consent of the Imperial Council, see Consent Decree 74, Session 8." The captain smirked, as if what he said was something to be proud of.

"I do not heed laws written by anguipeds," said Giufrio.

"You will," captain said, "and the shareholders of the Imperial Bay Company have sentenced you to death. You can make this hard, or you can make this easy. It's your choice."

Would the truth die with him? Giufrio would not die.

He heard a strange music. He would give into it utterly.

The captain charged first, and Giufrio struck to the imagined clink of a wine glass. The captain's skull was smashed, and his helmet fell from his head. He sank to the ground, into death.

He heard the soldiers screaming, but the imagined frenzied hymn was louder.

He a saw, the flash of an image, a bent mountain, a snowy peak.

He struck to the sound of the imagined kithara; he disarmed a soldier to the sound of an imagined double aulos. And as the double aulos began to blare in his mind, he was drunk, drunk with the power that now filled him.

As the soldiers screamed, he struck, and imagined the wine he was drinking in his mind. He struck, and felt Brecko's favor, and saw, in a flash of cognizance, that he was dripping with blood.

But all cognizance and reality was gone, as the frenzy overtook him, the blood red like wine, the screams like the sound of an orchestra on a high mountain.

He ferried his nightstick like a libation to Brecko's high house in Arkadion, striding from one edge of the battlefield to another in a fury of blows.

He thought he heard a voice, *My servant.*

And then he saw the trail of bodies, the bodies of the consulary soldiers twisted and contorted like they had died in the midst of a dance, blood everywhere — blood dripping from his head. How had his nightstick struck such blows?

What consulary soldiers remained were fleeing, screaming, "He is not a man! He is an ultra-man!"

And he counted fifteen bodies, motionless and contorted, strewn along the Corbian Way.

Chapter Forty-Five: Returning

Reev's new home was the spy room. Astarthe had begun to take him dinner there, and occasionally she would eat it with him.

The council was in session, and Reev did not know what day it was, only that it was the height of summer, and the Imperial government was not used to operating in the scorching heat.

The spy room, in addition to offering a hiding place from Barcho, was cooler than the Council Chambers or the palace, tucked away in the dark. And here he could be apprised of every action of the Imperial Council, whether good or bad.

The Imperial Council showed little sign of bucking the Amarothic emperorship. When or if it ended, Reev thought the Empire was done for.

Why did he know that?

He did not know what Verrus intended. He did not know what Valeria Verra wanted. But he knew that anyone who wanted power that badly would not use it for a good end. And they had striven their entire lives for power. What they had wanted, what they had spent all their energy on, was finally within their grasp.

It was so close, Reev could taste it, and it tasted like bitter poison.

"Members of the council," said Speaker Formusalis weakly. "Numera!"

What councilors were there indicated they were present or not.

"Ten are here," said Speaker Formusalis. "A quorum is not present. The council is thus dismissed."

The councilors began to exit from their seats. And the show was over.

The show was over, and the trouble Reev had been avoiding

could no longer be avoided.

~

The trouble found him as soon as he was back in the palace. Barcho was approaching in his full uniform, headed straight for Reev, looking straight at him.

And what would Reev say, and what could he do?

He had not come here with Astarthe. He had come with Fortunato of Ríva.

And he was a Telantine.

But amid the dark shadows of the hallway, a man pulled Barcho aside and began talking. Barcho began to converse, and Reev walked away.

Reev remembered the man with tawny hair and blue eyes, and the dark-haired man on the Great Porch, and he wondered if the three were connected.

He could not afford to worry. He had to survive… he had to find his necklace.

But he wondered if it was time to ignore the feeling, the urge to find it, and leave the last keepsake of Telantis in this world behind.

To do so seemed world-shattering. But could he really remain, now that the Imperial Palace was beginning to take notice of him?

And would Verrus take notice of him?

Valeria Verra and Verrus have not noticed you. When they do, the game's about to be up.

So had said the tawny-haired man on the Great Porch.

That night they served flamingo tongue on a bed of groats, followed by a serving of torte cake and bowls of flavored sweet ice, for it was Valeria Verra's birthday.

"Oh, Sextil the 11th, 1099… What a day that was," Valeria

Verra said, apparently happy to be the center of attention.

Wasn't that always the case?

At their tables, Astarthe and Reev fumed silently.

And Reev, having licked the bowl of flavored sweet ice of every drop, saw that Barcho across the room was looking at him.

"Come," Reev said quietly, "let's go to my room."

~

"Leave," said Astarthe in Reev's bedchamber, Appian's former workroom. "That bad feeling I have has only gotten stronger."

"The Amarothic emperorship holds," said Reev. "The Imperial Council holds back the chaos. Verrus still has no real power. We must find my necklace."

Astarthe shot him a sharp look. "Oh, I'd like to slap you. But I won't, Reev Nax, I won't... I have a strange feeling — that the Sons of Telantis will rescue us again, like they did before."

"Like they did before?" Reev said.

And he realized there was still so much about Telantis and the Telantines that he did not know.

Barcho knocked and he did not answer. At last, Barcho gave up, and Reev slipped off into sleep. He had a feeling, he would awaken.

~

When he awoke at the witching hour, it was a habit borne of Valeria Verra's nocturnal meetings. He thought it was only habit, and would soon go back to sleep, when Valeria Verra spoke in the room next door.

"The Imperial Bay Company has put together collateral for a

loan," said Valeria Verra. "Who could say no to one-hundred and twenty talents?"

"A man of honor," Thuban said, "of which many, sadly, are in the Imperial Council."

"We must find the weakest link," Valeria Verra said.

There was silence for a moment, and anxiety grew in Reev, at the thought of Verrus and Valeria Verra being so close to their goal.

"And we have our man at the urban cohorts," said Valeria Verra. "We're in control of the only legion of soldiers that operates in Imperial City bounds."

"Some paperwork remains to be filed," said Thuban. "A bit of red tape. But it's inevitable now, within days…"

Reev shuddered, and long after the conversation ended, he couldn't sleep. But eventually he slipped into a half sleep, beset by dreams and visions.

~

In the morning, Giufrio returned, and assumed to Barcho's grumbling command of the Imperial Guard.

Reev had evaded Barcho by wit and by the intervention of mysterious others, and now he felt comfortable and safe around Giufrio, a man he inexplicably trusted.

Giufrio gave this order and that, and at breakfast he seemed happy and confident, possessed of a strange energy. His hazel eyes had never seemed brighter. His brown hair had never glistened so completely in the sunlight.

And yet, Reev got the sense from him, that he had not been truthful about the illness of his grandmother. He had left for a different reason, and he had returned for a different reason.

In the dining hall, at breakfast, Valeria Verra was examining him, and her glances oscillated between glares and looks of suspicious distrust.

Chapter Forty-Six: The Speech

When Giufrio learned that Speaker Corvus Corbulo had been killed, he was not dissuaded from his task.

If anyone asked him about Corvus Corbulo's conspiracy, he would not tell them, truthfully, how he felt about it.

It was justified, he knew, and it was a shame it had failed.

But Giufrio now wielded the truth in his hands, the truth like a sword, and all the violence of the anguipeds had failed to quelch it. He would tell the world what Alessandro Sopis knew, and he would start with the Imperial Council.

In his bedchamber, he looked at himself in the mirror. He adjusted his red-half cape so that it contrasted perfectly with his breastplate, over his shoulder. He greased his hair, and played with it a bit, so that it stood up at the front, like he wanted.

He couldn't help but think he was a handsome devil.

He cleared his throat, washed it with a resinous fluid, and then departed. The Imperial Council was in session, and it was waiting for him.

The anguipeds had failed. Giufrio had won.

And no anguipeds stopped him as he walked through the palace, across the Sky Bridge, and at last passed through the open doors of the council chambers.

Valeria Verra and Verrus weren't in their seats.

He supposed it was a good thing — it would be awkward for the two hell-spawn.

The councilors were staring at him. The speaker, Mamerco Formusalis, loomed above him, directly ahead.

He would speak the truth boldly.

He spoke, and when he spoke his voice carried, and he was

confident.

~

What Reev heard Giufrio say in the comfort of the spy room was not an easy thing for the average Imperial citizen to accept.

A non-human species was on the threshold of controlling the Imperial government, and they yearned for the death of the Empire, so they could make a safe place for themselves.

But Reev knew things Giufrio did not know. He knew that anguipeds like Thuban and the kitchen maestro, Alsumo, were most focused on the extinction of the Telantines in particular.

Yet it was a piece of information Reev thought would be valuable, one he would hold to his heart and not forget.

Valeria Verra and Verrus were descended from anguipeds, a hostile non-human species. Their designs were not for the good of those they so desperately wished to rule.

Reev expected the Imperial Council to speak as one, in rage, perhaps complete the conspiracy of Corvus Corbulo in a justified killing their ancestors might have engaged in.

But instead, silence followed Giufrio's words, and Speaker Formusalis's weak eyes were looking to the other councilors for guidance, as Reev had witnessed him do before when he was nervous.

Reev wasn't sure what they would do, but he had expected a stronger reaction.

Then one spoke, a councilor Reev recognized as Malchus.

"Giufrio Vallo," he said, "your patriotism and devotion to your duties is admirable. But this is all a little far fetched. Do you know that Mania Kerius is my second cousin?

"Shall I tear my tunic, and show you I have no green scales on my chest?"

"The progeny lose the green skin and scaly complexion after

the first generation of intermarriage," Giufrio said.

There were a few scattered hisses amid the gathered Imperial Council.

Then there was silence, just silence.

"Giufrio Vallo," said Speaker Formusalis, and Reev knew he would say what he thought the other twenty-six gathered in the council chamber wanted to hear. "Consider this task resolved, and your Writ of Mandamus withdrawn. Any objections?"

No one spoke.

Giufrio bit his lip. To Reev, he appeared to be fuming.

Of everyone witnessing Giufrio, only Reev, it seemed, believed him fully.

And he wondered, beside Valeria Verra and Verrus, Thuban and Alsumo, who else in the Imperial Palace were descended from anguipeds? Who else in the wider world were descended from anguipeds?

Reev watched Giufrio storm off.

And Reev had a terrible feeling, a terrible sinking feeling.

~

In Astarthe's suite, Reev told her what Giufrio had told all the gathered council.

Astarthe seemed more credulous, less believing than he.

"It's a bitter medicine to swallow," Astarthe said. "They look just like average Imperials, and Valeria Verra is beautiful."

"A hard medicine to swallow," Reev said, "but Giufrio is intelligent, and he's a good man. And when he said it, it struck true to me."

"Intelligent, a good man," Astarthe said. "I agree with both those things."

"Perhaps, he would know where my necklace is."

~

In Giufrio's chamber, Giufrio smiled at the request.

"Reev Nax," he said, "I can tell you that the Imperial Guard is not in possession of your amulet, nor has it ever been."

So where was it?

"It's been misplaced," Reev said, "or someone took it."

Dare Reev look at Astarthe with new eyes, with suspicion?

No, he never would.

"I thank you," Reev said to Giufrio, "and I wanted you to know, I was in the spy room, and I believe you."

Giufrio's smile changed, and it became something somber, something no longer joyous, no longer a smile of its own self. "The truth," he said, "is what I declared to the Imperial Council."

"And they did not seem to believe," Reev said.

"The truth is what it is," Giufrio said. "It does not change with Formusalis's wrinkled brow."

"Or with Malchus's insecurity," Reev said.

"Insecurity," Giufrio said. "Do you think that is what we witnessed in him?"

Chapter Forty-Seven: Theme Night

It was Sextil, and Imperial City was no longer a furnace. It was something more.

If there had been dark figures with horns wandering amid Imperial Square, Fortunato might have mistaken it for Hell. But no, it was only the capital of the Empire, the largest city in Varda, at a time when anyone with means and opportunity fled for the relative cool of the outlying hills.

But Fortunato was not a rich man. He had no means to escape, nor should he.

Yet the oppressive heat, scorching like an oven, was weakening him, draining him of energy. It was so hot indeed that commerce had dwindled in Imperial Square and for the first time since Fortunato and Xan and the others arrived, one could call it sparsely populated.

Fortunato was eyeing the palace. He knew, in the wake of the attempted coup, the government had made a return to the city they ruled over. Reev was among them — Wrinn had confirmed it to he and Xan. And Reev had been alive and well, as recently as a few days ago, when Wrinn witnessed him at the Imperial Arena.

So why had he not escaped? Was he being held prisoner?

Fortunato knew the only one who wished to tread Seymus underfoot more than him was Reev. There had to be a cause for the delay, and what other explanation could there be, but that Reev was being held prisoner, or that he was otherwise unable to escape?

He eyed the palace, its complex of turrets and towers, battlements and bridges, a white horse rising above the urban sprawl. He wondered if there was a weakness he had missed, some method of entry he had looked past.

And as he found himself before the gate for the hundredth, or perhaps the thousandth time, he saw for the first time he was not cloaked in the crowds, and the guards were staring at him.

There were four soldiers posted outside the gate, and a small army behind. They were eyeing Fortunato in a way that indicated they knew he was. For they were sizing him up. They were sizing up Fortunato of Ríva.

They knew him, he sensed. They knew his name. In the eyes of the government behind that gate, he was a traitor to his country, though Fortunato would not call it as such.

They knew him — and yet in all this time, they had not arrested him.

Why had they not arrested him?

~

Spyke had been preparing for a new naval journey. The navy needed soldiers on a patrol of the Dark Continent. He had been reading and preparing for what he would encounter, even trying to learn the Sea Raider tongue — or at least bits and pieces of it — in his small bunk room in Fort Modestus, when there was a knock at the door.

"Signore," the door had opened, and a soldier he knew as Faunus was standing there, "Caro Hudnato has summoned you for a meeting in the Metropolitan."

Caro Hudnato was a name Spyke had not dwelt on. Though Caro Hudnato had not been a part of it, he reminded Spyke of a time when he had betrayed his country on behalf of Fortunato of Ríva, all in service of a young man whom his ancestors cried out against for blood-vengeance.

"I'll be right there," Spyke said.

He recalled with disgust that he had led Reev Nax's party so far, and that he had helped find quarters for their animals. He recalled, and was filled with fury, a fury to make things right, as he passed through the sparse crowds of Imperial Square in the now-baking heat, and found himself in the historical homes of the Metropolitan.

In the barracks, he located the chamber of the ward legate of the Metropolitan and pushed through. "Caro Hudnato?" he said.

But no, another man sat there, at the ward legate's desk, thin and emaciated, with skin of a greenish hue and flakes that resembled scales.

"I am Breckonisio Mawto," he said, "the new ward legate. Caro Hudnato has been promoted to legate of the urban cohorts."

The only legion of soldiers allowed to operate in Imperial City bounds, by law not under the command of the emperor, had a separate office.

Caro Hudnato... he had moved up in the world.

His chamber was painted a vibrant shade of green, and was festooned with maps and on one wall, a curved sword on which writing in an inscrutable language was embossed in gold.

Caro Hudnato, wrinkled and gray, with a wart on his nose, was now dressed in a breastplate with a red half-cape over his shoulder, but Spyke couldn't help but feel that it looked off, that it didn't look good on him.

"Spyke," said Caro Hudnato, "your ancestors need your help."

Spyke took a seat at the chair before the desk. "This is about Fortunato," Spyke said.

"No," Caro Hudnato said. "Some of us were of a mind to arrest him in Brenua, as the sailing season began, but we've been observing him closely all this time, and have come to believe he is searching for the one we are truly after, the Telantine. We had hoped he would lead us directly to him, but his movements seem baffling. We worry he knows where the Telantine is, and also knows we are searching for him. We worry if we do not act now, the Telantine will slip out of our grip."

"And what do you want me to do about it?" Spyke said.

~

The sun baked down Imperial Square, and Fortunato did not know where to go, or where to turn. He and Xan stood alone in the orange light, under the sun that had a hazy look. Fortunato had a bad feeling, that something terrible was about to occur, something that would change Varda forever, and that they were at its epicenter. He had a terrible feeling, and he thought the orange, hazy light would soon turn red.

If the skies turned red, what would that mean?

Did such a color to the sky have significance?

Fortunato had a strange feeling it did, inexplicable.

And the guards had not ceased staring at him.

Soldiers, too, no longer cloaked by swarming crowds, were clearly visible, eyeing Fortunato wherever he went.

He was not a traitor to the Imperial people. He was a fighter against those who ruled them. He served the gods, and the people.

But the sky — the sky, it troubled him, amid the baking heat that had not ended, the scorching heat that had not waned at all as the day grew late.

Xan with his butterfly blade, and Fortunato with his sword and his adamant knife, stood alone amid a wide berth in Imperial Square.

What did Fortunato want? To find Reev, and to be on his way. But Reev had been captured.

It took all his mental energy, all his strength, not to rush forward, and take the gates in his hands, and rip them open, despite the soldiers standing guard, and the small army standing in his way.

"What shall we do, now?" Xan said.

"What shall we do?" Fortunato repeated. He looked to the sky, orange turning ochre, then to the Council House towering in size. He fixed his eyes on the Imperial Palace, to where Reev was. And then, as soldiers at the gate looked on, he fell to his knees and prayed.

Xan then followed, falling to his knees, and laid a hand on his shoulder.

Fortunato prayed silently that Reev would come out of the Imperial Palace, right here and right now, before the skies turned red.

~

In the pit of the arena, the ochre light was filtering in. Wrinn had a bad feeling.

Scauro, however, was behaving as he always was, dabbing at Wrinn's hair with a damp cloth, massaging Wrinn's tender muscles and attempting to lift his spirits with all manner of positive talk.

Scauro paused his dabbing.

"Wrinn," he said, "it's a big day for you. A return to the afternoon games. You'll have your star power back in no time."

But Wrinn could not forget the Geath with the battle-axe, or how easily the Geath had defeated him.

Nor could Wrinn forget the poison dart, which Scauro had done his best to convince Wrinn that it had not been aimed at him.

"Tonight's theme is 'A Night in the Valley of Lotuses.' " Scauro picked something up from the table beside them — a pink tunic and a flower garland. "To fit with the theme, I think you should wear this."

"There is no way I will ever wear that," Wrinn said. "No price I'd accept, no payment high enough. No way, Scauro. Never."

Scauro frowned. "A shame. In the stands, they're serving lemon ice and honey wine to get the audience in the mood. A shame you won't make their day. But you're the boss, Wrinn. You're the captain of your own destiny."

Was that true? Wrinn didn't think so.

The gate began to crank open.

"Anyhow, Wrinn," Scauro said, "it's showtime. Get out there! Fight! Win!"

He rushed out, and saw in the orange light of the sun that the awning had been drawn over the seats, a behemoth of canvas, but that even with the barrier the seats were sparsely filled, amid the brutal Sextil sun.

He saw something else, the gate opening opposite him across the sand of the arena, and an enemy so large its head scraped against the gate.

His enemy was not human.

The elephant trumpeted as it stormed into the arena, to the scattered delighted howls of the audience. Yet the elephant was not an elephant of the usual kind.

Its hide was pink, and along its hide were the beginnings of mushrooms. It kicked off spores with each stride, but as it drew close, Wrinn saw they were not spores, but fairy dust.

When it stepped with its massive legs, its feet hovered above the ground, carried aloft by the fairy dust. It was not an elephant of the jungle, but some fey variation of it, a creature that could only be plucked away and found in the far reaches of Varda.

The audience howled its delight.

Yet Wrinn knew now, that the poison dart had been meant for him, and the Imperial Arena promoters had tired of him, and were trying to kill him.

Beside the fairy elephant, starved white tigers were racing out of the gate, all fixed on him. As the fairy elephant drew near, there was a flash of scintillating colors, red, white, blue, green, and it took all of Wrinn's inner strength not to be transfixed, to give in to fascination and then to death.

Wrinn could not win this fight. The Imperial Arena promoters knew it. He raced toward the seats where the audiences were sitting.

Just as the fairy elephant was swinging its tusks back to impale him, he leapt, and the traces of fairy dust now spilling around the arena gave light to his feet. He was lofted over the wall, to where the audience was sitting.

The audience was now spitting out their lemon ices and their wines and heckling him as he ran, fleeing up the steps, vaulting over the walls of one section to another. He had lost the audience's adoration, but he had gained his life.

He fled, realizing he no longer wished to be a gladiator, step after step, ascending section after ascending section, until he had climbed to the top, and was making his way down.

The gladiator's life was not for him.

~

"The Baths of Faustus," said Xan. "We haven't tried them."

Fortunato had given up on the coward's way out, of distractions like the hippodrome and the arena and the musical contests. Only breaching the gate would lead him to his goal.

But the soldiers were looking at him. Fortunato wondered if they would arrest him right here and now, if he waited.

"The Baths of Faustus," said Fortunato. "Let's go."

Fortunato did not disrobe. Now it was Xan, lingering unclothed in the hot waters of the bath.

Fortunato would wait tonight. He might sleep an hour or two. He would pray. Then, tomorrow, he would storm the gate.

He walked amid the Baths of Faustus, and saw that the marble floors were of rich hues of purple and red, and that along the ceiling were vivid celestial scenes of Heaven as the Imperials imagined it, Amara in war-dress and Alabaster with a lighting spear, enthroned.

He passed to the tepid pools, and saw beyond a glass wall there were tables, and people sitting in them. There was a bar, and wine bottles on display.

Sitting at a table, near the glass window, was the elderly man whose villa he had intruded upon when he shipwrecked off Dualmis. What was his name? Malchus.

Seated across from him was a man with sallow skin and soupy brown eyes, and long gray hair, whose very appearance seemed to declare, "You shouldn't trust me."

Fortunato wondered what they were discussing. He had a feeling, it wasn't good.

Chapter Forty-Eight:
The Oculus

Reev awoke when it was still dark.

He had a terrible feeling. And he stirred awake, and donned his trousers and tunic, and clipped Doomblade to his side. He had the sense he wouldn't be able to get back to sleep.

He also had a feeling he shouldn't.

When the door opened and Astarthe was there, standing in the doorway, he knew the terrible feeling he had was meaningful, that it was something much more.

"Reev," she said. "The Imperial Council has called a session. They are voting on the terms of the Amarothic emperorship. Verrus has made a motion…"

And Reev had a terrible thought that Verrus would not make such a motion were he not confident.

What had happened in the past night?

~

In the spy room they watched as the Imperial Councilors took their seats. They gathered in a ring around the council chambers, and there was an air of tension everywhere. Reev felt he was witnessing something that could not be revoked, a sense that the world of Varda's danger had never been greater, that its enemy was at the threshold.

When Verrus strode into the room and sat in the white seat, Speaker Formusalis cleared his throat nervously.

"Honorable members of the council," said Speaker Formusalis, "we are gathered here today for a moment of decision. Verrus has challenged the terms of his Amarothic emperorship, and we are here duty bound to consider it.

"I implore you, gathered members of the council, we have not completed the investigation. We have not determined whether illegality was used to install Verrus onto the throne. I implore you, gathered members of the council, do not revoke this safeguard prematurely. Work in the interests of the people."

The tension was palpable, something more than tension. Astarthe was acting like Varda's fate was being decided. And Reev felt woe, woe to the Empire, woe to Varda.

"The emperor has made a motion to end the Amarothic emperorship," said Speaker Formusalis. "I counter with a motion of continuance. Do any here object to the motion of continuance?"

There was silence.

Then, Malchus spoke. "I object," said Malchus.

Frenzied fear seemed to appear on the faces of some of the councilors. Astarthe gasped. Only Reev was calm.

Malchus had a diabolic grin on his face.

And Speaker Formusalis said, "The Amarothic emperorship of Verrus ends. Emperor Verrus begins his rule, this day, Sextil 12, 1155 Y.E."

Astarthe let out a wail, and Reev covered her mouth. He took her by the hand and guided her away, down the dark tunnels, until she was breathing harshly, and they were in the palace. He was half guiding her, half pushing her, as Imperial Guards ran this way and that, and a storm of people seemed to follow in the wake of Verrus's accession to emperor.

Fearing the crowds, Reev led her to the Great Porch where he thought they might be able to hide away, and ride through the storm.

And beyond the urban sprawl of harbor district, amid the glittering sea, was a red dawn, skies the color of blood, clouds the color of dark crimson, red, red, everywhere — red light bathing them, red light casting the statues of Emperor Claudio and

Emperor Numa in shadow.

Astarthe had fainted in his grip.

He heaved her slight form into his arms, and, having looked back once more at the red dawn, turned around and delivered her to her suite, and placed her in her bed.

He did not know what to say or do. He would try to ride out the storm.

Men and women hurried through the hallway outside his bedchamber. At some point, Reev became aware that they were all leaving, that they were going in one direction, toward the exit. The Imperial Guard was rushing them out.

And as Reev sat at his bed, realizing how impossible the task now would be to find his necklace. He saw a familiar form, and heard a familiar voice, "We're taking out the trash!"

Valeria Verra's voice was like fingernails scraping against chalk, a bitter howl that caused Reev's insides to twist.

"We're taking out the trash!" Valeria Verra said again.

And she had paused beside his door.

She was garbed, as always, in a black gown. Her face was not so heavily powdered with chalk and ochre, and all her grimace and fury was plain to see.

She looked to Reev.

Valeria Verra and Verrus have not noticed you. When they do, the game's about to be up.

"You," she said, "you're trash. You need to be out. Come with me."

Reev followed her, dreaming up what he would do, a blow to the head to save the Empire and Varda as a whole. But he would not strike her. He followed her through the hallway, through the winding corridors of the Imperial Palace.

And as they took a bend, and the exit to the stairs was in sight,

Reev saw Barcho standing their in his plate armor and half-cape.

"You're taking Reev Nax away from us, too?" Barcho said with an amused grin on his face.

And Valeria Verra stopped her monstrous gait. She turned and looked at Reev, and as she stared at him with her black pits of eyes, Reev thought he sensed a glint of fear in them, one that threatened to build to bottomless terror.

Yet she was the consummate liar, and she put on a bold face like a tragic actor might. "Your name is Reev," said Valeria Verra. "You must come with me."

Reev followed her, back the way he had come amid the droves of men and women now being forcibly expelled from what was now Verrus's court. Valeria Verra was huffing and puffing as she led him down a corridor, to a chamber, above it a nameplate, *Thuban*.

And Reev gasped in that moment, realizing she knew what his name meant, that she knew his identity, that he was a Telantine.

He had turned, when a panel of the wall seemed to shift, and a hand grabbed him. He went tumbling into the darkness.

He landed on his feet. He smelled chemicals and powder. He could see brick walls. And the man with tawny hair and blue eyes was standing before him. He was holding Reev's amulet.

~

Fortunato was standing at the gate. He was summoning up his energy to charge, to take on all of the Imperial Army at once, foolish as   he   knew   it   was. Who did he think he was?

Xan was standing behind him.

The day was a bit cooler, after the red dawn, and the crowds in Imperial Square were more numerous.

Someone was approaching — Spyke.

~

"Who are you people?" Reev said to the tawny haired man.

"We are unseen, by design," the tawny haired man. "I am Marius, Spymaster of the Oculus."

"The Oculus?" Reev said. He draped the amulet over his neck. He was glad to have it. "You had my amulet all this time."

"We wanted you to linger," Marius said. "We wanted you to fight for what was yours. For we know you and Verrus are opposed by your very blood.

"Come… let's go for a walk."

Reev followed Marius through the brick corridor. He realized that the brick corridor matched perfectly with the Imperial Palace above, that these rooms were directly underneath.

The Oculus… what had he meant?

~

"Where have you been, Spyke?" Fortunato said.

"I went searching for Reev in the north of Anthania," Spyke said. "I couldn't find him."

"Well, I must say, Spyke, you're a good liar, but I find that hard to believe," Fortunato said.

Spyke frowned, then gritted his teeth.

~

"What is the Oculus?" Reev said. "Tell me."

They had stopped at a window overlooking Imperial Square. The sunlight was catching on his amulet, and it was flashing.

~

"Do you know where Reev is?" Spyke asked.

Up above, in one of the Imperial Palace windows, there was a bright yellow flash.

And Fortunato saw in his mind's eye, Spyke with green skin and jagged pointed ears, yellow eyes and sharp fangs, and a forked tongue flicking out of sharp teeth.

"I've tried, in all this time," Fortunato said, "and I don't know. I have no idea where he's gone off to. We've checked everywhere."

Spyke seemed supremely disappointed. Something hovered on the edge of his tongue. Then he gave in to what he had wanted to say: "Reev is a Telantine. Do you know what the Telantines did?"

"What did the Telantines do, Spyke?" Fortunato said. "Do you know I am a Telantine?"

A shocked look appeared in Spyke's eyes, and his mouth hung agape. "I'd better go," he said, and left in a huff.

A bizarre encounter... and there was no way in Fortunato's estimation, that Spyke had been searching for Reev. He had something dark up his sleeve. He had a feeling, he was working for the enemy.

~

"What is the Oculus?" Reev said again, insistent, looking down from the window into Imperial Square below.

"Well, to begin with, few know about us," Marius said. "Most emperors aren't informed, only ones we trust. The last emperor to know about the Oculus was Marcus Amaranthius. Khandaraeus, we did not disclose our operations to, and we will certainly not tell Verrus. But there isn't a war, or an assassination, or a riot that the Oculus didn't have a hand in."

"You took my amulet," said Reev.

"Yes, we did," Marius said, "a talisman of a former kingdom, a kingdom now reborn. The memory of Telantis lives in that amulet, and as you have learned, Reev, there are many in this palace that hate it. Interlopers."

"The Sons of Nachash," Reev said. "Anguipeds…"

"Opposed by your very blood," Marius said. "And they conspired against your kind before, and you prevailed."

"There is so much I don't know about Telantis," Reev said.

"The Oculus can be your teacher," Marius answered.

Chapter Forty-Nine: Telantari

"He doesn't know where Reev Nax is," Caro Hudnato, legate of the urban cohorts, repeated Spyke's words in the privacy of his official chamber. "That is what he claims."

"And there's something else," said Spyke. "He is a Telantine." Caro Hudnato stirred, and in his eyes there was a touch of fear, which he squelched with serpentine grace. "Well," he said, "we cannot afford a Telantine to live. Your ancestors wouldn't like that, Spyke. We must make our move, and we must make it now.

"We will kill Reev Nax, and we will kill Fortunato. We will not cease until not a single Telantine remains in Varda."

~

Like a bull preparing to charge, Fortunato summoned a deep breath, and eyed the Imperial Palace gate. He did not know why he was so bold, so brash, to think he could succeed. But he thought he could walk through, and enter in, and rescue Reev. He thought the Imperial Army couldn't stop him.

But as the noon shadows grew, there was a commotion amid the square, Imperial soldiers in breastplates and red half-capes approaching, about a hundred in number, an entire century. Fortunato began to back away.

The chief of the soldiers spoke. "Fortunato of Ríva," he said, "you are charged with a count of treason. The penalty is death. How do you plead?"

Fortunato looked at the captain in stunned silence. He supposed this moment was inevitable. He had been traipsing about the city freely. But in the end, they had delayed this for a reason

Fortunato did not know.

"Innocent," Fortunato said, and the Imperial soldiers seized him by the arm, as Xan looked on.

~

Xan watched as the Imperial Guards took Fortunato away, to the place of his trial. They had called him a traitor and all manner of dark names. But Fortunato was not a traitor to his people. He had fought against the ones who ruled over them — men like Verrus, whom the people hated.

Xan uttered a prayer to whichever god would hear him, as the shadows of noon turned to the long shadows of the afternoon, that justice would somehow prevail with an unworthy man on the Imperial throne. He prayed that somehow true justice would prevail amid a people under threat, amid a captured Empire.

The sun was glistening on Fortunato's hair as he was led away, and at last disappeared down a road.

Chapter Fifty:
Primus and Secunda

Though Reev was directly under the floor of the Imperial Palace, he felt he was a world away.

The entrances were sealed, and neither the Imperial court, nor Verrus, nor his mother, knew anything about the Oculus.

As the spymaster Marius led him through a red-brick hallway, he explained: "The Oculus has operated for all of the Empire's more than a thousand years, and longer."

"Longer?" Reev said. "How much longer?"

Through a doorway appeared the dark-haired man who had intervened when Barcho tried to question Reev. His green eyes flashed, reflecting in a distant lamplight.

"This is Agent Numerio," said Marius. "His specialty is in forgetfulness powder and jungle terrain."

"Jungle terrain?" Reev said.

"The reach of the Oculus is all over Varda," Marius said. "Long ago, we were sworn — we could intervene outside the bounds of this palace, but go up the stairs, and all is sacrosanct. That is, until we met you."

Marius led him through an open doorway.

He saw a stone table, and on it projected an image of the dining hall.

"There is a tiny hole in the floor of the dining wall," said Marius. "A camera obscura reflects its image onto this table. Every room in the Imperial Palace has a hole for a camera obscura, and the acoustics are such that everything can be heard, even a whisper."

What would a cruel emperor like Verrus, or a slothful emperor like Khandaraeus, do, if he knew the Oculus was operating in such a manner?

The Oculus had to be incredibly skilled not to be discovered for these more than a thousand years.

"You've never been discovered," Reev said.

"We've had some close calls," said Marius. "But every time, we've managed to pull the shade of secrecy back. Sometimes, it takes blood."

Reev watched the reflection of the camera obscura, and saw that as servants wiped down the tables, painters were lathing green paint over the once-purple room.

"What are they doing?" Reev said.

"Foreigners, interlopers, you called them." The voice that spoke was not Marius's, it was female. Reev turned and saw a woman standing there with her black hair tied in a bun. "You are correct."

She wore a leather vest, and had a dagger at her side.

"Agent Secunda," said Marius. "She is best for her silver tongue. She is a master of disguises."

"And what is the purpose of the Oculus?" Reev said.

"Well, for one," Marius said, "we've been waiting all this time, for you."

~

When Wrinn reached Imperial Square, having given up the life of a gladiator forever, and he did a diligent search for Fortunato and Xan, he couldn't find them anywhere. But as he walked about, he overheard, a public trial was set to begin for Fortunato of Ríva, the crime treason, the penalty death.

It was to take place in Voluscan Square outside the Metropolitan. And Wrinn had a feeling, the Empire would rig the jury, and Fortunato would be sentenced to death. How, then, could the party have any hope of resuming its journey to *Naron Da*, and treading Seymus underfoot?

As Wrinn traversed the streets, more to ease his building nerves than for any other reason, he came to a white temple with a triangular roof. He saw words on its lintel.

THE TEMPLE OF JAINE

One door was open, and Wrinn entered in.

Beyond the vestibule was the smell of incense. Beyond another open door, beyond pews and a marble walkway, was a statue of a god with two faces, each faces having a long beard.

Before the statue was an altar and an offering plate. Along the statue's pediment were words, "What he opens none shall close."

Wrinn did not know what to do. He was worried about his friend and the terrible odds he faced. The offering plate was empty and it seemed the parishioners were not generous with their wealth.

Wrinn had a little left. What could he do? He would give the gods his all, so that the impossible might happen.

He strode down the pews. He took his coinpurse and emptied it into the offering plate.

"Open the gate, Jaine," Wrinn prayed aloud.

Perhaps, the gods would hear him.

~

"For me? The Oculus is for me?" Reev said to Agent Secunda.

"Not for you in particular," Agent Secunda said. "But our origins go back to your homeland and your people. The first of us was a Telantine, Agent Primus. It was he who wrote the laws and bylaws, the rules that govern us to this day."

"But what is it, that the Oculus wants?" Reev said.

"The maintenance of order," said Marius. "The holding back

of chaos. To weaken the Sons of Nachash, what Giufrio called anguipeds, until such time as a hero would arise."

"Am I that hero?" Reev said.

"So, we think," Marius said.

"And why do you not strike dead and kill Verrus now?" Reev said.

"That's your job," Marius answered.

"And as we said," Marius added, "we abide by the regulations of our founder Agent Primus. We may not harm any in the Imperial Palace. We may only manipulate the world at large. We may provoke the emperor to act, but we may never bring harm to him. Our hand is always to be unseen."

"You took my necklace from Astarthe's room," Reev said.

"Our bylaws do not extend to the hero Agent Primus promised us," Marius said.

And so, perhaps, Reev wasn't safe here, after all.

~

In the Metropolitan Prison, Fortunato had been beaten with a rod, his sword and adamant knife taken from him, and rough brown clothing of horsehair forced upon him. He was an Imperial citizen, so certain tortures and gruesome deaths remained beyond the powers of the Imperial government, but the Imperial government now wanted his blood.

The Imperial government, now in the control of someone unworthy, a man some in the Imperial crowds had called "hostile to the human race."

But Fortunato would enter with bravado. He had not betrayed his kinsmen. He had battled the ones who oppressed them. The legions sent to Gallia had been sent under Khandaraeus, unworthy of the throne.

He had fought against the legions, but he had not fought against people like his father Petro and his mother Alessa. No, if his mother Alessa knew, he suspected she'd be proud that he had fought against those oppressing them for generation unto generation.

In the dank cell, there were pools of water. The only light came from a narrow window high above, which was sealed with iron bars.

In the dark, he prayed, to whatever god would hear him, the gods of the household he had been taught to revere from an early age.

He would stride forth. He would bear the Imperial government's blows with his head upraised.

He had a feeling, he would prevail.

Chapter Fifty-One:
A Higher Justice

Late at night, Reev began to explore the Oculus chambers. In each room, as Marius had said, was a camera obscura projecting what was happening in the room up above. Following his recollection, he made his way to Astarthe's suite.

As he looked, he saw that the walls, once painted with clouds and cupids, were now a jungle green. Rugs and carpets now covered the floor, and braziers burned, lending heat.

He walked to the camera obscura below Astarthe's room, and saw the sheets had been changed to green as well, and that Astarthe was no longer sleeping there.

Valeria Verra was standing beside the bed. She was not alone.

Thuban stood there beside her, his soupy brown eyes visible in the projected image of the camera obscura.

Valeria Verra had recently bathed and was combing her hair with a triumphant look on her face.

Their conversation carried perfectly to Reev, in the room below.

"Oh, Thuban," she declared, "now that the *mugush*-folk are gone, I shall heed my physician. Doctor Alqarfo says if I take a bath every day in the milk of five hundred she-asses, I will never have a wrinkle. I will retain my beauty forever."

"Ah!" she continued, "I will light six candles each sunset and say the Prayer of Alafeo. I will ask the Tannin that I die before I ever lose my looks!"

Valeria Verra had painted and taken over Astarthe's suite. Where, then, was Astarthe? Had she been expelled with the others?

Reev began to walk around the Oculus's rooms, seeing a projected image in every room of the Imperial Palace above.

In the Imperial Guard's suite, Giufrio was sitting at his desk with a worried look on his face. Barcho sat in the background, eyeing him with what Reev thought was jealousy.

He tried to find the projection of the Great Porch, but he realized the Oculus's chambers did not go that far, that there was no such projection to be found. But as he lingered near the edge, he heard a scream from the other room.

He rushed into the room where he had heard the voice, and saw a projected image from a camera obscura. In a dim room lit by lamplight, Astarthe was tied to a pole, her mouth tied tightly with a cloth to muffle the scream. Even with it muffled, Reev had heard.

He turned — to flee to her, perhaps, when he saw Marius standing in the doorway.

"We are managing the situation, Reev," Marius said.

"We must rescue her," Reev said.

"*You* must rescue her," Marius answered.

~

When the trial began, stands had been set up on either side of Voluscan Square, and they were packed with people. Fortunato, sitting in the seat of the accused, made out Xan and Wrinn sitting there to watch, and lend him their support.

There was a seat for the judge, and a box for the jury that obscured sight. In the Empire, trials were public entertainment, and public executions were entertainment, too. But as an Imperial citizen, Fortunato did not have to worry about death in the Imperial Arena.

Only Wrinn had to worry about that. But the afternoon games had begun, and he was here — had he given up on the gladiator's life?

The prosecutor strode forward, a man with salt and pepper hair who despite the gray hairs on his head appeared young, not much older than Fortunato. Between him and Fortunato was a witness stand, and according to Imperial law he was also given a defender. The judge was the referee, and the jury, of ten Imperial citizens, would decide his fate.

"We have before us a traitor to his country," said the prosecutor. "Fortunato, the son of Alesso and Petro. Born in Ríva to a family of the common classes. Some of the common exhibit noble characteristics and mimic those higher than them. But it was not so in Fortunato. For at an early age he showed signs of the treason to come. As a boy, he learned to enjoy poppy's milk, against all law and regulation. He stole fruit from a farmer's orchard, and it was the commission of that crime that caused him to flee, away, to Gallia, where his penchant for lawbreaking continued."

Fortunato eyed the crowds, who were stirring uncomfortably. They didn't seem impressed, but Fortunato had a feeling, a captured Imperial government had acquired a captured jury. There was little hope for justice to be done.

~

They were managing the situation, Marius said, but in the morning Reev returned to the room below Astarthe, where her projected image was beamed down. As he watched her now limp against her restraints, no longer having the strength to struggle against them, Reev couldn't help but give her all his focus and his attention. He felt, somehow, duty-bound to protect her.

But he couldn't protect her.

And as he watched, he saw the door to the dim room open, and Valeria Verra enter. She was carrying a whip.

Astarthe looked at Valeria Verra in terror.

"The harlot queen dares to look me in the eye," said Valeria Verra. "She will learn not to make such mistakes in the future."

There was a cracking of the whip, and there was blood,

spraying. Reev saw a wound had been opened up on Astarthe's leg. Tears then began to drip from Astarthe's eyes.

"The harlot queen, simpering and sobbing, yet she looks at the Telantine with lust in her eyes," said Valeria Verra. "She knows what the Telantines have done, not least to her kind."

What did Valeria Verra mean?

"She simpers, coquettish. Such a harlot queen is she, that she calls a Telantine her consort," hissed Valeria Verra.

One thing Reev noticed, Astarthe wasn't bucking. She wasn't responding. She wasn't bowing to Valeria Verra's torment.

"Ah," said Valeria Verra. "What would her ancestors think? They had ample opportunity to be a consort to a Telantine. But I think they had more pride. They had more love for their own kind. They had dignity. They loved themselves, and their families…"

Valeria Verra uttered madness.

But Astarthe wouldn't buckle. Astarthe said nothing, only endured the pain and the threats.

"You know where he went off to, don't you?" said Valeria Verra. "I will get it out of you, if I have to remove your fingernails and all your flesh…"

Marius said he was managing the situation, but he clearly wasn't.

~

"In Gallia, Fortunato began to think of himself as a Gallian," said the prosecutor amid the heat of Voluscan Square. "He began to identify no longer with his blood, but with those he had surrounded himself with. He began to be seen in the company of unsavory characters — not least the Green Wizard, Gastreel."

To call Gastreel an unsavory character seemed almost a sacrilege to Fortunato, and surely to anyone who knew him.

"Gastreel the Green Wizard was a wonder-worker, and a cunning meddler in Gallian affairs," said the prosecutor. "Though his speech was crafty, I believe he had a hand in Gallia's intervention in the war in the west, and then our defensive war against them. When war at last came to Gallia's doorstep, Fortunato helped massacre our soldiers in Highrock Abbey, and even designed the trap that led to the deaths of so many of his blood..."

There were a few angry faces in the crowd.

So often did the prosecutor use the words blood and kin, but Fortunato had not fought against them. He had fought against those who ruled over them.

He had fought against people like the prosecutor. He had fought against people like Verrus.

"So much blood was spilled, that day," said the prosecutor, "at the Abbey of Highrock, that if it were possible, I would ask that Fortunato be executed three thousand times. Yes, three thousand Imperials were killed that day, and Fortunato had a hand in the planning of that event."

What could the defender do, what could the defender say, to assuage the angry faces in the crowd? The only ones not moved by the words were Wrinn and Xan. No, fear was dawning in Wrinn and Xan's faces.

"It would be a miscarriage of justice not to sentence Fortunato of Ríva to death," said the prosecutor. "I yield the floor."

~

Reev watched Astarthe and Valeria Verra, transfixed, in the room just below them.

"Your husband Appian was a delight," said Valeria Verra. "You should know how pleased he was to be in my embrace.

"And in the end, a child was born that now rules over you. So we do have some things in common, Astarthe."

She gripped the whip, as if to strike her again, but a figure appeared behind her, one Reev recognized — Thuban. They walked away, down a corridor, and Reev followed the sound of their footsteps as they echoed down below.

The footsteps stopped at an antechamber, and a lamp Thuban was carrying spread light.

"Now that we have full control," said Thuban, "we were making changes to the dole."

"Verrus and I agreed, giving them money is so distasteful," Valeria Verra said. "The common *mugush*-folk do not know what is good for them. We do. And they are such drunkards."

"It is Verrus's belief that they that go to taverns should only be allowed a thimble full of wine every night," said Thuban.

"I concur," Valeria Verra said. "What a brilliant son I raised..."

But Reev knew that son had been trying to kill her. Had Valeria Verra already forgotten?

~

"Well," said the defender.

A positive start.

"While it is true that Fortunato had a hand in killing three thousand Imperials, and while it is true that he took up arms against his own blood and people — "

Blood, people, over and over — all untrue.

" — let's consider the mitigating factors. He had lived in Gallia by then for some sixteen years. He had learned barbarian ways and barbarian customs. By then, he was a barbarian himself."

At that point, Fortunato knew the defender was working for Verrus and the ones who wished to put him to death. Not just the content of her speech, but as she walked about, black hair glistening in the sun, she seemed to be reacting not to a positive response but looking for grimaces and frowns.

So what hope was there, then, in a trial designed for Fortunato's defeat? The Imperial government would have their execution, one way or the other.

What hope was there that the jury would see through the lies?

"I yield the floor," the defender said.

The judge, sitting in his chair, his long gold tunic and blue sash shining in the sun, made a motion with his hands. "The defender and the prosecutor have spoken. Tomorrow, the prosecutor shall call witnesses. The defender has elected not to call witnesses of her own."

And Fortunato knew the Imperial government intended there to be no justice. But there was a higher justice, Fortunato knew, the justice of the gods and of Heaven.

Chapter Fifty-Two: The Monster

Giufrio woke from his half-sleep to the sound of screaming.

By the time he had donned his breastplate and grasped hold of his nightstick, the screaming had ceased.

He knew where the screaming was coming, Astarthe's former suite, which Valeria Verra had taken up residence in.

He sprinted through the now-green halls. He thought it had to be the witching hour.

Still a bit tired, he swept open the door, and saw a scene of blood — blood, everywhere, and drooping off the bed, the body of Valeria Verra torn and stabbed in multiple places, but she had left a trail of her own.

The bodies of two assassins lay near the bedside, and they bore marks too. Barcho was already standing beside the body of Valeria Verra, looking in horror at the aftermath.

"The assassins slipped through the window," Barcho said.

And Giufrio felt a cool breeze — and saw shattered glass.

Barcho was in denial, but Giufrio knew who had sent these assassins, the monster who occupied the throne.

He stooped down, and saw what looked like claw-marks and bite marks on the two dead assassins. "Did you do this?" Giufrio said.

"No," Barcho said.

Valeria Verra had bitten and clawed these men to death. Who was Valeria Verra? What was Valeria Verra?

Giufrio, and Alessandro Sopis knew.

Giufrio knew something else, that Barcho had allowed the remaining assassins to escape. Perhaps, he had shattered the windows himself. But Giufrio knew Barcho was in on the conspiracy.

That left Giufrio alone in a nest of anguipeds and their allies, and what a terrible thing that was for the world.

But Giufrio would try to be the bulwark that the Imperial Council had failed to be. Giufrio's ancestors, in Heaven, would expect nothing less.

Giufrio couldn't stop looking at the mauled bodies of the two dead assassins. Valeria Verra, now limp, was bent over the bed, and even in death, had a rabid look.

Who and what was Valeria Verra?

She and her spawn were anguipeds.

~

At dawn, they dressed Valeria Verra's body for the funeral. Giufrio stood guard outside the chamber of the Maestro of Undertakers, Insalaco.

Insalaco, whom Giufrio suspected was an anguiped.

Giufrio wouldn't succumb to fear, he promised himself. He would fight, and try to stop the worst from happening to the Imperial people. But he had made a vow, not to harm the emperor. He would honor that vow.

For vows were not things to be taken lightly, or in the spur of the moment. A vow was something the gods expected you to honor, even if it led you to such a place — such a place as this.

Verrus appeared through the corridor, looking sheepish and timid.

Speak of the devil.

And he was one.

"May I see my mother one last time?" Verrus said.

"You're the emperor," Giufrio said coldly.

Verrus nodded weakly.

He entered into the undertaker's chamber, and Giufrio heard

the sound of soft weeping.

"Why, O Tannin?" Verrus said beyond the door.

What in Varda was Tannin?

There was silence a while. Then, Verrus strode out.

"I did not know my mother was such a looker," Verrus said.

And Giufrio's disgust was enough to destroy worlds.

Chapter Fifty-Three: The Tough Guy

The trial was set to resume, but Wrinn was hungry.

He was hungry, and he had left all his money in the offering plate at the Temple of Jaine.

He had all those earnings from his gladiatorial matches. Scauro had said they were held in a bank, and were accruing interest, but Scauro seemed a conman, not to be trusted.

Wrinn's empty stomach, though, was a matter of emergency. And when Xan stirred awake at the inn, he saw the party's collective coinpurse had also dwindled to nothing.

The dole would be distributed tomorrow, but Wrinn couldn't wait until tomorrow for such an emergency.

He was hungry now.

~

Scauro lived in the west side, amid the slums, where a con artist should live. Wrinn remembered seeing the address 12 Emperor Corvus Way.

He had fought quite hard for those earnings, risked life and limb… and it would be a shame if he had nothing to show for all the entertainment he had provided for the audience, the audience whose love he had lost.

In the parks of the west side, Haroon spice users would gather at night to undertake their illegal activity, but in the daylight only the remnants could be seen — the silken packets discarded, the excreta after they hadn't bothered to use the public latrine, caught up, as they were, in manic feelings of euphoria and vivid hallucinations.

The concrete apartment blocks were dirty, and some of their roofs were sunken in. There was graffiti on some of the walls.

Yet after a few conversations with unsavory characters, he found himself at the sign reading Emperor Corvus Way, and walking down the rows of houses, some of which were marked with numbers and some of which weren't, but he counted, and found himself at 12 Emperor Corvus Way.

The house he saw had broken windows, and a caved-in roof. None had lived in it for years.

Scauro hadn't been who he said he was.

Were Wrinn's earnings also illusory?

His stomach growled, but Fortunato's trial was set to begin.

He would be there to support his friend, amid the great injustice.

Xan had bread when Wrinn reached Voluscan Square, bread Xan had purchased last night, before the money ran out. Together, they sat, Wrinn and Xan, watching the trial unfold, praying constantly in silence.

~

"The prosecutor has called Vitto Khandulis, called Spyke, as witness to the stand," said the judge from his seat.

When the judge and the prosecutor spoke of traitors, there was none worse than Spyke, for he had betrayed the gods and all goodness and light. He had betrayed the mission he had been sworn to. Fortunato had fought against the Imperial government, but he would never betray the gods like Spyke had.

When Spyke sat in the witness's chair, Fortunato gave him a

look of bottomless contempt.

"Spyke, I understand this is the name you prefer," the prosecutor said, walking up to him. "We will use it. You bear witness to the fact that Fortunato was a traitor, even calling himself the general of the Gallian Army, fighting against his own kin and blood."

There it was again. *Kin. Blood.*

"I do testify," said Spyke. "I fought alongside him, I admit, and I deeply regret my choice, though I spilled the blood of no Imperial. I always considered myself a loyal citizen, and would never willingly fight against the Empire or the emperor."

"There you have it," said the prosecutor. "He witnessed Fortunato taking up arms against his own, and calling himself a general. He witnessed Fortunato shed the blood of his own."

The prosecutor paused, and the audience did not seem as impressed as before, as it had been with the statement of three thousand Imperials dead.

"Is there anything you wish to add, Spyke?" the prosecutor said.

"If you want to bear a sword, Fortunato," Spyke said, "you should sign up at your local barracks. If you want to be a tough guy, there's a recruiting officer in every town in the Empire. When I participated in the Pan-Vardic Games and met Fortunato for the first time, I couldn't believe how he walked about in public with a sword, openly, without being a proper soldier. If you want to be a tough guy, sign up for the Imperial Army. That's all I have to say."

The judge stirred. "The accused may respond," he said.

Fortunato reached for a sword that wasn't there. He let his anger fuel his words. "I bear a sword, and I do not bear it in vain. But I am a much better man than cowards like you, Spyke, or cowards like the men who arrested me. I am a man who has used violence, but I used it with the threat of the law bearing down on me. You risk nothing when you pillage the towns of Gallia, or oppress your own people. I risked everything, and I have always prevailed. I do not expect that to stop now."

There was a howl of fury from the prosecutor, and a hiss from the defender, the one who was in theory supposed to speak for Fortunato.

But the effect of his words was evident everywhere, from Spyke's pouting face and defeated posture, to the audience that was stirred, not to condemnation or to anger, but sympathy.

Sympathy — *has this man, whom the government accused, been fighting for us all along?*

~

At dawn again, Reev monitored Astarthe, bound to the pole. Thuban had brought her water and some dry bread.

Reev did not expect him to keep her alive for much longer.

And Marius said it was Reev's task to rescue her.

But as he stared and prayed silently, the door opened, and Marius was standing there.

Speak of the devil.

"Reev," he said, "you are a dutiful watchman. Come with me… I wish to show you something."

In the palace shrine, a funeral was underway for Valeria Verra.

Verrus was in attendance, and lingering in the corner of the room was Giufrio. Barcho was nearby the body, staring at her wounds, which cosmetics had failed to cover up.

"What happened?" Reev said, staring at the image projected by the camera obscura.

He noted the shrine had changed, that there was no altar, and instead a table with candles, and what looked like some kind of charm fashioned of gemstone and metal wires. The paintings of the gods, worth a fortune, had been covered up with lurid green paint.

It was a crime against art. It was also a sacrilege.

"What happened?" Marius said. "In the night, Verrus sent assassins to kill her."

"His own mother?" said Reev, stunned.

And he was stunned that such a monstrous man now sat on Varda's most powerful throne, now without any opposition.

Reev supposed there was opposition — himself included.

"Of anyone remaining in the palace, who has not been purged," said Marius, "only Giufrio is not under Verrus's thumb. Verrus as emperor can now run roughshod over the Imperial Council. Woe to the Imperial people."

But Reev thought there was still some fight left in them.

There was fight in them — but Verrus was a dreadful foe.

"And what are his designs?" Reev said. "What does he intend?"

"The end of Varda as we know it," said Marius. "The end of the Empire, changed from a bulwark against chaos to a safe place for anguipeds."

"Will he prevail?" Reev said.

"It is up to the Sons of Telantis to defeat the Sons and Daughters of Nachash," said Marius, "as it was, long ago."

~

Fortunato's words, as Wrinn watched, had caused the prosecutor and the supposed defender to erupt in fury. Spyke had exited the square, somewhere between fuming and pouting.

And Wrinn had cheered it on. He wondered if the jury, hidden in their box, was affected as strongly as the audience had been.

But as the prosecutor grumbled, the judge made a motion with his hands, and said, "The trial ends for deliberation. Jurors, discuss it among yourselves, and then go home. Bring your verdict at dawn."

"There's no money," Wrinn said.

"I know," answered Xan.

Wrinn hadn't given up hope that all those gladiatorial earnings were real, that Scauro — though a con artist — had managed to speak truth.

"I've gone hungry before," said Xan. "They'll give us the dole tomorrow. And then we'll eat well, for a while."

But the quest seemed to be foundering. Fortunato would be convicted — then executed.

Would he really? Could Fortunato really die? It seemed unfathomable. But the forces of the Dark One seemed to be winning. How could they possibly find a way out of this mess?

Wrinn tried to summon hope.

In the end, he told Xan to return to the inn, while he continued his quest to locate Scauro.

He hadn't lived in the abandoned house he claimed. Where did he live, in truth?

He inquired in Imperial Square about "a man name Scauro."

"I don't know anyone by that name," said a rich woman draped in a silken shawl.

He inquired further.

"Scauro? Who's that?" said a poor man, bedraggled, as he passed Wrinn by.

Wrinn cast a wide net, and had asked anyone in sight, from one edge of Imperial Square to the other. He pressed into the Suburro, and asked more people to no avail as the sun set, and it was night.

When he returned to the inn's room, feeling not just defeated but hungry, he saw Xan had some bread. "I begged a priest," Xan said. "He gave me a little of the sacramental bread."

And they ate, and it was the best bread Wrinn had ever eaten.

Wrinn would not give up on Scauro.

But how could he possibly rescue Fortunato from his plight?

He had a feeling in his heart, the jury had already made up their minds.

Chapter Fifty-Four: Hope

It was still dark when Reev was awoken. Outside his small room in the Oculus chambers was a window looking down into the streets below. He had a plush bed.

Marius was standing there, and behind him Agent Secunda.

"Reev Nax," he said, "we have something planned for you."

And Reev was not sure that he trusted Marius or Agent Secunda, but the founder of the Oculus was a Telantine — and so he would try.

He donned his tunic and trousers, and Marius seemingly eyed him in disapproval.

Why?

He followed them through the web of chambers, down a corridor, to a window baring a vista of the city below.

"The windows are visible from the outside," said Reev. "How has anyone not noticed there is a complex beneath the palace floors?"

"The windows are designed perfectly to trick the eye," said Agent Secunda. "An ancient art of architecture, learned from Telantis."

"Telantis," Reev breathed.

"Telantis," said Agent Secunda. "You bear its blood in your veins. You will also bear its sigil."

"What do you mean?" Reev said.

There was a flash, a lamp carried in Agent Secunda's hand, the smell of ink. And as Reev peered into the urban horizon, he felt a stinging on his neck, a continuous stinging. Tears welled in his eyes at the pain, but he bit his lip and endured it.

Marius walked over, and held a mirror up to Reev's face.

Reev saw that black lightning marks had been tattooed on his neck.

"How do you like it?" said Marius.

"I like it," Reev said

"And you shall bear the sigil of Telantis, wherever you go," Marius said.

Reev's gaze turned to a square below, where — as dawn began to make itself known — crowds were gathering, and beginning to filter into wooden stands.

"What's happening there?" Reev said.

"The trial of Fortunato of Ríva," said Agent Secunda.

He heard footsteps behind, and sensed the presence of Agent Numerio.

"They've arrested him," Reev said. "They're trying him for — "

"Treason," said Agent Numerio. "The penalty, death."

"I've got to go there — rescue him," Reev said.

"No," Agent Numerio said. "Let justice be done. It is better. The Imperial government is not all-powerful. The juries are selected by lottery, and the Oculus has learned, nine out of ten members of the jury are Telantines."

~

Fortunato sat in his seat, not knowing what to expect. He felt nervous, now, tension and fear — a thought that perhaps, his journey would end now, and he would see the gods soon. But perhaps... perhaps, not.

He had hope, inexplicable.

Wrinn and Xan had taken their seats. The tension was over all, and Fortunato was not sure what the audience was hoping for. As the prosecutor sat, the jury began to filter into their secret box. The judge stirred in his seat. The defender examined the audience's eyes, hoping perhaps to see a glimpse of bloodthirst for Fortunato, because she could not see the jury.

Then a man strode out, dressed in a black tunic with a white sash. "The jury has made their decision," he said.

He ventured behind the box, and when he returned, he returned with a parchment scroll.

"All rise for the reading of the verdict," said the man in the black tunic.

The audience stood up. Fortunato could see that Wrinn and Xan both were uttering silent prayers.

"We the jury," said the man in the black tunic, "find Fortunato of Ríva not guilty of the crime of treason."

The defender gasped and hissed. The prosecutor let out something like a howl.

There were happy faces in the audience, but not a few angry ones.

Fortunato could see the relief in Wrinn and Xan washing through them like waters through a mountain meadow. Then, Fortunato felt his knees give out. He had almost fainted.

He realized — he hadn't expected this.

He thanked the gods in Heaven. Now, one task remained — Reev.

How good it would feel, to have his sword and his knife in hand again.

~

As the sun rose over Imperial City, Giufrio stood guard over Emperor Verrus in the dining hall, remembering the vow he had made, never to harm a hair on the emperor's head.

A vow was not something to break, and though his ancestors would wish for the death of Verrus, breaking a vow was a much more serious crime.

Emperor Verrus was sitting at his table, once purple and now green, with a stew of dormice cooked in honey and poppyseed.

Giufrio thought he'd rather skip breakfast than eat such fare.

As Emperor Verrus devoured his dish, with Barcho seated next to him, a man strode in, one Giufrio knew but now called his enemy, one of long gray hair and soupy eyes, Thuban. A curved saber was now clipped to his side.

"Your Worship," said Thuban.

The term of address for emperors was "Your Excellency."

"The jury found Fortunato of Ríva not guilty," Thuban continued.

Verrus spat out his dormice.

Then a look of fury appeared on his face. "This cannot stand," he said. "Fortunato of Ríva is a Telantine…"

"According to ancient Imperial law, a man cannot be tried twice for the same crime," said Thuban. "But the Imperial Bay Company has its own courts and can sentence men to death. When the Imperial Bay Company tries people, there are more people like us on their juries."

People like them… *anguipeds.*

Giufrio tried to put on a brave face, not to give away his burning fury at the lawlessness of the suggestion.

"Preparing a writ of arrest," said Thuban, "will, however, require a meeting of shareholders before the majordomos can issue it."

"Get to work on that," said Verrus.

There was a pause, and a dark grin appeared on Thuban's fate. "A surprise for the *mugush*-folk today."

"They don't know what's good for them," said Verrus.

"And if they resist, we control the urban cohorts," said Thuban.

For the first time since Giufrio had been in Verrus's presence, he saw Verrus smile.

And the urban cohorts were designed, with many safeguards, to never be in the control of the emperor, for they were the only legion of soldiers allowed to operate in Imperial City.

But it was possible for an outside force to install a lackey.

And Giufrio suppressed a gasp, as he realized that — judging by what Verrus and Thuban had said — the leader of the urban cohorts was likely an anguiped, a member of the Qab of Thuban.

The only legion of soldiers allowed to operate in Imperial City would do whatever Verrus wanted.

~

When Fortunato was found not guilty, and given back his sword and knife, in addition to his tunic and trousers, he had not expected much more.

But the prison maestro informed him he would be paid, that having been found not guilty, that he would be compensated for the trial costs.

As he exited the prison outside the Cloaca, he was ten denara richer, and Wrinn and Xan were there to greet him, their faces radiant with joy.

They ate, then, at a cook-shop outside Imperial Square. Inside the cook-shop, the walls were painted in a red and gold theme, with scenes on the wall depicting urban life. Along a masonry counter, jars were set in holes, under which coals were burning to keep the food hot. In one jar was a red stew, in another jar a black stew, in another a concoction of chicken and boiled wheat, in another sweet cream mixed with dried fruit.

Wrinn, Xan, and Fortunato ate well, and they still had nine denara.

"What will we do now?" Wrinn said.

"We rescue Reev, of course," Fortunato said.

Chapter Fifty-Five:
The Telantines

As Reev walked down the Oculus's corridors with Agent Secunda and Marius behind him, now bearing the tattooed sigil of Telantis on his neck, he heard voices through a door.

He ventured in, followed by Secunda and Marius, and saw in the camera obscura's projection, that in a dark room, Thuban and Alsumo were gathered.

"Astarthe has outlived her usefulness," said Alsumo. "The Telantine is not coming to rescue her."

"I will walk down there," said Thuban, "and cut her throat."

Reev looked to Marius in a panic.

"Now is your time, Son of Telantis," said Marius.

Through a door Agent Numerio was approaching. He was holding something.

Marius said, "You must re-enter the place of danger, and make war against the Sons of Nachash. You now bear Telantis's sigil on your body, but you are not yet attired like a warrior of Telantis."

Reev saw that Agent Numerio was holding a leather loin cloth.

"Shall I wear a loin cloth in place of trousers?" said Reev.

"A loin cloth is all you will wear," said Marius.

~

Now clad in a loin cloth and nothing else, with Doomblade drawn and in his hand and the tattooed lightning marks of Telantis on his neck, Reev stormed through the corridors of the Oculus chambers, and Marius, Agent Numeria, and Agent Secunda followed.

At last, they had come to a door. Reev opened it, and saw a

stairway leading to the palace up above.

"Stride forth as a Son of Telantis," said Marius. "Speak boldly or stay silent, but do not tell a lie. Enter through the bold gate, for doors and gates belong to the Sons of Telantis, and no door or gate can hold against you.

"Go forth and conquer!"

~

It was the fifteenth of Sextil, Fortunato remembered, and the dole was being distributed.

Fortunato would get even richer.

As he saw the lines in Imperial Square, he was near the front, waiting for the distribution he was entitled to, as an Imperial citizen, from the Imperial treasury.

As he stood in the heat, a man in a tunic and a blue sash strode amid the tables, now set up before Imperial Square.

He began to speak loudly, shouting so as to allow everyone to hear. "His Worship, the Emperor Verrus, has made some changes for your good! He has noticed you do in Imperial Square do not eat healthily! Instead of entrusting you with fifteen denara to spend as you desire, he will ensure you have an adequate diet!"

More men appeared at the tables, and they were heaving onto the surface of the tables sacks filled with broccoli and lettuce, carrots and leeks and onions.

"You shall have vegetables to carry you through the remainder of the month!" shouted the man in the sashed tunic. "And moreover, Emperor Verrus has issued a regulation, that no tavern may serve any more to one person than a thimble full of wine each night!"

There was stunned silence amid the crowds, gathered in the tunics.

The Imperial government had crossed the mob. Anger was

building, fury. Amid the silence, shouts broke out. Not a single man or woman went to the table to gather their vegetables.

There was the sound of shattering glass. Someone had thrown a rock through a window.

~

Reev strode out in his loin cloth to a palace that had changed. The walls were painted green, and it was so hot, he had already begun to sweat.

Braziers had been set up in every room, to add to the heat. And as he stood in the midst of the sweltering heat and the green color, as it seemed he was in the midst of a steaming jungle, he was also not alone.

Alsumo stood there, bearing a dagger in his hands.

"Signore!" he said. His face had gone white. He was terrified. "You are — you are — "

Reev turned to him, now yards away down the hall. He brandished Doomblade.

"Do you know where the Telantine is?" said Alsumo. "Surely you are not he... if you were, my face would melt, and I would be a puddle."

"The Telantine is here," said Reev.

"I will go search for him!" Alsumo howled and ran off.

And Reev shouted, "It is I! I am the Telantine!"

But Alsumo, in terror, was in no state to listen.

Reev rushed down the hall in his loin cloth, down a path he knew well. He knew, by the path he had trod in the floor below, where the anguipeds were hiding Astarthe.

He rushed in, and he kicked down the door.

Astarthe cried out, in desperation, in love. Thuban had a saber up to her neck.

And Reev brandished Doomblade.

In Thuban's face was a look of bottomless terror, but unlike Alsumo, he reacted like a cornered rat.

He drew his saber and struck at Reev, metal clashing against metal.

He stabbed and Reev blocked. He slashed and Reev leapt back, with a mobility that his loin cloth allowed.

A storm of blows ensued, anguiped against Telantine, Son of Nachash against Son of Telantis. He pitched back Doomblade.

He felt an energy fill him.

~

Astarthe watched as her hero pitched back his blade, and as he pitched it back, sunlight seemed to glitter upon it, though there was no window. He struck a mighty blow, and the blade cut through Thuban's neck, all the way down through his hip. Thuban had been sliced in two.

~

Reev saw the body of Thuban fall to the ground in two bloody pieces. "Milady," said Reev, "I will cut your binds."

With a flick of his *estirion* blade, Astarthe's binds were cut and drifted waiflike to the floor. Astarthe fell, hitting the marble softly. Reev sheathed Doomblade and heaved Astarthe in his arms.

"My heroes," said Astarthe, "are all Telantines."

He carried Astarthe, then, through the Imperial Palace's winding corridors. Alsumo caught sight of him and screamed, fleeing into another room. Reev descended down the stairs, toward the ground floor, to the city.

He would ensure his consort got safely home.

~

The mob was setting fire to buildings, and chaos had consumed the streets. The advertisement for Regulo's Potions above Imperial Square was now a burning inferno. Imperial Square was a scene of pandemonium, and Fortunato saw — in that moment — that the guards who stood watch over Imperial Palace's gate had abandoned their posts.

"Wrinn, go fetch Tyra," said Fortunato. "Xan, go fetch the horses. I'll rescue Reev…"

As Wrinn and Xan sprinted into the distance, amid the pandemonium, Fortunato charged ahead. He laid a hold of the posts of the gate. He pulled and the hinges wined. He yanked and the hinges seem to buckle. Then he pushed forth boldly, and the Imperial Palace gates burst open.

As he rushed toward the front doors of the complex, he saw he was not alone. Reev was standing there in a loin cloth, carrying a woman in his arms. On his neck were tattoos of black lightning marks.

"Reev, what happened?" said Fortunato.

"I am dressed a warrior of Telantis," Reev said. "I am a Telantine, and so are you."

~

In the Harbor District, they found Astarthe's ship, and her servants had been waiting for her.

"Pandemonium has consumed the city," said the ship's captain, a Khazidee like her.

Reev set her to her feet. "Milady," he said, "find refuge in Khazidea. There, await the dawn."

Astarthe gazed into his eyes with bottomless love. "The dawn?"

she said.

"The dawn is coming," Reev said. "Tell everyone you know."

Reev and Fortunato stood by as the sails of *The Northward Star* caught the winds and took off through the harbor, setting sail for the land of Khazidea far away. Astarthe would be borne to safety. But behind them, as Reev turned, he saw fires were burning all throughout the city, as the city mob let its anger at its rulers be known.

~

As Xan led the Elvish horses Cobalt and Asté by the reins through Imperial Square, in light of the fires and spreading destruction, he saw that the stage where once Sylvia and Rufo had performed their plays was now occupied.

A man stood there with brown hair, garbed in trousers and nothing more, on his neck a tattoo of lightning marks. He was holding a rope to Spyke's neck, and strangling him.

Xan rushed forth, ignoring the sight, and at the harbor found Reev and Xan. "Where to?" Fortunato said. "You said, a port on the Empire's southern coast. That is where we will find the desert road to *Naron Da.*"

"A port called Calabar," Xan muttered.

~

When Wrinn had tried to pluck Tyra Jade out of her kennel, she had whined and whimpered, not wanting to leave. The kennel had toys and balls, and other wolves to play with. In a city as large as Imperial City, there was a space dedicated to those who had great wolves as pets.

But now Wrinn, with a bit of coaxing, was leading Tyra through the shops and markets of Emporia, and passing now through the slums of the west side.

Everything was burning, and the fires were spreading through the city, as the city mob ransacked homes, threw rocks through windows, and assaulted anyone who stood in their way. Emperor Verrus had not respected the Imperial people, and now they were lashing out.

He had broached Imperial Square. Small fires were burning throughout it. Wrinn began walking due southeast, in the direction of Harbor District.

Someone was approaching.

It was Scauro.

~

"A port called Calabar," said Ivan Xandrast to a pair of sailors walking down the way.

"We are headed to Bregantium," said one of the sailors.

They disappeared down the street.

Everyone, it seemed, who was able, was fleeing the city and the raging fires, the city mob now running loose through the streets.

"A port called Calabar!" Xan shouted to a man standing beside the docks.

"We are headed to Nichaeus," he said dismissively.

Fortunato and Reev, not least Wrinn, were depending on Xan. He recalled from his ill-fated first journey to *Naron Da,* where he had gone, and where their feet should tread.

"A port called Calabar!" Xan screamed, but now he was screaming to the wind.

~

"I looked for you at 12 Emperor Corvus Way," Wrinn said.

Scauro's expression twisted, to embarrassment, to shame.

"I admit," said Scauro, "I did not tell you my state. I am homeless. I have been staying at the Temple of Amara on Narrow Way with others like me."

Wrinn looked at him with no judgment. No, he felt the stirrings of pity in his heart.

"I heard you were searching for me, scouring for me," Scauro said. "And now people like me have no hope, with Verrus on the throne."

"There is hope," said Wrinn. "Heroes have arisen to make war on Verrus."

"Truly?" said Scauro. Wonder touched his eyes.

"Were my gladiator earnings made up, too?" said Wrinn.

"No," said Scauro. "They are held at the Mother Amara Bank on Crow Street. I could not withdraw them without you."

Wrinn knew the situation in the city was spiraling out of control, that fires were spreading and the mob was running rampant. He knew Fortunato, Reev and Xan were waiting for him in the Harbor District. But he knew something else, that they were about to go on a long journey, and any money helped.

"Let's hurry there!" Wrinn said.

And Scauro led him down toward a narrow avenue.

~

"A port called Calabar!" howled Xan, and this time gesticulated with his hands.

The southron sailor looked at him squarely. "This ship is going to Saidoon," he said.

Xan grumbled curses.

Was there a single ship in the harbor going to Calabar? Xan worried, for Calabar was not much a town. There was an inn, a trading post, and a well for water.

But he would do his best.

He prayed, and continued to search.

"A port called Calabar!" he screamed again, louder than ever.

~

The Mother Amara Bank was a chamber inside a temple. Wrinn strode up, and the woman at the desk inquired, "Would you like a withdrawal or a deposit?"

"Withdrawal," Wrinn said, and remembered what Scauro had told him, "for Wrinn Finnis, gladiator. The passphrase is 'Jaine the Opener.'"

The woman passed beyond a columned chamber. Wrinn eyed Scauro. The woman returned moments later and said, "Wrinn Finnis, you have fifty libra waiting for you."

"Fifty libra?" Wrinn said in disbelief.

Fifty libra was a small fortune, more than most workers would see in ten years or more. But Wrinn had risked his life, he supposed, and he had entered into an endorsement agreement with Regulo's Potions at the behest of Scauro.

Scauro, he remembered, would get forty denara for every hundred he made.

Forty out of every hundred. That left Wrinn sixty out of every hundred, he remembered.

He did the arithmetic in his head.

"I'll have thirty libra," said Wrinn, "and the man behind me gets twenty."

Scauro strode up to the desk. "I'll take it from here, Wrinn," he said.

~

"A port called Calabar!" Xan screamed.

"Just talk like a normal person," Fortunato said as sailors passed Xan by in disgust.

But Fortunato thought that Xan was growing afraid at the fires spreading throughout the city, and was reacting to that fear.

Xan seemed to gather in himself all his strength. "A port called Calabar," he said to an easterner walking by him in a red tunic.

The easterner passed him by silently with a sneer on his face.

"See?" Xan said. "Shouting works."

~

When Scauro dropped the gold coins, into Wrinn's coinpurse, Wrinn counted them one by one.

"I said thirty, this is fifty," Wrinn said.

"You are a warrior against Verrus," Scauro said. "I, on behalf of all the anger you see today, give you it all. Pray for me and people like me, that we may wage war too."

And Wrinn, wishing to give Scauro more but realizing time was running out, thanked Scauro profusely. He rushed outside the doors of the temple and found Tyra Jade where he had tied her. He unlatched the rope and mounted astride her, his coinpurse jingling with fifty gold coins.

~

"A port called Calabar," Xan said, and it was almost a whisper.

Before him was a buck-toothed sailor with a pipe in his mouth. In the colors of the late afternoon sunlight, his eyes had a red glint.

"We're headed there, signore," he said. "Straight to it."

"We would like to board," Xan said. "There are four of us, and three animals."

"Twenty-five denara," the sailor said.

"You're robbers!" Fortunato snapped.

They only had nine denara in the party's coinpurse.

"The captain of the ship sets the price," said the sailor, and his pipe flared. He opened his mouth, and a cloud of smoke wafted out.

Yet there was commotion through the docks, Wrinn riding astride Tyra Jade, his white shift and quarterstaff and longknife glistening in the waning sunlight. He had a happy look.

"This man wishes to extract twenty-five denara from us for passage to Calabar," Xan sneered.

"Twenty-five denara is one gold libra," Wrinn said with a triumphant look on his face. And he took his coinpurse, and flipped a gold coin directly into the sailor's hands.

The sailor had a disappointed look, like he could have asked for more. "A captain's word is his bond. Come, gather your animals, and climb aboard…"

Chapter Fifty-Six:
A Memory of Blood

Night had set in across Imperial City. Giufrio, in the dining hall, could see that the fires set in the Imperial City, which were growing and not shrinking, and had made the streets below almost as bright as day. Below him, the urban cohorts attacked the people with their swords, shedding their blood, on behalf of a captured government. The anguipeds were fully in control.

For now.

Verrus was not in his usual place, at the usual hour. Giufrio wondered where he was as Barcho ate his fish sauce-smeared bread.

Giufrio wondered, and felt his hand, despite his vow, going to his nightstick. He passed through corridors, drawn it seemed by a spirit, and then, by the sound of the kithara.

Then, he was at the Great Porch.

~

The statues of Emperor Numa and Emperor Claudio on the Great Porch had been beheaded.

Their marble heads lay on the ground, and Verrus stood before a vista of the burning city, as soldiers below slaughtered the people.

He was not singing but chanting, and at the end of each verse he would strum his kithara violently.

Amid gray ash-land
Rule and regulation
A memory of blood
Rule and regulation

Blood was spilled, it was
Rule and regulation
I stand in ash-land
Rule and regulation

There was a roar as a concrete apartment block in some far-off district gave way to the fire and tumbled into ruins. Giufrio knew below there were screams, as the only legion that could operate in Imperial City, now headed by an anguiped, slaughtered the people.

Giufrio cursed Verrus as he stood there, strumming his kithara as Imperial City burned.

Verrus continued to chant, and to tear at his kithara at the end of each verse.

Take back what they took from us
Rule and regulation
Take back what they took from us
Rule and regulation
Take back what they took from us

"Take it back!" Verrus screamed, no longer chanting, and as his kithara fell to the floor from limp fingers, Giufrio fully expected him to levitate and his eyes to turn to black marbles.

Giufrio tore his half-cape from his breastplate, cast his helmet to the ground, and fled.

~

As Giufrio fled Imperial City, he made another vow, that he would announce the truth in every town square in the Empire, starting with the towns surrounding Imperial City.

He had removed his pauldrons by the time he had reached the west side. He had removed his breastplate by the time he had reached Imperial City's outskirts.

He was in his civilian clothes, then, as he exited city bounds.

The Empire was no longer Imperial, and he would tell everyone.

He would tell everyone the truth about the anguipeds, he vowed, as he sprinted into the night, and into the cool of the Anthanian hills.

Chapter Fifty-Seven: Telantis's Son

Aboard *The Storm Skipper*, on the top of the deck, Reev reflected on all that had gone on, and all that now faced him.

He could see Imperial City in flames behind him, but it was quickly disappearing into the darkness, amid the darkness of the sea, amid the sultry summer night.

He did not trust the sailors aboard *The Storm Skipper*. He thought there was something they were not telling Reev and Fortunato, Xan and Wrinn.

Even Cobalt had bucked at the touch of the ship's captain, as he was led into the ship's stalls.

To *Naron Da* they would go, to tread their enemy, Seymus, the Dark One, under their feet.

That had been their goal all along.

As the lights of the flames at last disappeared, and they were in the open ocean, Reev caught sight of the ship's captain in the moonlight, the reddish glint of his eyes, and thought better of standing on the deck.

~

In a room below deck, Reev found Fortunato, Wrinn and Xan. The ship's captain had provided four bottles of wine, and they were sharing them in cups.

Reev thought he had earned the wine, standing in the threshold of the doorway in his loin cloth, his amulet of Telantis firmly around his neck, his neck now tattooed with Telantine lightning marks.

But wine, he supposed, was for a later time, when he heard the snap of the Dark One's neck underneath his foot.

Would Seymus's neck snap, when Reev tread him underfoot? Reev did not know. He only knew what the prophecies said, prophecies that he trusted, prophecies that said he had to complete this voyage, and begin the journey to *Naron Da*.

He watched the others clink their glasses, and enjoy, in the privacy of their room, red wine bubbling into cups. The sailors of *The Storm Skipper* were not to be trusted, but Reev trusted these four with his whole life. He would trust them with all he had.

In such a circumstance, trust was imperative for all of them. A dangerous journey lay ahead.

Five had shipwrecked off the coast of Dualmis; four had left Imperial City.

One had been winnowed out.

Spyke, Reev sensed, was dead.

They would trust each other, these four, Reev knew.

He watched their smiling faces as they drank their wine.

Where would they go? Only the gods knew.

Xan had a better idea than anyone. A desert road, traveling to *Naron Da*.

The journey, Reev thought, would be long and arduous. He had never traveled through a desert before. The lands south of the Empire were wild, and it would be hard going for them all.

But for now, they were smiling. They were glad, those three to *Naron Da*, and Reev was glad with them, though he would not drink their wine.

Wine was for when the victory had been achieved, when all Seymus's power was gone. Wine was for the light of the dawn.

"What a journey it's been, so far," Fortunato said with a smile on his face, and took a deep sip of wine. "What a journey…"

"And there is a long journey ahead," Xan said, and took a sip of wine, of his own.

Xan had been down this road before. But for the others, the voyage was uncharted. Reev supposed he would do what he could, to pray, to hope, to use all shrewdness to defeat the enemies they would face.

The darkness had spread to Imperial City fully, and Shadow now had its champion on the throne. But Reev had seen inklings of their defeat. He knew, Telantis was about to be reborn.

He was Telantis's son. He was a Telantine.

So, Reev knew, was Fortunato.

"You didn't want me in those games," said Wrinn, and clinked the glass. "But now, we have ample coin."

"To the games," Fortunato said, "and Wrinn."

They took a sip, a deep sip, first Wrinn, then Xan, then Fortunato.

For now, they had each other. But danger lay ahead. As soon as they docked in Calabar, the journey would begin in truth.

Fortunato's eyes glistened, and his smile brightened, and his happiness was evident as he fixed his gaze on Reev. "What shall we drink to, Reev?" he said.

"To the dawn," Reev answered.

"To the dawn!" said Fortunato, and in unison the three drank.

Wrinn smiled, and his joy too seemed to be overflowing. His eyes glistened as he looked to Reev. "What else shall we drink to, Reev?" he said.

"To the treading of Seymus underfoot," Reev said.

And as the three drank, and Reev watched, and the ship tossed slightly in the waves, Reev knew it was true.

He knew in his mind, these four to *Naron Da* would tread Seymus under their feet.

THE END

Continued in Book Seven, *The Doom of Qadirra*...

Glossary

Times and Dates

	Vardic Calendar	Julian Calendar Equivalent
1.	Albos	January
2.	Kaldsil	February
3.	Primrane	March
4.	Tidusca	April
5.	Brenua	May
6.	Aurelios	June
7.	Odens	July
8.	Sextil	August
9.	Harona	September
10.	Brightleaf	October
11.	Anthanos	November
12.	Candlebright	December

Currency

Aesa: A copper coin, worth an eighth of a denara.

Denara: A silver coin, worth about a day's wages for a typical laborer.

Libra: A gold coin, worth twenty-five denara.

Talent: A unit of measurement in gold, worth eighty-four hundred denara.

Imperial phrases

Lupa: A female wolf, used as a curse.

Foreign phrases

Mugush: Shame.

Terms

Actors Guild: Officially called the Venerable Brotherhood of Mimes and Pantomimes, a representative body defending the interests of actors and entertainers throughout Imperial City.

Adamant: A blue-colored metal, hard enough to pierce stone, named after Emperor Adamantus.

Alabaster: The god of thunder and kingship.

Anthania: A peninsula bordering Gad on its north, home to Imperial City and the Imperial government.

Amara: The goddess of motherhood and war.

Amaroth: A temple city on Anthania's south coast, controlled by the priestesses of Amara.

Archon: Historically, the elected leader of an Eloesian city-state.

Black wolves: Large, intelligent wolves of the Dragonteeth Mountains. They are often captured and forced into the service of rokahn. They are one of the three divisions of great wolves, along with white wolves and brown wolves.

Brecko: The god of wine and frenzy.

Breckonalia: A celebration of the god of wine and frenzy, marked my drinking copious wine and dancing to frenzied music.

Camera obscura: A box with a lens, capable of projecting the image of an adjacent room onto a surface.

Corbian Way: A famed road leading from Imperial City in the north to Nichaeus in the south, crossing the southeastern Anthanian peninsula's urban sprawl.

Dark One, the: A name for Seymus, the enemy of the gods, the king of the Abollaren or demons.

Dark Continent, the: A mysterious land far south from the Empire, past the South Seas, covered in jungle.

Dualmis: An island along the Anthanian peninsula adjacent to Imperial City.

Dó Kentari: A practitioner of *Dó Kentas*.

Dó Kentas: Literally, "the Way of the Staff." The elves' most ancient martial art, focused on mastery of the quarterstaff. A practitioner of *dó kentas*, called a *dó kentari*, is mandated to only.

Easterner: An inhabitant of the easternmost parts of the Empire, especially Eloesus.

Elders: The Imperial term for elves.

Eloesian: A native of Eloesus.

Eloesus: The easternmost province of the Empire, famed for its rich history, philosophy and former power. It was once a disunited region of warring city-states.

Elves: Long-lived beings whose kingdoms and settlements lie in the north of the world. They are divided into several tribes, including the Lamen, the Umen, the Lonen, and the Nurnen. In recent years, the Lamen kingdom lost a war to the Kingdom of Zarubain and untold thousands of elves were brought into forced servitude.

Elvish horse: A kind of warhorse bred by the elves for speed and bravery. They are known by the bony horns that grow on their noses.

Estirion: "Star-iron" is the hardest and sharpest metal known to man. The means of the making of star-iron swords are lost to history; they were said to be forged by Danthelon, the so-called "Wonder-Smith." Only twenty are known to exist; they are considered priceless.

Fharese-Eloesian War: One of many wars between what is now the Imperial province of Eloesus, and the Kingdom of Fharas west and south of them.

Forgetfulness powder: A tasteless substance that causes a target to forget recent events within a an approximately half-hour time range.

Gad: The northernmost province of the Empire, often considered rustic and uncultured.

Galiope: A large city of the Northern World, called by those that love it the Queen of the North.

Gallia: A region east of Zarubain and west of Kardir, a place of mixed forest and farmland. Its greatest city is Galiope.

Getan: *Sense 1* — A gladiator bearing a breastplate and two sabers. *Sense 2* — A native of Gad.

Gypsies: A wandering folk who traditionally roamed the world in colorful wagons. In recent years, they were welcomed by the Gallian government and allowed to settle in Galiope.

Imperia: The most ancient representation of the Empire, portrayed as a woman in a war-helmet, often considered to represent the people rather the Imperial government. She contrasts with Imperium, who is more associated with the emperor and the Imperial government.

Imperial: To those outside the Empire, a citizen of the Empire. To those within the Empire, a man or woman originating in the coastal provinces associated with its founding.

Imperial Bay Company: A powerful consortium of merchants controlling much of trade throughout the Empire.

Imperial City: The largest city in Varda, with a population of more than a million, the capital of the Empire.

Imperial Council: A body of thirty men, representing Imperial City's thirty wards. Originally the most powerful part of the Imperial government, over centuries their power has waned.

Imperium: The god said to embody the Empire. The Magisterium has denied his existence.

Jaine: The god of doors and gates.

Kav: A feudal principality south of Gallia.

Kavan: A native of Khav.

Khopesh: A sword, shaped like a sickle, common to Khazidea.

Khazidea: A province in the south of the Empire, consisting of farmland along a river called the Khazan. The Khazan floods annually.

Khazidee: *Sense 1* — A gladiator attired in chainmail and bearing a khopesh. *Sense 2* — a native of the Imperial province of Khazidea.

Kronos: A malevolent supernatural entity, considered a foe of the gods.

Myrmidon: A gladiator wearing heavy armor and wielding a trident and a net.

Nichaeus: A large city southwest of the Empire in the province of Anthania. It is the home of the Imperial Navy.

Noricum: A small region in the center of the Imperial province of Gad, named after the River Nor. Its administrative center is the village of Tancreda.

Norwood: A small village in the region of Noricum in the Peregothian Empire, in the province of Gad.

Queen Varae: The Imperial transliteration of the Elvish *Warë*, a girl who after the heresy of Loni traveled from Lamdar to Londor on her knees to prophesy against them. The king noticed and married her. She died of old age, in peace.

Quorum: A two-thirds majority of the Imperial Council, necessary to be present for the Council to be in session.

Rokahn: Humanoid creatures known to dwell in the Dragonteeth, considered creatures of shadow. When their population swells, they will often raid the lowlands for food. Breeds include kehrad, toltar, and the standard species simply known as rokahn.

Solarias: An elf of ancient days, born in the early years of the Second Era, who received a message of the gods and paid the ultimate price.

Sea Raiders: A confederation of seafaring peoples. Their homeland is far south of the Empire, in the South Seas.

South Weald: A large forest in the south of Gallia.

Southron: A native of the lands south of the Empire.

Speaker of the Council: The chief Imperial Councilor, elected by a majority of the Imperial Council.

Suburro: A sprawling urban area abutting Imperial Square. Although impoverished, many famous Imperials have hailed from the Suburro.

Thartan: *Sense 1* — A gladiator in light chainmail, wielding a spear and shield. *Sense 2* — A native of the historical city of Tharta, now called Imperiopoli.

Urban cohorts: The only legion of Imperial soldiers allowed to operate within city bounds.

Valley of Lotuses: An area of fey influence on the island of Saidonia, in the middle of the South Seas.

West side: An impoverished urban area beyond the Suburro.

Wilderlands: A sprawling region southeast of Gallia.

Wilderman: *Sense 1* — A gladiator only allowed to wear vambraces and pauldrons and wield a shield and a heavy barbed spear. *Sense 2* — A native of the Wilderlands.

Wizards: Powerful magic weavers of the northern kingdoms. They are governed by a council and have their own nation-state within the walls of Galiope.

Zarubain: A large kingdom of the north, west of Galiope. Its legal ruler is the king of Zarubain, who dwells in the capital city of Zarubad; outlying regions are governed by dukes (duchies), counts (counties) and barons (baronies).

APPENDIX 6: MEMBERS OF THE COURT

- Khandaraeus, emperor (age 62), reigning since 1151
- Khandaraeus's wife, Flavia Karbo (age 46)
- Nnubi aka Khando, Khandaraeus's son (age 25)
- Astarthe, wife of the late Appian (age 74)
- Appenina the Younger (age 42)
- Giufrio, Marshal of the Guard (age 35)

Former members of the Imperial court
- Appian, now dead, who leaves a long shadow
- Appenina the Elder, formerly, now lives in Eloesus (age 45)
- Reekee, former Maestro of the Treasury, killed in the Emporian Riots
- Marcus Amaranthius, emperor before Khandaraeus, died in suspicious circumstances

And then there is Valeria Verra and Verrus…

- Verrus, aged 30 at the New Year's party
- Valeria, aged 56 at the New Year's party

About the Author

Cursed at birth with a wild imagination, Andrew Cooper spent his youth dreaming of worlds more exciting than Earth.

He is a graduate of the Odyssey Writing Workshop. His stories have appeared in Morpheus Tales, Fear and Trembling, Residential Aliens and Mindflights, among others.

He is also a graduate of the Creative Writing program at Western Michigan University.

Visit **www.aj-cooper.com** to sign up for the newsletter and stay up-to-date on new releases.

Find him on **x/Twitter** @ajcooperwriter.